The Gentleman's Scandalous Mermaid

Rumor Has It Book Two

by

Lora Darling

This is a work of fiction. Names, characters, places, and incidents are either the product of the author's imagination or are used fictitiously, and any resemblance to actual persons living or dead, business establishments, events, or locales, is entirely coincidental.

The Gentleman's Scandalous Mermaid

Contact Information: info@thewildrosepress.com

Cover Art by *Diana Carlile*

The Wild Rose Press, Inc.
PO Box 708
Adams Basin, NY 14410-0708

Visit us at www.thewildrosepress.com

Publishing History
First Edition, 2022
Print ISBN 978-1-5092-4019-7
Digital ISBN 978-1-5092-4020-3

Published in the United States of America

Shocking scandals, dangerous enemies, and the rules of London Society are no match for true love...

Henry sighed. "My inner voice is telling me to walk away and leave you to muddle through this on your own."

"But?"

"*But* when have I ever listened to my inner voice in regards to you?"

"Does this mean you will give me directions to the study?"

"No, it means, in spite of the impending sense of doom that has suddenly come over me, I will escort you to the study and help you search."

"Thank you." Without thinking, Ren laid her hands on Henry's shoulders and leveraged herself up to give him a kiss on the cheek. The act was as natural to her as breathing. Warning bells sounded in her mind the moment her mouth touched his skin, but they came too late.

She jerked away from him, but he caught her in his arms and prevented the escape. She dipped her head and stared at the contrast of her black-gloved hands pressed to his white shirtfront. "Please let me go, Henry."

"Ren—"

"Please."

She nearly cried out at the soft glide of his gloved finger under her chin. He tipped her head upward. As always, her breath caught as she looked into his eyes. Perhaps they were merely brown to most people, Henry included, but to her, they were pools of chocolate laced with rich honey. The thick fan of coal black lashes only enhanced their allure. He had offered her the opportunity to look into those eyes for the rest of her life, and she had said no.

"Before I risk my freedom and possibly my life searching Lord Sumner's study, perhaps you should tell me the circumstances that led to his possible possession of your ship registration."

Chapter One

London, 1810

Henry Westhaven led Miss Annabelle Parish to the center of Lady Sumner's conservatory, where her ladyship's most prized roses bloomed with an explosion of rich color and heady fragrance. He'd whisked Miss Parish away from the dinner hour on the pretense of wanting her to enjoy the conservatory while the other guests were engaged. She had clapped with delight at the idea and presently flashed him a bright smile as she stopped to give her attention to a large, pale pink rose.

He took the opportunity of her distraction to drop to one knee and extract the small ring box from inside his waistcoat. As he waited for Miss Parish to finish admiring the rose, he carefully considered his words. He had done this before under very different circumstances involving a very different woman, and the outcome had not been pleasant. He was determined to do it correctly where Miss Parish was concerned.

"It smells heavenly," Miss Parish exclaimed. She turned, glanced down, then lifted both gloved hands to her mouth to smother a gasp.

Henry cleared his throat and pushed all thoughts of the *other time* from his mind. "Miss Parish, will you do me the honor of consenting to be my wife?" Bloody hell, he could have tried for a bit of enthusiasm. After all, he had thought of this moment for nearly a year.

While Miss Parish gaped at him, he opened the ring box and lifted it to present the large, square-cut, pale sapphire, and gold ring.

"Oh, Henry, it is beautiful." She sighed, just as he predicted she would when he had chosen the stone. After all, it matched her eyes perfectly.

Henry got to his feet and slipped the ring from its case. He reached for Annabelle's hand—

"I cannot."

He froze, then looked in her pale sapphire eyes. "Pardon me?"

"I cannot marry you."

"I see." He returned the ring to its case and closed the lid. The *other time* had taught him the valuable lesson that no meant no, so he saw no point in attempting to change Miss Parish's mind. Assuming he wished to change her mind. Strangely enough, her rejection seemed to have very little, if any, impact on his emotions.

"Of course, I *want* to marry you," Miss Parish said in a rush. "I hold you in such high regard, but I must be practical and secure an advantageous marriage." Her wide eyes slowly narrowed the longer he remained silent. Did she wish him to beg? "My mother would be furious if I did not hold out for a title. Surely, you understand?"

Henry put the ring case inside his waistcoat. "Of course, I understand." Ah, the irony to be rejected for not being good enough. The *other time* he'd been rejected for being too good. Life really loved a lark, did it not?

He bowed to Miss Parish and offered his arm. He

might not possess a title, but he possessed manners, and even after one's proposal was rejected, a gentleman did not abandon a young lady. "Shall we return to the ball?"

"There is no need for you to play the gallant. I imagine the last thing you wish to do is spend another moment in my company, so I will take myself off to the withdrawing room." She made it seem as though he needed a moment alone to dry the tears of rejection, but with her rejection had come a realization.

He did not love her. A man in love would feel something, but he felt nothing.

No disappointment.

No hurt.

No loss.

Nothing.

He met Miss Parish's wide, blue gaze and offered another bow. "I bid you good evening." Then he turned and walked away. Each step increased the sensation that he had just narrowly missed making the biggest mistake of his life. Perhaps, in the morning, he would send round a thank you note to Miss Parish.

My dear Miss Parish,

I wish to thank you for your rejection of my ill-advised proposal. Had you said yes, I fear we would have lived a life of abject misery as man and wife...

He rounded a corner and halted beside some large, exotic, flowering tree that seemed to have outgrown its pot. The marriage would, indeed, have been a disaster. They had nothing in common. Hell, she was afraid of horses. How could he marry a woman who was afraid of horses? And water. She had told him once that she was deathly afraid of the water, going so far as to confess the city of Bath made her nervous simply because of its name and she could never, *ever*, live near the coast.

He owned a yacht, well a former smuggling schooner that was in the process of being refitted into a personal yacht to allow him to enjoy a great deal of time on the water. He also spent his time away from London in Cornwall, which very much possessed a coast, and he loved his horse, Poseidon. Why the devil had he proposed to Miss Parish?

"Men do questionable, sometimes damaging, things when running from personal demons." That bit of wisdom, delivered some time ago by his best mate, Bramley Venton, flitted into his mind. As much as he would like to deny it, it was true. He had fixated upon Miss Parish in an attempt to forget a personal demon by the name of Morvoren Teague, the woman responsible for the *other time*.

"Hello, Henry."

He whipped around so fast he entangled himself in the large leaves of the tropical tree and had to smack himself free, as if traversing an undiscovered jungle. Once the deed was accomplished, he gaped like a fish out of water. "Ren?"

Had he summoned her with his thoughts? Think of the devil…or was it, speak of the devil and he shall appear? Not that Ren was the devil. Lilith, perhaps, but not the devil.

"What the devil are you doing here?" He was not sure if his question referred to her presence in London or Lady Sumner's conservatory. In a moment of clarity, he scanned her person and realized she was not dressed to attend the ball. In fact, given the form-fitting, black trousers that were tucked into black boots, the black shirt buttoned up to her chin, and the black gloves, she appeared ready to either fight a duel or burgle the place.

He snapped his gaze to hers. Bloody hell, had her eyes always been quite that pale green or was it a trick of all the black clothing and surrounding green foliage? "Why are you here, Ren?"

"I heard you the first time." She sounded more than a bit irritated.

"And?" he prompted after an infuriating few moments of silence.

"*And* I would rather not say."

She would rather not say? Well, too bloody bad, because he was in no mood for riddles. "You suddenly appear before me after three years of no contact, dressed as though you mean to steal Lady Sumner's jewelry collection, and you would rather not say?"

"Exactly." She made to brush past him, as if, in her mind, the encounter was over.

"Not so fast." He snared her arm and hauled her a few meters away to an iron bench. "Sit. Please." She'd always been too stubborn for her own good.

She sat and glared up at him. "It's lovely to see you again, Henry, but I really don't have time for this."

He squatted in front of her, which seemed the safer option, given the small size of the bench. If he sat next to her, their bodies would be pressed against one another, shoulder to thigh, and God help him, he did not need that level of torture at the moment. Seeing her was bad enough.

"This little interrogation will end quickly if you answer one simple question. Why are you slinking around Lady Sumner's conservatory dressed like a thief?"

"I am not slinking."

He waited for her to deny the accusation she was dressed as a thief, but it seemed such a denial was not forthcoming. "What are you here to steal?"

"This is none of your concern, Henry." She suddenly stood, which put a certain part of her anatomy directly in front of his face. He stared at the fastening of her trousers and slowly, very slowly, counted to ten, then again, then backward, but nothing would reverse the blood flow to his groin.

She had had such an effect on him from the first moment he laid eyes on her across a crowded pub, but it was not lust. It had never been lust. It was something more, something he had never been able to define or deny, but it was very real and still very present between them. Given the increasing ire upon her face and the tightness of her jaw, she felt it, too.

He took a deep breath and got to his feet. "Just answer the damn question, Ren, or we will be here all night, and you damn well know it." That was the thing with them, *both* of them were too stubborn for their own good and they'd butted heads more than once in an attempt to control certain situations.

****

Ren inwardly scowled. Henry had always been too stubborn for his own good and too handsome. Three years had not altered either characteristic. In fact, the passage of time may have enhanced the latter. Heaven help her.

She should have turned and run from the conservatory the moment she saw him step around the corner. He hadn't seen her. She would have had time to escape. But, oh no, why do the sensible thing? It made much more sense to speak and draw his attention so he could interrogate her in his usual "why must you do what you are doing" fashion while awakening feelings she had long suppressed.

Oh, really, Ren? More lies? You haven't suppressed a bloody thing where Henry is concerned.

In an effort to ignore her annoying inner voice and to distract Henry from his prying, she made an attempt to appeal to his ego. "You look good, Henry."

Despite the motivation behind the compliment, it was true. He was decked out in perfectly tailored black and white evening wear. His nut-brown, unruly, too-long hair eclipsed his left eye as always, and her fingers itched to push it behind his ear like she'd done so many times.

He rolled his eyes. "I will not be distracted by your attempts to flatter me."

Had she really believed he would not see through the ruse? She had never been able to fool or manipulate him, and it seemed time and distance had not altered the fact.

"What has brought you to Lord and Lady Sumner's home like a thief in the night?" He crossed his arms and braced his legs apart in a stance she knew all too well. He'd faced down foul weather, irate crew members, penny pinching merchants, and a few customs officials with that particular stance.

"Do not speak to me as if I am a mutinous crew member."

"Then cease acting like one and answer my question."

Really, did she possess the patience to go round

and round all blasted evening? She relented with a sigh. "I believe Lord Sumner has something that belongs to me, and I want it back."

Henry's golden-brown eyes narrowed. "What do you believe Lord Sumner has?"

She hesitated. Not because she did not wish him to know the answer, but because she felt like a bloody fool for having landed in her current situation.

His eyes narrowed a bit more, and he arched a brow, indicating she was close to exhausting his limited patience.

"My ship."

"Your *ship*?" He shook his head and uncrossed his arms to rake a hand through his hair. "Why do I very much doubt Lord Sumner has your ship stored in his wife's conservatory?"

Ren barely stopped herself from stomping a foot in frustration. "Do you think me an idiot?" She quickly held up a hand. "Do not answer that. Lord Sumner is in possession of my ship's registration, which technically makes him the owner. I'm here to take it back."

"You said you *believe* Lord Sumner has it, or did I mishear you?"

Ren was tempted to rake a hand through her own hair in frustration, but it was so tightly plaited, the gesture would fail to bring even a sliver of satisfaction. "Can we discuss this at some other time? This ball will not last forever, and I need to locate Lord Sumner's study—"

"Why the devil did you begin your search in the conservatory?"

"Because, obviously, I am lost." She did not, unlike Henry, have years of experience traversing the corridors of London's finest mansions. Were such large homes really necessary? Her quaint, two bedroom cottage in Cornwall had always served her needs just fine.

Henry sighed. "My inner voice is telling me to walk away and leave you to muddle through this on your own."

"But?"

"*But* when have I ever listened to my inner voice in regards to you?"

Ren could remind him of the night he left her. He had listened to his inner voice then. Well, after she had provoked it a little. *Ah, a rare moment of honesty*, her inner voice chided.

"Does this mean you will give me directions to the study?"

"No, it means, in spite of the impending sense of doom that has suddenly come over me, I will escort you to the study and help you search."

"Thank you." Without thinking, Ren laid her hands on Henry's shoulders and leveraged herself up to give him a kiss on the cheek. The act was as natural to her as breathing. Warning bells sounded in her mind the moment her mouth touched his skin, but they came too late. His achingly familiar citrus scent filled her nose as the feel of his skin imprinted itself upon her lips.

She jerked away from him, but he caught her in his arms and prevented the escape. She dipped her head and stared at the contrast of her black-gloved hands pressed to his white shirtfront.

"Please let me go, Henry."

"Ren—"

"Please."

He did as she asked, and the sudden absence of his arms made her heart cry. She hadn't felt so bereft since the night he left her. In all fairness, she had told him to leave. Or rather, she had ordered him to leave, and there may have been a gun involved, but she never would have shot him. Surely, he knew that. Shouldn't he have at least tried to convince her to allow him to stay?

She nearly cried out at the soft glide of his gloved finger under her chin. He tipped her head upward. As always, from the first moment she had seen him, her breath caught as she looked into his eyes. Perhaps they were merely brown to most people, Henry included, but to her, they were pools of chocolate laced with rich honey. The thick fan of coal black lashes only enhanced their allure. He had offered her the opportunity to look into those eyes for the rest of her life, and she had said no.

"Before I risk my freedom and possibly my life searching Lord Sumner's study, perhaps you should tell me the circumstances that led to his possible possession of your ship registration."

"Oh." She had expected him to make some sort of sentimental declaration or voice regret about the time they had spent apart, but maybe those were emotions only she possessed. Maybe he felt nothing for her anymore. Well, if that was the case, then she needed to get herself together so she would not make a bloody fool of herself at the first possible moment.

She stepped back, forcing him to withdraw his finger from under her chin. There. Yes. She could think better without physical contact. It would be even better if he would move to the other side of the conservatory so she could no longer smell him, but *c'est la vie*.

"I do not see how the details of how the registration came to be in the poss—"

"Ren." He crossed his arms again and pinned her with a steady *I'll not tolerate anything but the truth* stare.

"I got drunk and lost it in a damn card game."

"You do not drink."

He was right. She did not drink. Didn't possess the head for it. But that night she'd been drinking, and she prayed to God he did not ask—

"Why?"

"Why what?" Her question made his nostrils flare in annoyance.

"Why were you drinking?"

"Why does it matter? I was and too much, and one thing led to another, and now here I am trying to fix it." If he would cease with his questions and allow her to carry on before the bloody sun came up.

"Let me get this straight," he said, and she nearly groaned out loud.

"Henry," she interrupted before he could begin some long-winded speech more suitable to Parliament. "Can we discuss my moment of stupidity later and perhaps search for the document now?"

He did not answer. He seemed to be doing some sort of figuring in his head, which made her a little nervous, but it wasn't likely that he would actually determine that she'd been drunk because it was—

"My birthday," he announced then laughed softly. "You were drinking to celebrate my birthday?"

Celebrate? Not exactly. More like drinking to numb the memory of his existence. The previous two years she'd simply passed out and woken up the next day with a foul stomach and devilish headache. Obviously, this last time hadn't gone as well. Instead of passing out, she'd lost her bloody ship to some starched London lord who may or may not be Lord Sumner. After all, Sumner had been one of four gentlemen plying her with drinks and encouraging her to deal one more hand. She had briefly been in possession of one of their country estates until the final hand had cost her everything.

"I do not recall telling you when this card game took place."

He continued to smile like a satisfied cat. "No, but knowing how important your ship is to you, I can assume you wasted no time chasing after Lord Sumner. His lordship arrived back in London from his Cornish sabbatical yesterday so as not to miss his wife's annual ball. He was overheard complaining about the conditions of the roads due to the recent rain and having to spend a full day sitting on his arse while the coachman dug the carriage out of the mud."

Ren rolled her eyes and crossed her arms. "Is there a point to this long-winded presentation?"

"By my calculations, Lord Sumner left Cornwall eight days ago." His smile broadened, and she had to resist the urge to knee him in the ballocks. "Nine days ago was my birthday."

"And you naturally assume the two events are related?"

"Yes," he said without a bit of hesitation or doubt. "And, knowing you as I do, you probably blame me then for your current predicament."

"In a roundabout way, yes." Why deny it? After all, if he had never been born, she never would have fallen in love with him only to lose him and then have cause to drown herself in alcohol upon the occasion of his birth in an effort to numb the pain.

Chapter Two

Henry allowed Ren's admission to go unremarked, because to do otherwise would be to open wounds best left closed. The feel of her lips upon his cheek had been dangerous enough, and what had he been thinking to catch her as she attempted to escape that moment? Kissing her would have been a disaster.

"Shall we?" Ren gestured in what he assumed *she* presumed was the direction of the conservatory exit. She was wrong, of course. She was one hell of a smuggler and could read the stars better than anyone he knew, but once on dry land she had the directional skills of a dead fox. It was little wonder she hadn't found herself on the roof while searching for Sumner's study.

"Follow me." He led the way in the opposite direction of her gesture and smiled to himself as she huffed behind him.

"I am curious," Ren suddenly said, after a few moments of silence. "Why are *you* in the conservatory, alone, during a fancy ball?"

Henry silently cursed. Ren had always possessed an uncanny ability to read his moods and ascertain his thoughts. It was damned annoying at times.

He glanced over his shoulder. "These affairs can be rather trying, and sometimes a moment of solitude is needed."

"In other words, you were hiding? Interesting. I always believed London rogues, such as yourself, thrived during such events."

"I was not hiding, nor am I a London rogue." He turned back around to realize they'd reached the double doors that led to a rather expansive corridor. He hadn't a clue how they were going to get to Sumner's study without being seen. There were at least one hundred guests at the ball, and even in a house the size of Lord Sumner's, strays could be found in every nook and cranny. Most of them were couples looking for a bit of privacy.

He shot a look over his shoulder again. "This would be easier if you were dressed appropriately." Then they could simply walk, arm in arm, through the corridors.

"Oh, pardon me for not wearing my best thieving gown."

He rolled his eyes and glanced down the corridor. It was empty, but who knew for how long. He grabbed her hand and yanked her along behind him. No doubt she was none too happy to be towed along like a becalmed ship, but needs must, and he refused to allow her to traipse about Lord Sumner's home with no idea where she was going or likely any idea what to do if she managed to get there.

They reached a turn in the corridor, and Henry peered around the corner. The study was located at the end. He knew because he'd recently been inside to partake in a lovely brandy during a discussion about Cornish mining investments with Lord Sumner. Why his lordship believed Henry to be some sort of expert on the topic was a mystery, but he'd managed to offer some answers that seemed to satisfy Sumner.

"Do you know where you are going?" Ren asked as she pressed against his back to look over his shoulder.

He clenched his jaw and gritted his teeth. Her chosen attire did nothing to mask the feel of her breasts flattened against his shoulder blade. Of course, the sensation was made more intolerable by his knowledge of what those breasts felt like in his hands and under his mouth and pressed against his chest… *Christ!*

He took several deep breaths and forced himself to think of something—anything—other than Ren naked. The prospect of Miss Parish having accepted his proposal flitted through his mind, and the fire in his blood cooled instantly. She was a lovely young lady, but not once had he imagined making love to her. Yet more proof that he had never been in love with her.

His friends had attempted to snap him out of his foolish infatuation, but he had ignored them, so intent was he upon believing Miss Parish to be *the one*. He owed them all an apology for making them tolerate him for the past year.

"Well? Do you?" Ren shifted her weight against his back and laid a hand on his shoulder, actions which effectively ended any and all thought of Miss Parish.

"Yes, I know where I am going." He jerked his chin. "The study is the last door on the right."

"Good." She straightened and released him from the agony of physical contact. "What are we waiting for?"

Before he could stop her, she brushed past him and stalked down the corridor.

"Bloody hell." He darted after her and caught her just before she strolled past the billiard room. The smell of smoke wafted out from within, followed by the sudden bellow of an amused gentleman. He yanked her close and put his mouth to her ear. "Wait for me to distract them and then make your way to the study."

She nodded, then flattened against the wall the moment he released her. They made brief eye contact, nodded at one another, then he left her and stepped into the room. "Gentlemen!"

All eyes swiveled in his direction, and he casually moved away from the door and farther into the room, prompting the occupants to follow his movements.

"Westhaven." Lord Holt was the first to speak. They were acquaintances but far from friends, and his lordship's tone was a tad unwelcoming.

Henry nodded to acknowledge Holt's greeting and saw Ren dart past the door. "I thought Venton might be hiding in here, but I see that I was wrong."

"You needed to prowl the room to ascertain that? Did you think the devil might be hiding under a chair or perhaps in the fire, eh? Be right at home there, I'd say." Holt laughed at his own wit, then scowled at the assemblage when no one else joined him. Most were wary when it came to mocking Venton, Earl of Cragmoor, otherwise known as The Demon Earl, but Holt was too much of an idiot to be wary of anything.

Deeming it best to simply ignore the buffoon, Henry bowed. "Pardon the interruption, your lordships—"

"No need to run off, Westie," this from Lord Bolton who sat ensconced in a deep leather chair with a large snifter of brandy propped upon his knee. Given the loosened cravat, he seemed keen to remain right where he was for the duration. "How is your old man, eh?"

Bolton and Henry's father had been at university together and, to Henry's knowledge, had maintained minimal to no contact since. After all, a high-ranking earl would have little to say to an honorary baron. "The baron enjoys good health, I am happy to say."

"Good, good." Bolton nodded, sipped his drink, then lost interest.

Activity and conversation resumed as if Henry had already left, and he was reminded of the fact that, although his father was a baron, he, himself, was a mere gentleman and every man in the room viewed him as a lesser entity. Of course, not all titled gentlemen possessed equal degrees of arrogance, and Henry called many a lord, friend, but none of them were present. He bowed, though no one paid the gesture any mind, nor did they so much as glance in his direction as he crossed the room to leave.

He found Ren outside the door to Sumner's study focused upon the task of picking the lock. As he joined her, she shot him a triumphant smile, then opened the door. He preceded her into the room, and she closed the door behind them. The room fell into complete darkness.

"Bloody hell," Ren cursed.

"Do not move. I will find a lamp."

"Oh, you will, will you? Have you acquired the ability to see in the dark since last we saw one another?"

"No, but I've been inside this room before. I have a vague recollection of where things are, so I believe I can locate the desk without crashing into anything."

"Hmph."

Henry smiled into the dark as he imagined Ren crossing her arms and scowling at him. He took a moment to recollect his visit with Lord Sumner. His lordship had occupied a large desk with his back to a garden window.

Henry looked to his left and detected the faintest hint of light, which he deduced to be moonlight showing between a slight gap in the curtains. He fixated upon the light and cautiously moved toward it. Aside from his right leg bumping into something, he reached his destination without mishap and soon had his hand upon the desk lamp.

It was a bit more difficult to locate something with which to light the lamp, but after some rummaging around, his fingers touched the recognizable feel of a flint box. He struck it, lit the lamp, then turned and found Ren right by his side. She'd crossed the room as silent as a cat.

"I *told* you to stay put."

"You know I don't fancy taking orders from anyone, Henry, least of all you." She sidled by him to take a seat in Sumner's chair. "In which drawer would a fancy gent hide his important papers, hmm?"

"There is no rulebook for such things, Ren, but I would look in the top left." He recalled Sumner locking that particular drawer as Henry had entered the room. "It will be lock—"

"That was easy." Ren shoved both hands inside the drawer to lift out a great quantity of papers and two slim ledgers. She set all of it atop the desk and glanced up at him. "Are you going to help?"

"There is no need." He nodded toward the pile of papers. "Your ship's registration is not within those documents." He knew because the quality of paper used for the registration was much less than the fine quality of all the documents spread before Ren.

She did a cursory search but conceded to him with a nod, then returned to the drawer the papers and the ledgers. After all, Sumner was not likely to house a registration document haphazardly within a ledger like some overworked secretary, and it seemed as though Ren had concluded as much for herself.

"Kindly relock the drawer." He knew she could. Ren possessed alarming skills with a set of lock picks. He'd teased her once that if she ever grew bored of smuggling, she could retire to London and make a fortune letting herself in and out of all the Mayfair mansions. Wasn't life ironic?

She did as he asked, then moved on to another drawer. Only the one had been locked, which indicated she wasn't likely to find anything of value in the others. Though how valuable would the registration be to Lord Sumner if he'd won it on a whim during a card game? His lordship could have placed the document anywhere while emptying his pockets from that evening and forgotten all about it.

"Ren, this is a waste of time."

She looked up from a stack of papers she'd been rifling through. "If you wish to return to the ball, do not let me stop you."

"I do not wish to return to the bloody ball." He planted both hands on the desk and leaned down to look her in the eyes. "What I mean to say is this search is a waste of time. The likelihood of finding the document is slim, and you are not even certain the document is here."

She sat back in the chair and crossed her arms. "And? I should simply give up? To hell with my ship? My livelihood? The livelihood of my men? Is that what you are saying?"

"No." Henry straightened and raked a hand through his hair. "I am simply stating there must be a better way to go about this endeavor than rifling blindly through a man's desk."

"Oh, aye, my original idea was to gather all the fancy lords from that night and hold them at gunpoint until one of them coughed up the document."

"Dare I ask what made you change your mind?" Though thank God she had.

"Well, it's pointless to threaten someone with a gun if you do not intend to shoot them, and I didn't fancy being hanged for murder, so this way seemed safer."

"Safer perhaps but not efficient."

"How would you go about it then, hmm?"

"You say you lost this document in a card game, yes? Then a card game is the perfect way for you to win it back."

She narrowed her eyes at him. "I lost, Henry. Did you forget that not so minor detail?"

"You will not be the one playing, my dear." He'd probably lost his bloody mind suggesting what he was suggesting, but in for a penny in for a pound, and he knew if he did not see this through to the end, Ren would find some other dangerous means to accomplish her task, and then he'd be bargaining to get her out of prison or off the gallows.

"And what if you lose?"

"I will not."

21

Now she arched a brow. "Oh? You can guarantee such a thing?"

"Of course not, but I have a friend who possesses unnatural luck at cards. I need only convince him to join me in this particular game, and you will have your ship back." He did not feel the need to inform her that it would be more difficult to convince Sumner and the others to play a game against Venton. Assuming he could convince Venton to help him.

Extinguishing the lamp, he rounded the desk and parted the curtains to check if the garden window was locked. It sprang open and filled the room with crisp, damp air. He held his hand out to Ren. "Shall we?"

He led her into the garden, careful to avoid the lanterns lit for strolling guests. He expected a barrage of questions from her, but she seemed lost in thought and he was hesitant to intrude.

A lifetime later, or so it seemed, he was alone in his carriage, having dropped Ren at her lodgings with a promise to contact her the moment the card game was arranged. She had nodded, extracted a slip of paper from her pocket to give to him, then exited the carriage. He put his head against the squabs and let out the breath he felt as though he had been holding for hours.

For reasons that escaped him, Fate had brought Morvoren Teague back into his life, and he did not have a blasted idea what to do about it. His revelations surrounding Miss Parish's rejection of his proposal proved, quite inarguably, that he still possessed feelings for Ren. His reaction to her proximity did nothing to counter the fact. It had been hell being so close to her and not being able to touch her or kiss her, but the real hell would come when she inevitably left London to return to her life in Cornwall.

The life that did not include him.

He stared out the carriage window but saw nothing as he cursed Fate and its damnable sense of humor.

****

Upon arriving in London, Ren had gone to visit an old friend from Cornwall who kept a small set of rooms above a confectioner's shop in Piccadilly. Anne had been shocked and delighted to see her, but she'd also been in the process of packing up her things to move to a "lovely little" country cottage where she would enjoy *carte blanche* as the mistress of a man she referred to only as George. Ren pressed for long enough to establish it was not *the* George as in the king. Anne had laughed, then implored Ren to make herself at home for as long as necessary.

Henry had arched a brow when she'd given him her direction, then nodded when she had explained about Anne. That had been the only conversation between them until she stepped down from the carriage and he promised to contact her about the card game. They had parted with mutual nods and nothing more.

Ren recollected all of it while she stood with her back against the apartment door. At the memory of Henry's perfunctory nod, she sucked in a sharp breath and slid down the door to sit upon the floor. She wrapped her arms around her raised knees and took several rapid, shallow breaths in an attempt to stave off the incoming tidal wave of emotions. She shouldn't feel so strongly. She had ordered Henry out of her life. She was not supposed to want him back.

A shiver worked its way through her body, and she clenched her teeth as her eyes began to burn. No. She would not cry. She was Morvoren Teague, captain, smuggler, leader…

The room blurred, and she dropped her forehead to her knees and surrendered to the pain that had clutched at her heart since the moment Henry appeared before her in the conservatory. Seeing him, being with him, arguing with him, almost kissing him, all of it had stoked the inner fire she had so desperately tried to put out since the moment he left. It burned hot as ever, and, Lord help her, she wanted to bask in the heat forever as it fed her soul and ignited her passion.

But all of this would end. She would get her ship back, because she knew Henry, and he would not fail her. Then she would have no reason to stay in London. They would say goodbye and return to their separate lives, and she wondered if his would be as cold and empty without her as hers would be without him.

Chapter Three

Dearest Readers,

This Season has been equal parts Scandal and Success. I did not believe it could become more exciting after last month's "secret" wedding of the false Vicomte B and his Lady of Great Wealth, but alas, it has. It seems Mister H.W., whom we all know has been pining for the oh so lovely Miss A.P. since last season, finally proposed during Lord and Lady Sumner's annual Floral Ball. The dashing gentleman got down on one knee, in the conservatory, amidst Lady S's prized roses and offered his heart and a ring set with a pale sapphire to match Miss A.P.'s eyes. So romantic, yes? Sadly, Miss A.P. did not seem to think so. The young miss refused the ring, the proposal, and Mister H.W.

Rumor has it, she is holding out for a title, a common enough endeavor to be sure, but this author cannot help but wonder if that was the only reason behind the rejection. Far be it for me to disparage a gentleman's reputation, especially one as charming and well-liked as Mister H.W., but events that took place after Miss A.P. rejected him leave this author wondering if Mister H.W. has been living a lie more damning than that of the oh so false Vicomte B.? Is no one who they seem to be? Are all the fine gentlemen of London wearing masks we dare not look behind?

It would seem so…

Henry nearly choked on his tea as he reread the column. "What the bloody hell is this writer insinuating?"

He had passed a horrible night of little to no sleep, plagued by dreams of Ren, only to awaken fatigued and in a foul mood. The last thing he needed was a bloody gossip column insinuating… Well, he did not quite know what the devil it was insinuating.

"Good morning, Henry old boy." Bramley Venton, the Earl of Cragmoor, simply Bram to Henry, and *only* Henry, strolled into the room without the benefit of having been announced.

Henry glanced up, and the adage misery loves company sprang to mind at the sight of his friend. Bram, not known for his sunny disposition, seemed in a particularly dark mood.

"Dear God, you didn't murder my butler, did you?" Danvers, although a very good, loyal servant, was bloody terrified of Bram. The man made himself scarce as a mouse in an alley full of cats whenever the earl called, which was often.

"Why the devil would I murder your butler?" Bram crossed the room and took a seat to Henry's right. As he did so, he gestured to the paper held aloft in Henry's grip. "Did you see the bit about you? Riveting, eh?" Bram helped himself to a sip of Henry's tea, then instantly spat it back into the cup. "Damnation, that's awful."

"Perhaps you should act like a civilized human being and wait for me to ring for a fresh pot?" Henry set down the paper, belatedly realizing it was a tad early for his friend to be up and about. "Why the devil *have* you emerged from your crypt earlier than normal?"

"You have that wrong, my friend, I've yet to return to said crypt."

Henry glanced at the mantel clock. "It's half ten, for God's sake."

"Maintaining my status as Dark Lord of the Nobility can be rather exhausting." Bram's tone oozed with disdain. Henry knew how much his friend loathed the moniker and the other equally non complimentary ones that plagued him. "But I'm not here to discuss me." Bram pinned Henry with one of his infamous, coal-black, unblinking, and damn unnerving stares. "You've been the topic of some rather interesting conversations these past few hours."

"Bon matin, mes amis."

Both Henry and Bram looked in surprise as their friend Adrien Cloutier, formerly known as Vicomte Benoit, strolled into the room. The man, recently married to one of the wealthiest women in the realm, should be rusticating with said woman in the country.

"What the devil are you doing here, Adrien?" Henry demanded as his friend took the seat opposite Bram. He looked well, not that Adrien had ever looked poorly, but there was a depth of happiness in his eyes that hadn't been there prior to his marriage.

"That thrilled to see me then, eh?" Adrien nodded toward Bram without taking his eyes off Henry. "I am here for the same reason as Venton."

"To murder my servants, drink my tea, and ravish my maids?"

Bram scoffed. "When have I ever ravished your maids? And I did not murder your damn butler."

Henry waved away the protests and looked to Adrien. "Why are you in London? Tired of married life already?"

"Not at all." Adrien reached for the tea pot.

"I wouldn't," Bram warned.

Rolling his eyes, Henry stood to ring for the elusive Danvers.

"I am in London," Adrien began, "because Lady Dunston cornered us in our lair, convinced my wife of some long-standing relationship with her late grandfather, then proceeded to coerce Eirene into agreeing to attend her annual ball."

"How in blazes does anyone coerce your wife to do anything?" Bram inquired.

"It startled me as well, *mon ami*, but Eirene has been acting strange of late. Not poorly but restless. She's of the mind now to have the unused guest rooms refurbished. That is no less than six rooms, gentlemen." Adrien shook his head. "As for the rest of the place, she wants all new carpets and drapery installed before winter and the south block of the stables to be turned into a gallery of sorts." He held up his hands in surrender. "I have no idea what has come over her."

"You, my friend," Bram said with a wink. "Or rather, *in* her, I should say, because it sounds as though your wife is breeding."

"*Mon Dieu*, Venton, my wife is not a horse, and it is much too soon for her to be with child. We have only been married—"

"Only takes one time, my friend," Bram informed him.

Adrien sat back in his chair with a rather stunned look upon his face. *"Mon Dieu."*

Henry reached over to clap him on the back. "Relax, this is good news."

"Perhaps we should leak it to the papers to distract the gossips from Henry's exploits." Bram's suggestion seemed to snap Adrien out of his shock.

He looked to Henry. "The very reason I am here. I overheard Venton's remark about the rather interesting conversations as I walked in, and he is not wrong. No less than three gentlemen accosted me on my ride here to ask if I had heard. When I inquired what I was meant to have heard, they filled my ears with rather shocking tales."

Henry looked at the paper next to his plate. He'd grown accustomed to being gossiped about in the society column, but one did not wish to be the topic of "some rather interesting conversations" among peers. He glanced back and forth between his friends. His stomach already churned with the prospect of what he might hear. "Tell me."

Bram shook his head. "Before we relay what I presume is utter nonsense, perhaps you should simply tell us if you were, indeed, skulking about Lord Sumner's corridors with a young gentleman in tow who may or may not be the type of young gentleman to encourage other gentlemen to engage in practices they should most definitely not engage in outside the privacy of their own abode."

"Bloody fucking hell." Henry's foul curse echoed about the room. But really, what else could he possibly say to such an accusation? "I believe you had better tell me *exactly* what you heard."

Bram shrugged. "I basically just did. You were seen, hand in hand, moving about Sumner's corridors,

29

in a rather covert fashion, with a young, comely, tight-arsed gentleman, and it has led to much speculation about your supposed infatuation with Miss Parish this past year." Bram narrowed his eyes. "Is it true that she rejected your proposal?"

"Yes," Henry answered through gritted teeth. "She wishes to marry a title, and I cannot inherit my father's honorific."

"Ah, pity that." There was not a drop of sympathy in Bram's reply. After all, he'd been the most vocal in the anti Miss Parish campaign. "Perhaps she would wish to marry mine?" The earl was in great need of a bride in order to secure his recent inheritance, but the common born Miss Parish would do him no good, and they both knew it. Likely, he'd made the suggestion simply to test Henry's reaction.

"Even if she was a lady born and said yes to you, you would destroy her inside a fortnight."

"Oui, c'est vrai," Adrien murmured.

Bram clapped a hand over his heart in a dramatic display of mock offense. "Are the two of you suggesting I cannot be trusted with the delicate sensibilities of a virgin?"

"No," Henry countered, "but Miss Parish is too young and too naive to marry a cynical bastard such as yourself. She'd likely throw herself from Cragmoor Keep's battlements simply to escape your dark moods."

"Cragmoor Keep does not technically possess battlements, nor am I a bastard, much to my late father's eternal disappointment, but your point is valid." Bram arched a brow. "And yet you deemed her good wife material for yourself? Though allow me to observe you do not seem all that bothered by her rejection."

"I was wrong about the first, and you are right about the second. I am unmoved by her rejection, because it made me realize I never loved her."

"Well, hell," Bram murmured. "I could have told you that one year ago and saved you the price of a ring."

"You did tell me. I simply did not listen."

"You did not listen to any of us," Adrien reminded him.

"Yes, yes, lesson learned." Henry flicked his gaze to the door as Danvers suddenly appeared. "Where the devil have you been?"

"Begging your pardon, sir, for my delay, but there was a small fire in the kitchen."

Henry waved away the excuse, mumbled an apology for his temper, then requested fresh tea and a small pot of coffee for Adrien. Danvers bowed and scurried away without once glancing in Bram's direction.

"Why is that man so convinced I mean to do him harm?"

"Because rumor has it you possess a dungeon at Cragmoor filled with the corpses of servants who have displeased you," Adrien supplied.

Bram's raven-wing brows flew upward. "These rumors become more colorful by the day, do they not?" He returned his attention and the conversation to Henry. "Speaking of, how did this rumor of you and a young gentleman actually start?"

Henry had been trying to answer a similar question since reading the not so heavily veiled accusation in the gossip column, but he'd yet to come up with any—Bloody hell!

"Ren," he announced.

Bram looked at him as though he'd suddenly gone mad. "Owl."

"Quail," Adrien added.

Henry glared at both of them. "No, you bloody fools, not the bird. Morvoren Teague."

"Ah. Her." Of course, Bram knew all about Ren. Whether he wished it or not, he'd been the sole recipient of Henry's drunken laments about their doomed relationship and his shattered heart and lost soul and whatever other drivel he'd spouted that night. Bram might have profited as a romantic poet had he thought to write it all down.

"You have me at a disadvantage, *mes amis*. Who is Morvoren Teague?"

"The Mermaid," Bram said simply.

"Aaaah."

Bram met Henry's dark glare and shrugged. "What? He asked why you were skulking about, so I told him you'd had your heart broken by a female smuggler known as The Mermaid."

"Her ship is called the Mermaid, not her," Henry clarified.

Bram waved a hand. "And you boarded both, so I see no difference."

Adrien barked out a laugh, then shot Henry an apologetic look.

Henry chose to ignore Bram's idea of humor. "I was with her last night."

Bram shook his head and held up both hands in surrender. "You've lost me, Henry. Why were you with Ren, of all people, and what does that have to do with you being a rumored—"

"Do not," Henry interrupted before his friend could give voice to the damning rumor.

Bram acquiesced with a nod. "I trust you will explain how all of this is related?"

"Ren was dressed like a man."

"Of course, she was, being the unnatural creature that she is." Bram directed the latter at Adrien.

"Ren is not unnatural," Henry protested.

Bram ignored Henry and continued to address Adrien. "The woman runs her own smuggling gang, dresses like a man, and lured our friend in like a siren, then spit him out when she'd had her fill. What do you call that if not unnatural?"

"Independent?" Adrien offered, and Henry gestured and nodded in agreement.

"Yes, well," Bram continued, "if that is what helps you sleep at night, do not allow me to dispel the myth. Might I inquire why Ren was at Lord Sumner's ball dressed in breeches?"

"Trousers, actually, and I would prefer not to relive the foolish reasons behind her behavior."

"And I prefer not to leave until I have the full story, and I imagine Adrien feels the same, *oui*?"

Adrien concurred with a nod just as Danvers entered the room with a tray bearing the requested tea and coffee. The butler did not offer to pour, and Henry allowed the man to escape without comment or reprimand.

Bram helped himself to a steaming cup of fresh tea. "I believe you were about to explain the foolish reason behind Miss Teague's behavior?"

Henry sighed. "She was there to burgle Sumner's study."

"Of course, she was. And you, being who you are, offered to help her. Am I close?"

"You are not close. You are annoyingly correct." Henry had rarely known his friend to be wrong.

"And what, pray, did the two of you steal?" Adrien asked as he sipped his coffee.

"Nothing. She was searching for the registration for her ship, which she lost in a card game to one of four lords. Sumner was one of them."

"And the others?" Bram and Adrien asked the question in unison.

"Holt, Wexler, and Keene." The names had been on the paper Ren had given him before exiting the carriage.

"Three of the most insufferable men to ever exist." Adrien's opinion received a nod of agreement from Bram.

Henry nodded as well. "Yes, quite, and it was Ren's plan to break into all of their homes until she found her registration."

"Or until she was caught and thrown in prison," Adrien offered. He arched a brow at Henry. "I assume you convinced her to abandon her plan?"

"Yes. I told her I would get the registration back for her."

"How?" Bram asked, and then, before Henry could reply, he shook his head. "No."

"I haven't requested anything of you yet."

"But you mean to. You plan to win the damn document back in a card game, and you want me to make certain you succeed. Am I close?"

"Again, you are annoyingly correct."

Bram shook his head with enough vehemence to

send his long, black hair cascading over his shoulder. "You could fleece those fools with your eyes closed. Why do you need me?"

"As insurance. I do not trust them not to cheat."

"The three of them combined do not possess the cunning needed to cheat at cards," Bram snarked.

"Bram."

His friend cursed. "Why should I help that woman? She destroyed you, Henry."

He chose to ignore Bram's latter observation. "You would not be helping her. You would be helping me."

"It is the same bloody thing." Bram shoved a hand through his thick, black hair. "Bloody hell, if I say no, you will do it without me, and Lord knows how that will end. Already, the woman has destroyed your reputation and all but put a noose around your neck. Why not land you in debtor's prison as well?"

"What happened to me being able to fleece those three gentlemen with my eyes closed?"

"Under normal circumstances, yes, but involve Ren and your common sense and instinct for self preservation seems to go on holiday." It was logic Henry could not argue.

"You will owe me for this, Henry," Bram went on. "In fact, you can repay me by supplying the funds to fix Cragmoor Keep's roof."

"Done," Henry agreed without hesitation.

Bram nodded. "And do not forget the gargoyles."

"There are no gargoyles on Cragmoor Keep," Adrien interjected.

Bram reached for his tea and smiled for the first time since entering the room. "Not yet there aren't."

"*Touché.*" Adrien saluted Bram with his coffee

cup, then turned to Henry. "All of this is rather fascinating, *mon ami*, but what of your more pressing problem? These gentlemen will not agree to share a gaming table with you if the vile rumors are not dealt with."

"Yes, I know." Henry raked a hand through his hair. "How the devil am I going to fix this?"

"Ah, well, that's simple, isn't it?" Bram spoke up. "Put Ren in a damn gown and squire her about to a few functions. It shouldn't be difficult for you to summon a proper display of infatuation."

"I am not infatuated with Ren."

"Of course not," Bram agreed. "You are in love."

"You would not know love if it bit you on the arse, Venton." This from Adrien.

"Perhaps not, but I might learn to love a woman willing to bite my arse."

Henry glared at Bram in exasperation. "Not a visual I wish to have at my breakfast table, thank you very much."

Adrien laughed at the exchange, then brought the conversation back around. "Your Ren can accompany us to Lady Dunston's ball. I believe she and Eirene will get along famously."

"It is a kind offer, but Ren will never agree to any of this."

"She will if she wants her ship back," Bram said, and Henry, again, could not argue the truth of the statement.

****

After a restless night of little sleep and unwanted dreams, Ren carried a pot of very strong coffee to Anne's small breakfast table along with the paper,

36

which had been delivered with a resounding thump at the door. She hoped the combination would clear her head and distract her from persistent thoughts of a certain tall, too handsome for his own good, insufferable, stubborn, meddling, honey-eyed—

She flicked the paper open with enough force to tear the page. Sipping her coffee, she skimmed for something diverting and found the gossip column. Normally, she would not read such drivel, but she hoped it would provide some amusement and it did not disappoint. Whoever Mister H. W. was, he had not had a very good night either. First, a rejected marriage proposal, and then he had obviously engaged in some form of behavior that led the author to suggest he had been living a lie that may or may not have been the reason for the rejected marriage proposal.

Ren tried to reason out what the author might be insinuating. Perhaps the man was already married? A fellow smuggler had attempted to keep two wives, one in England and one in France, but the whole ordeal had, quite literally, blown up in his face when his French bride discovered the truth and met him at the coast with a gun. The story had made its rounds as a cautionary tale against marriage and a warning never to allow women near firearms. Ren had rolled her eyes at the latter but had been assured by her men that she "weren't no natural woman, so the rule didn't apply to her." How thoughtful of them.

She returned her attention to the column, which went on to mention a few more amusing anecdotes about the guests at Lord and Lady Sumner's floral—

Ren's eyes flicked over the name again. *Sumner*.

She was no expert on British nobility, but she

assumed there were measures in place to avoid duplicate titles, which meant the article gave reference to events that transpired within the home of *the* Lord Sumner. Which meant…

She read the article again, and her earlier amusement diminished.

The dashing gentleman got down on one knee, in the conservatory, amidst Lady S's prized roses…

Ren set down her coffee with a bit more force than necessary.

The conservatory.

Mister H. W.

She stared across the room at the small red and green floral pattern of Anne's wall covering. Henry had been in the conservatory and very deep in thought as she recalled. Had he been contemplating Miss A.P.'s rejection? The column claimed the lady in question wished to marry a title. Henry did not possess a title presently, but she did not know if he would inherit his father's title. She had never asked, because her feelings for Henry had not depended upon such things. Obviously, Miss A.P. felt differently and had rejected Henry because of it.

Assuming Mister H.W. was, indeed, Henry.

She read the article again.

It seems Mister H.W., whom we all know has been pining for the oh so lovely Miss A.P. since last season, finally proposed…

Pining? Ren knew from experience that Henry did not *pine* or beg or make a fool of himself in any way for a woman. She flicked the paper closed, satisfied the Mister H. W. of the very bad evening was *not* Henry. After all, it was not as though Henry was the sole owner of the initials, H. W. There were likely dozens of gentlemen with those initials.

Feeling foolish for her momentary unease over the gossip, Ren reached for her coffee just as a knock sounded at the door. Without thinking, she went to answer it. The sight of Henry robbed her of speech. She would have been less shocked to see Napoleon.

"We need to talk," Henry said in lieu of a more civilized greeting, then brushed by Ren to enter the apartment.

Ren closed the door and scowled at the way Henry filled the small space with his presence. He shed his riding cloak, hat, and gloves, and she saw he was attired quite casually in brown trousers, a plain, black waistcoat, white shirt, black cravat, and black riding boots in need of a good polishing. It also appeared as though he hadn't taken the time to shave that morning, and her lungs burned as she forced herself to breathe normally.

This was Cornwall Henry. *Her* Henry.

She gripped the door handle a bit tighter as if seeking an anchor in a storm and forced herself to speak. "I assume you've arranged the card—"

"You assume wrong." He raked a hand through his already tousled hair.

"Did you ride here?"

He looked at her as if she'd gone mad, and she could not blame him given how asinine was her question. She knew well Henry's preference to be on horseback in lieu of "staring at a horse's arse from a bloody cart," as he'd once told her.

"How is Poseidon," she asked as she conjured an image of the large, white stallion that Henry treated with more affection than most people gave their own children.

"He is well and currently costing me a king's ransom to be held by an enterprising urchin."

"What did you promise the lad?"

"The lad is a lass, and she's got her eye on some fancy frock in the shop across the street not to mention a sweet tooth for nearly every type of candy in the confectioner's shop."

Ren smiled. "A gown and a few bits of candy are a small price to pay not to have Poseidon stolen."

"Aye, normally you'd be right about that, but she hasn't got her eye on a gown. She wants to blend in with the lads, so she says, and to do that it obviously requires a suit of fine black wool, a new pair of boots, and silk hat."

"A girl after my own heart."

"Yes, well, your preference for trousers has created a situation I would very much like to have go away."

"You are speaking in riddles, Henry. You know I do not like riddles." She brushed by him. "Do you want coffee?"

He snared her arm and spun her to face him. "Listen to me. We were seen together last evening at Lord Sumner's, and it has created a very damaging rumor." The seriousness of his tone got Ren's full attention.

"What sort of rumor?"

He released her arm and raked his hand through his hair again. "The type no gentleman wants to have attached to his name."

"I will need a bit more than that, Henry."

He sighed. "Gossip is putting it about that I have

been living a lie, and that tidbit has grown into a rather outrageous tale that you were a young gentleman entertaining me in a most inappropriate fashion last evening."

"I see." She turned away and returned to the breakfast table where she proceeded to pour a fresh cup of coffee. Her hand trembled, and the pot knocked against the cup. Coffee splashed onto the white linen tablecloth, and she thought how upset Anne might be if she could not remove the stains.

All the while blood roared in her ears as she replayed Henry's words in her mind. Her gaze fell upon the paper and its exposed gossip column. She mustn't jump to conclusions. The paper had said nothing about a young gentle—

"Ah, so you've seen the gossip." He reached around her and took up the paper, then grunted and tossed it back onto the table. "According to my friends this little *on dit* has made me the talk of the clubs." He pointed directly at the column she'd read no less than six times.

Ren wrapped her arms around her body. She'd become very cold all of a sudden. Henry had been in the conservatory to propose to another woman. The reality of that left Ren debating if she should smack him, order him to leave, or cast up her coffee all over his riding boots. She pressed a hand to her stomach, fearful her body would make the choice for her.

"Good Lord, Ren, what the devil is the matter? You've gone green all of a sudden." Henry reached for her and guided her to a well-worn sofa in the sitting room. He did not sit beside her but instead went down on one knee before her. As he had evidently done in order to propose to Miss A.P. He'd not done so three years ago when he proposed to her. He hadn't even gotten out of bed. He had simply pulled her naked body on top of his and said, "Marry me."

Her first reaction had been to laugh until she had realized he was serious. Then she had said, no and told him to leave…

"We are on a bloody ship. Where do you want me to go?"

"Just leave." Ren rolled out of bed and took the sheet with her. She didn't want to be naked in front of him. Not now. Not when she felt like he'd just exposed the very core of her being with his stupid proposal. Why did he have to ruin everything?

"I refuse to leave until you explain why you said no."

"What is there to explain? You asked. I said no. Is that not how proposals work?"

He left the bed and stalked toward her in all his naked glory. Damn him. He took hold of her arms. "Generally the answer is yes when two people love each other, or are you going to claim you don't love me?"

Ren wriggled free. "Of course, I love you, and you damn well know it, but I cannot marry you."

"Why?"

"Why? My God, Henry, are you daft?" She gestured around the cabin. "I am a smuggler."

"As am I."

"No," Ren shook her head. "No, you are not. You are the son of a baron playing at being a smuggler. There is a difference."

"This is not a game to me, Ren." His tone had

gone hard.

"Nor is it your way of life," she countered. "If this ship is taken, you return to a life of privilege while my men and I hang."

"You are wrong. I would be just as guilty as you and the men."

"As if your father would hang his only son." She shook her head. "We are different, Henry. Too different."

"If that is your only excuse for rejecting my proposal, I do not accept it."

"I do not belong in your world, you stubborn fool! You are a gentleman. How would it look if your bride was a smuggler? Marrying me would ruin you."

He took hold of her again and gave her a little shake. "Not marrying you will ruin me." His words were like a dagger through her heart.

"Please go." Again, she wriggled free and stepped back to put some distance between them. Though, at the moment, the entirety of the bloody English Channel would not have been enough distance. Not when she could see the reflection of her breaking heart in his eyes and knew he felt the same pain that was trying its damnedest to choke her.

He crossed his arms and braced his legs apart. The stance was made no less intimidating by his nudity. "I am not going anywhere. I proposed. You said no. Very well. Nowhere in there do I see a reason to bloody leave."

Ren reached behind her and felt the pistol that lay atop the desk. She drew it forward and aimed it at Henry's bare chest. "Go."

He laughed. "Or you will shoot me?" He sobered

when she cocked the pistol. "Bloody hell, Ren, have you gone mad?"

"I swear to God, Henry, go."

"Ren, you are being ridic—"

"I will count to ten."

Without a word, but with a glare that seared her soul, he pulled on his trousers, grabbed his shirt and boots, and stalked to the door. He turned at the last moment. "If I walk out this door, you will never see me again. Is that what you want?"

Ren struggled not to cry and struggled harder to hold the gun steady. "Go."

And so he had.

True to his word, she hadn't seen him after that. Not on the ship. Not at the dock. Not anywhere. Well, she had seen him nightly in her dreams but not physically until she had accidentally entered Sumner's conservatory.

The room swayed around her as she looked up from the floor and into his concerned gaze. "Do you love her?"

He blinked and drew back in obvious confusion. "Who?"

"Miss A.P." *The woman you bloody proposed to.*

"Oh, her. No. Not at all."

"The gossip claimed you pined for her for a full year." Good Lord, why did she insist upon having this conversation? What did it matter how he felt or did not feel about Miss A.P.? She had literally forced him out of her life at gunpoint. She had no right to question any involvement he may or may not have with another woman.

"I believed myself in love, but I was not." He stood

up. "You look well enough now."

Did she? Because she felt as if she were drowning in the stinking Thames.

"To return to the matter at hand…" he began, as if the subject of Miss A.P. had been closed. "Seeing as how helping you landed me in my current predicament, it only seems right that *you* help *me* get out of it."

Ren blinked and tried to clear the fog from her mind. "How?"

"Simple." He smiled, but it did not quite reach his eyes. "From this moment forward, I am officially courting you."

Surely, she had misheard him. "Say that again."

"I am officially courting you."

All right, so she had not misheard him. "Is this part of your plan to get my ship's registration back, because if it is, I cannot see how—"

"Have you not been listening, Ren?" He shoved a hand through his hair in agitation.

She really wished he would cease with that oh so familiar gesture, because each time he did it, she wanted to throw herself in his arms and kiss him until the world ended.

"Ren." He snapped his fingers in front of her face, then stalked away. He returned moments later and thrust a steaming cup of coffee beneath her nose. "I've never seen you so out of sorts. Maybe this will help you remain focused."

She took the coffee and glared at him. "I am perfectly focused, thank you very much, and waiting for you to explain what your ludicrous announcement has to do with my ship."

"There are more important matters than your

bloody ship at the moment."

"I beg to differ."

"My life, Ren." He hunkered down in front of her. "Do you deem that a tad more important than your ship?"

"My ship is all I have."

"And whose fault is that, hmm?"

Ren battled with the urge to throw the hot coffee in his face. "I appreciate your flair for dramatics, Henry, but your life is not in danger because of a silly gossip column full of vague suggestions and ambiguous initials. I cannot imagine anyone actually believes any of it."

"You would be surprised how many people take what they read in the gossip column as gospel, and I do not care to be the topic of such lurid, damaging speculation."

"Those who know you would never believe such talk."

"Of course not, but it is not that simple." He strolled into the kitchen and returned with a cup of coffee. He sat next to her on the sofa, as if it were the most natural thing in the world to do. "In Society, one is guilty until proven innocent, and such speculation will not only ruin me but also my family." He looked at her. "If you agree to this farce of a courtship, all of this can be put to rest."

"And would it be?"

He narrowed his eyes in confusion. "Would what be what?"

"A farce?" She gripped her coffee cup a bit tighter and tried to decide if she wanted him to say yes or—

"Yes, of course. It need last no longer than it takes

to clear my reputation, and once I am no longer *persona non grata*, I can make good on my promise to regain your registration."

"In that case, perhaps we should simply make love in the street right now." She tossed that salvo in his face in lieu of the coffee, but it seemed to have the same scalding effect. He gaped at her as if he could not understand why she might be angry, and really, why the devil was she angry? Did she want a real courtship? Of course not. She did not want any of this, and that included Henry. All she wanted was her bloody ship.

You continue to tell yourself that, Ren, and perhaps you'll come out of this ordeal only slightly wounded.

Chapter Four

"So, I am to finally meet the infamous Ren, eh?" Bram lounged in a plush armchair within Henry's bedchamber as Henry attempted to perfect his cravat. The silk seemed determined to thwart his efforts.

"Yes," Henry said as he lifted his chin to check the knot. Dissatisfied, he scowled and tugged at the silk to begin the process again. "I hope I do not need to tell you to be on your best behavior." He met his friend's gaze in the mirror. "In other words, Ren need not know that you have any prior knowledge of her existence."

"Ah." Bram's lips spread into a slow, somewhat devious grin. "Very well. I shall refrain from revealing the details of your drunken confessional."

Henry trusted Bram with his life, but he did not trust him not to make his life more of a living hell than it was at present. "I have enough problems, so kindly do not add to them."

Bram held his hands up in surrender. "You have my word." He scoffed and left the chair. "For God's sake, we shall be here all night at this rate." He batted Henry's hands away from the mangled cravat, then quickly tied an expert, but far from ornate, knot. "You should invest in a valet or have Danvers trained to do more than run and hide when guests arrive."

"Danvers only hides when you arrive." Henry smoothed the ends of the cravat and frowned. "This is a rather informal knot."

"Yes, and you are welcome."

Henry let the matter go. He did not have time to argue knots with Bram. He gestured to his small jewelry box that contained four pair of cufflinks and three cravat pins. "Which pin to do you suggest?"

"Do I look like bloody Beau Brummel to you?"

"Honestly?" Henry selected the ruby cravat pin. It would be a nice bit of color in his otherwise black and white attire. "You look like a highwayman."

Bram nudged Henry out of the way so he could use the mirror. He smoothed a hand over his long, black hair, tugged at the bottom of his expertly tailored black evening jacket, shot the cuffs of his black shirt, then adjusted the knot of his black cravat. A diamond cut onyx winked from within the folds. "I shall don my mask later to complete the look." He winked at Henry. "Perhaps I shall lie in wait outside the ladies withdrawing room and kidnap a bride."

"Considering your failure to secure one by traditional means, I fear you may have to." It wasn't that Bram lacked female admirers. Quite the contrary, the problem was none of them wished to actually marry him. Perhaps it was a lack of desire to become mistress of the crumbling Cragmoor Keep, or perhaps it was a lack of desire to become the countess of an earl rumored to have been born of magic.

Bram scowled at his reflection. "I will do what I must, because I refuse to allow my father, may he burn in hell, to win this round."

"Before you don your mask and resort to kidnapping, have you given any thought to any of Lord Worley's daughters? The man has six. He must be desperate to marry them off." If Henry recollected correctly, four of them were passably attractive, perhaps even pretty. He had danced with a few of them, though he could not recall their names or their personalities, but surely, one of them would be able to tolerate Bram and all that came with the marriage.

"Oh, aye, the Worley litter as they are so affectionately called within the clubs." Bram turned from the mirror to look directly at Henry. "My father made it perfectly clear in the will that my bride is to be a lady born *and* virtuous. Worley's daughters can lay claim to the former, but none of them can claim the latter."

Henry arched a brow. "Do you know this through personal experience?"

"Of course not. You know I don't dally with virgins, but Holt likes to boast about his conquests, and it seems he deflowered three of the six sisters."

"Clearly, half the Worley females lack taste. And what of the other three?"

"Two of the three are engaged and the remaining sister, the eldest, resides in the country to be close to the child she had two seasons ago. Rumor has it, Wexler is the father. He denies it, of course, but it wouldn't be the first bastard he's fathered and abandoned during his hunt for a wealthy bride."

"How is it that I do not know any of this?"

"Because, my friend, you spent the last year following Miss Parish around like a whipped hound."

"Yes, thank you for the reminder."

"Do you suppose Miss Parish will be in attendance this evening?"

"I have not given it a thought." His mind had been

consumed by one thing and one thing only. Ren. She plagued his thoughts during the day and haunted his dreams at night, which left him in a constant state of frustrated hunger.

"Well," Bram went on, "if it's a title she fancies, she won't likely miss tonight's ball. Lady Dunston is known for coercing the who's who of London to her affairs." He met Henry's gaze in the mirror once more. "I still cannot believe she managed to lure Adrien and his bride from their country nest."

"Nor can I." Henry's thoughts drifted, once more, to Ren who was currently in the care of Adrien and his bride. Adrien had assured Henry that his wife would delight in having Ren accompany them to the ball. He'd gone on to say the two women were likely to get along famously. Oh, aye, Henry had thought, two strong-willed, independent, alluring females.

God help London Society and he and Adrien as well.

"Will you make introductions?" The question scattered Henry's musings. "Miss Parish and Ren," Bram clarified.

Henry recalled Ren asking if he was in love with Miss Parish. At first, she had seemed ill, but then her temper had flared, and he had ended his visit in haste given Ren's tendency to brandish weapons when angry. At the time, he'd assumed her anger had been prompted by the necessary delay in his plan to retrieve her ship registration, but perhaps he'd been wrong about that. Perhaps she'd been angry about Miss Parish, though he had assured her he had never loved the girl.

"I suggest you do not."

He narrowed his eyes at his friend. "Do not what?"

"Good God, Henry, cease your woolgathering and pay attention. I suggest you keep Miss Parish and your Ren well away from one another."

"For God's sake, Bram, you sound as if you believe they will engage in a bout of fisticuffs to win my affection."

"Or your Ren will simply shoot Miss Parish," Bram suggested, then looked thoughtful. "Lady Dunston would delight in the publicity, and it would certainly alleviate the boredom of another tedious ball."

"She is not *my* Ren, and I appreciate your desire to have something exciting happen at this evening's ball, and perhaps it shall, but it will not involve Ren, Miss Parish, or myself." After all, both women had made their feelings quite clear upon being proposed to. Ren had even emphasized her rejection with a gun. No, Bram, for all of his rumored intuition and ability to divine the future, was wrong.

Miss Parish and Ren had no cause to be enemies.

****

"Cease fidgeting." Lady Eirene Rowe-Weston smacked Ren's hands. "You will upset the lay of the fabric if you continue to pluck at it in such a fashion."

Ren dropped her hands and stared at her reflection in the mirror of Lady Rowe-Weston's, or Eirene as she insisted upon being called, lush bedchamber. She had liked Eirene instantly, recognizing a kindred, independent soul. When Eirene assured Ren she had the perfect gown for Lady Dunston's ball, Ren had trusted her. However, three days later and faced with her reflection, she had begun to have doubts about the gown and a few about Eirene's intentions.

She frowned at her reflection and attempted to

pluck at the bodice again, but Eirene captured both her hands and secured them behind her back as one might do to a criminal.

"I said no more fidgeting, and why are you frowning? The gown is beautiful. You are beautiful. The combination is breathtaking. Stop frowning."

Ren could not help but smile at the militant tone of Eirene's voice. The woman ran her household the way Ren captained a ship. "The gown *is* beautiful, but—"

"No, no, no. I will not allow you to have doubts." Eirene released Ren's hands, then moved to her side so they were both reflected in the mirror. Eirene stood several inches shorter and possessed the russet coloring of a fox, a smattering of fetching freckles, and a bosom that made Ren more than a little envious. The woman was like a rich, vibrant painting come to life, and standing beside her, Ren felt very pale and very flat.

"Eirene, be reasonable." Ren returned her focus to the mirror. "I may not know all the rules and whatnot of proper society, but my gut warns me this gown is scandalous."

Eirene scoffed. "I would never purchase a gown that would be deemed scandalous."

"And yet you have never worn this one."

"No, I have not, because I, unlike you, do not possess a willowy frame that allows the fabric to cascade the way the dressmaker intended."

"But the color—"

"Was never right for me, but it is perfect for you," Eirene interrupted. "With your black hair and those green eyes and your milk-white complexion"—she fanned herself—"men will collapse in agony as you walk by."

Ren laughed at Eirene's dramatics, then studied her reflection again. The gown was, indeed, beautiful, and Eirene was correct about the scarlet fabric acting as the perfect complement to Ren's coloring. She wondered what Henry would think— No! What Henry did or did not think did not matter. If she allowed it to matter, she would find herself on a path she did not wish to walk ever again.

She focused on the gown once more. She did rather like the way the draping of the bodice enhanced her subtle curves and the drop sleeves drew attention to her swan-like neck, to quote Eirene, and yes, the fabric did cascade like a scarlet waterfall of wispy muslin down the length of her legs to then form a short train.

"Admit it," Eirene said as she smiled. "You look beautiful."

"I will admit I look different. None of my men would recognize me if they saw me now."

"And Henry? Has he ever seen you in a gown?"

Ren recalled the one time she had donned a gown per Henry's request. The dress had been plain, modest, and black and had led to a rather exhilarating evening spent in bed with the gown on the floor. "Yes, he has," she finally answered.

"Hmm, I sense a story there, but keep your secrets if you wish." Eirene winked, then clapped her hands. "You need jewelry." She vanished from the mirror's reflection, and Ren turned to track the woman's progress across the room. She rummaged in the box from which she'd chosen her own jewels for the night, a pearl choker with matching earrings and bracelet that proved the perfect complement to her midnight blue gown.

"Ah ha!" She returned to Ren's side with a strand of small black pearls that she dropped over Ren's head in a way that created a slim choker and a fall of beads against her bosom.

Eirene stood back and clapped her hands. "Perfect!"

Ren ran her fingers over the beads. They were probably worth more than anything she'd ever worn and the sort of treasure she likely would have sought had she lived during the golden age of piracy. She met Eirene's gaze in the mirror. "They are beautiful."

"Yes. My husband had them in his possession when he arrived from France." Eirene fussed with the fall of the necklace, the beads of which seemed to change color as they moved "I haven't any matching pieces, but I believe the necklace will suffice alone." She stood back and gave Ren a thorough onceover. "If Mister Westhaven does not fall to his knees and profess his love for you, then he is either blind or the most foolish man alive."

Ren had no idea what to say in response to Eirene's words. They had talked about Henry, though Ren had made certain to reveal nothing of the regret and longing she felt for the past three years, but perhaps Eirene had perceived it. The woman seemed to possess unnatural powers of observation when it came to reading people's expressions and body language.

Eirene suddenly took hold of Ren's hands, and their gazes met. "I know what it is like to pretend you do not feel what you are feeling. I tried so desperately to convince myself that I was not falling in love with Adrien." She laughed and shook her head. "It was like trying to ignore a military invasion." She squeezed

Ren's hands. "My point is, if it is meant to be, it will be, no matter how much you fight it."

Ren extracted her hands. "Henry and I are not meant to be."

The hollowness of the words rang around the spacious room and the emptiness in Ren's heart.

Chapter Five

Lady Dunston's ball was a maddening crush, and yet, Henry stood alone. Bram, despite his excitement to meet the "infamous Ren" had gone off after the scent of a potential bride, leaving Henry to deflect the sideways glances and not so subtle whispers. He sipped his champagne and pretended not to notice, but his patience nearly snapped as a gamboling gentleman careened into him and stepped heavily upon his left foot. To make the moment worse, the man wore heels as if it were the bloody eighteenth century. Henry gave the man a light shove that set him back on course without so much as an apology.

"Brave of you to make a showing, what?" The words came with a solid thump to Henry's back, and he turned to find Lord Wexler smirking at him. The man was dressed in shades of orange from his jacket down to his stockings, and Henry wondered if he had overlooked some fine print upon the invitation that stated all men must dress as buffoons.

"Wexler," he said with a nod. "You look…interesting."

"Ah, yes, quite." The man smoothed his hands down the orange waistcoat. "We all know Lady Dunston loves a bit of color." He eyed Henry's traditional black and white attire. "I can understand your desire to go unnoticed, however, what with the rumor and all." He winked and thumped Henry on the shoulder again. "Never believed it for a second, Westhaven." Wexler shook his head. "But still, it's a damn bloody jam to be in, and I thought perhaps I'd show a bit of support for you, eh?"

Henry was not certain if Wexler's tangerine-colored person was the sort of support he needed or wanted, but he merely smiled and nodded to acknowledge the offer. After all, he might glean some useful information from the man, seeing as how he was one of the four gentlemen in possible possession of Ren's registration.

"It might please you to know that talk has shifted a bit," Wexler went on. "Seems there's a bit of a debate as to the identity of your young friend, eh?" Wink. "As you might imagine a few blokes sat up a little straighter at the mention of a tight-arsed young gent."

Oh, the hypocrisy, Henry thought as he took another much needed sip of champagne.

Wexler, of course, continued to talk, seemingly unaware that he was engaged in a one-sided conversation. "Of course, the running bet is Kilby—"

"Kilby is currently with family in the country and is a friend of mine, so I suggest you choose your next words very carefully, my lord." It was known only to a select handful of Kilby's friends, Henry and Bram among them, that Kilby did not fancy female companionship, but as the only male child in his family, he was determined to do his duty, find a bride and produce an heir or two. A task which would be near to bloody impossible if Wexler and his crew destroyed his already fragile reputation.

Wexler's blond eyebrows flew upward, and he

clapped a hand to his chest. "You mistake me, my friend. I merely pass along information."

"Then see that you pass along whatever information necessary to remove Kilby's name from the conversation and perhaps mention he is close to proposing to Lord Huxley's daughter."

"Huxley's daughter, eh?" Wexler looked mildly impressed. "The girl is a bit bookish, but that should make her easier to manage, eh? It's the beautiful ones that run wild." Another wink. "Kilby and Huxley's daughter, eh? It's a good match, and the family properties join up there in the wilds of Yorkshire if I'm not mistaken." Wexler rubbed his chin. "Aye, very good match. Keane will be disappointed to learn the gel is off the market. Had his eye on her, he did. He hopes to snare an obedient wife who won't fuss about all the other women he keeps."

Henry made a mental note to send word to Kilby about Keane's interest. The match was as good as settled between Kilby's father and Lord Huxley, but it did not need Keane stepping in to throw around his ridiculous wealth and arrogance.

"And who do you have your eye on?" Henry asked out of mild interest.

"Ah, well, I'm not dressed like this for nothing, my good man." Wexler thumped Henry on the shoulder again, and the gesture not only irritated but it had begun to cause pain given the proximity of the thumps to a gunshot wound that had never really healed. "It is my hope Lady Dunston will permit me to court her niece."

"I see." Henry, who had not known Lady Dunston possessed a niece, suddenly felt sorry for the girl.

"Rumor has it, she is a fetching little piece with

dark hair, blue eyes, and large…" Wexler gestured and winked. "Not to mention the fortune her aunt is likely to settle upon her."

"She sounds lovely. I hear you were in Cornwall recently?" If Henry must be made to suffer Wexler's company, he might as well steer the conversation into useful territory.

Wexler arched a pale brow. "I was, yes. It's good to take in a bit of sea air now and then, eh? But I don't have to tell you about the benefits of the sea, now do I?" Another wink, then Wexler looked around and moved a step closer. "Is it true you are no longer in the game, as they say?"

"I haven't a clue as to what game you refer."

"Oh, come now, Westie. We are mates, yes?"

No, but Henry held his tongue.

"It's common knowledge you did a bit of—" Wexler glanced around again before continuing in his hushed tone—"smuggling."

"Ah, that game." Henry sipped his champagne while Wexler stared at him in anticipation. Rather like a spaniel awaiting a treat. After several moments of silence, Wexler nodded and chuckled.

"Yes, yes, it's best not to admit to such things out loud, eh?" The man moved another step closer, and Henry felt the weight of a few interested stares. Thankfully, Wexler's reputation as a womanizing cad would prevent gossip from using the man's proximity as more proof of Henry's supposed indiscretion.

"I might have a go at it myself," Wexler all but said into Henry's ear. "Smuggling, I mean. I recently acquired a ship."

Henry had never been so grateful of Wexler's

annoying need to talk about himself.

"And," Wexler went on in his conspiring whisper, "it's full of goods."

Henry stepped back so he could look Wexler in the eyes. "Is that so?"

"Oh, aye, though I barely had time to take a peek. The crew was a bit testy." Wexler tugged on the bottom of his orange waistcoat. "I plan to return to Cornwall as soon as possible and take possession of the vessel. Won it in a card game if you can believe it."

"Is that so?" Henry said again, merely to keep Wexler talking, though it was unlikely his lordship would reveal the whereabouts of the registration.

"Oh, yes, from a *lady* smuggler, no less. A real beauty she was, too. Can't recall her name." He tapped index finger to chin. "Not a real name of course. Ah! The Black Mermaid." Wexler frowned. "Maybe that is the name of the ship. Regardless, the lass almost took Holt's country estate off him, but he managed to win it back. Poor thing, the lass, I mean, couldn't hold her alcohol, and it was almost too easy when she dropped her ship's papers onto the table. Felt a little bad for winning that final hand."

"But not bad enough to refuse the winnings."

"Lord, no. A bet is a bet, Westie, and a gentleman always—" Wexler broke off as his gaze wandered. "Bloody hell, how did Lady Dunston manage to lure Lady Rowe-Weston and that fraud of a husband out of hiding, and who the bloody hell is the raven-haired goddess with them?"

Henry followed the direction of Wexler's wide gaze and saw Adrien at the entrance to the ballroom with his wife on one arm and Ren on the other. At least

Henry assumed it was Ren. The raven-haired goddess, as Wexler so aptly called her, bore little resemblance to the Ren Henry knew. She wore a gown of striking scarlet that made her skin look like poured moonlight. He winced at the ridiculousness of his analogy.

"If there is a God," Wexler breathed into Henry's ear, "that woman will be wealthy and in want of a titled husband."

"How quickly you forget Lady Dunston's niece."

Wexler shook his head. "No matter how large the gel's tits are, she cannot possibly hold a candle to that"—he gestured toward Ren—"sort of beauty." He proceeded to smooth his waistcoat and shoot his cuffs. "Wish me luck, Westie, old mate."

Henry shoved his champagne glass against Wexler's chest, halting his forward progress. "Sorry, Wexler, but she is spoken for."

Henry released the glass, and Wexler had no choice but to take possession of it or have champagne spill down his orange breeches.

****

Despite the crowded ballroom, Ren found Henry instantly. Their eyes met, and she was transported back to the first moment she'd ever seen him. It had been in a crowded pub in Cornwall. She and her men had stood in the back, drinks raised in celebration of a particularly successful run, when she'd glanced toward the bar and been snared by a pair of dark eyes. The voices around her had become nothing but a monotonous roar of noise. Her heart had stuttered hard against her chest, and she had struggled to breathe normally.

All the while, Henry had continued to look at her in a way that made her feel as if no one existed in that moment but for the two of them. And then he had moved toward her, and she had ceased breathing until he reached her, took her hand, and said, "Where have you been my whole life?"

Her men had hooted, unaware that, in that moment, Ren's heart and soul had dropped anchor as if finally finding a safe harbor in an everlasting storm.

He moved toward her now just as he had then with focus and determination. The crowd parted and stared after him in avid curiosity. It did not take long for their gazes to lock upon Ren, and her skin prickled at the sudden rush of unwanted attention.

"It seems Henry has seen us," Adrien remarked at her side. She heard the humor in his voice, but she could not take her eyes off Henry.

He looked incredibly handsome in his black and white evening attire with his unruly hair flopped over his left eye. Most men would have tamed those wayward locks with pomade but not Henry. He detested the smell as much as the idea of trimming his hair short, and she was glad of it. She loved the feel of his silky hair sliding through her fingers as it resisted her attempts to tuck it behind his ear while they—

She ended the thought abruptly, but not before it caused a wave of heat to creep over her skin. She snapped open her black, feathered fan and waved it in front of her face, grateful to Eirene for the lessons that had seemed silly at the time.

Henry reached the stairs, climbed them two at a time, and halted before her. Without a word, he held out his hand.

Ren ceased the movement of her fan as Adrien let out a huff and spoke quietly. "Henry, this was not the plan."

Several guests boldly edged closer.

"The plan has changed." Henry answered his friend without looking away from Ren. "Wexler is on the hunt, and I'll not have Ren act as unwitting prey."

"Wexler?" Ren scanned the ballroom beyond Henry's shoulder.

"He is the one in orange," Henry supplied.

"Oh…my." The last time she had seen Wexler, he had not been dressed quite so…brilliantly.

"The man is a fool," Adrien said, "but why is he dressed like that?"

"He hopes to gain the affection of Lady Dunston's niece," Henry explained.

"By dressing like a mango?" Adrien laughed. "The woman is obsessed with peacocks not tropical fruit."

"Lady Dunston does not have a niece." This bit of information was given by Lady Rowe-Weston who caught Ren's attention behind her husband's back, then rolled her eyes and mouthed the word, "*Men.*"

Henry turned his attention to Eirene and bowed. "Allow me to say how beautiful you look this evening, my lady."

Ren resented the whisper of jealousy that coursed through her as Henry paid court to Eirene. Why had he not said as much about her appearance? She worked her fan again out of irritation, and the snap of the feathers seemed to catch his attention. She looked away from his gaze and unfortunately clashed with that of Wexler. The man smiled and bowed then moved in her direction.

"Blast it! I made eye contact." She looked at Henry. "Will he recognize me?"

"I barely recognize you." He frowned as he said it, and Ren refused to allow the expression to concern her.

"Perhaps you should ask Ren to dance, Henry," Eirene suggested, "before Lord Wexler has the opportunity to beg an introduction."

Ren would have preferred to swim among sharks than dance with Henry, but she smiled, accepted his arm, and allowed him to lead her away from Eirene and Adrien.

As they walked through the crowd, Ren's attention was caught by the avid, unblinking, wide-eyed gaze of a petite blonde dressed in a high-waist, white, gossamer gown that enhanced her ample bosom and the natural rosiness of her complexion and doll-like features. The woman's pale, golden hair was piled artfully upon her head and woven through with white ribbon. She needed only a pair of large, white wings to complete the angelic presentation.

Ren offered a smile but did not receive one in return. It seemed the angelic appearance only went skin deep. As she and Henry moved away, she felt the heat of the woman's stare searing into her back, and she glanced over her shoulder just as the woman turned to address an older woman by her side.

"I was not expecting you to choose such a bold gown for your first foray into Society." Henry's comment drew Ren's attention from the two women.

"Eirene assured me the gown is quite appropriate."

"For a siren, perhaps," Henry muttered.

Ren scowled at Henry's profile. "Do not be ridiculous."

Given that she had already seen no less than four women in gowns so transparent as to reveal details she would rather not know about their bosoms, she found his remark rather unjustified.

"Everyone is staring at *you*."

She glanced around to find not *all* but a great many pairs of eyes fixed in her direction. "Perhaps they are staring at you? After all, you are the flavor of the week in the gossip column."

He flashed an irritated look at her, then returned his attention to maneuvering them through the crowd without incident. Not an easy task, Ren realized, as she held her gown's train close to her legs to avoid the more careless and unobservant guests.

"Are these events always this crowded?" She sidestepped a woman, apologized for nearly bumping into a gentleman, and almost screamed as she found herself confronted by a...peacock? "What the devil?"

"Lady Dunston harbors a fondness for peacocks."

Ren stared into the bird's black, glass eyes. It had been mounted on a small pedestal that allowed it to stare directly back at her. Its impressive multi-colored tail had been immortalized in full display.

"Her ladyship is quite renowned," Henry went on, "for the larger than life sculptures that grace her garden and the half dozen or so peacocks that reside in her conservatory." He shook his head before she could speak. "Guests are not permitted inside the conservatory during a public event, but it is where Lady Dunston receives callers."

"And you have had cause to be received by Lady Dunston?"

"Of course. She and my mother are dear friends."

"Henry, darling!" The enthusiastic greeting interrupted them and preceded the appearance of a striking, older woman dressed in a breathtaking gown of emerald green and deep blue. The tall peacock feathers arranged in her silver coif gave her away as none other than, Lady Dunston.

Henry smiled and bowed gallantly over the woman's hand. "You look ravishing as always, my lady."

Lady Dunston blushed like a young debutante and playfully smacked Henry's arm with her peacock feather fan. "Your mother raised a dangerous rogue, she did." Her sky-blue eyes narrowed as they suddenly settled upon Ren. "And who do we have here?"

"Morvoren Teague, my lady." Ren curtsied just as Eirene had trained her to do. Personally, she detested all the bowing and scraping necessary in such company, but she detested more the idea of embarrassing Henry.

"Hmm. Teague, you say?" Lady Dunston's tapped her closed fan against her chin. "Any relation to Jack Teague of Cornwall?"

"I am his daughter, my lady."

Lady Dunston nodded as if Ren had confirmed a suspicion. "You have the look of him about you, though, I imagine, those eyes of yours came from your mother because the Jack Teague I know has eyes as brown as English soil."

"I had no idea my father had such illustrious friends."

Lady Dunston laughed and playfully batted at Ren's shoulder with her fan. "In fairness, I was not born illustrious, but I was born in the same Cornish village as your father, my dear. I hope he is well?"

Henry's arm stiffened beneath Ren's hand. "Sadly, he passed some years ago."

"Oh, my dear, forgive me." Lady Dunston laid a hand upon Ren's arm. "Is it safe to assume you and Mister Westhaven claim a long-standing acquaintance?"

"Yes, my lady."

Lady Dunston nodded, then turned to Henry. "I shall never forgive you for hiding her away for so long."

"It was not intentional, my lady," Henry countered with a bow.

"Perhaps, but now I must consider whether or not to forgive you." Lady Dunston returned her attention to Ren and scanned her person. "You are a veritable siren in that gown, my dear."

"Yes, Henry accused me of the same."

"Ren," Henry said under his breath.

Lady Dunston laughed, then focused on Henry. "What is this I hear about you and a young gentleman?" A few of the nearest guests cocked their heads in obvious anticipation of his response.

He cleared his throat. "It was nothing more than a—"

"It was me," Ren interrupted.

Lady Dunston's gaze widened and shifted to Ren. "Pardon me?"

"It was me. I was dressed in men's clothing, and Henry did nothing more than escort me from Lord Sumner's home." It seemed close enough to the truth.

"Dare I ask *why* you were dressed in men's clothing, my dear?"

"I lost a wager, my lady." Again, not too far from the truth.

Lady Dunston looked to Henry. "Is this true?"

"As unbelievable as it sounds, yes, Miss Teague is telling the truth."

"Hmm." Her ladyship gave Ren another thorough onceover. "I do not find it unbelievable at all to imagine Miss Teague engaging in a wager that would lead to a lark involving men's attire."

Ren hadn't a clue as to whether or not the lady's words were an insult or compliment, and she was not deaf to the sudden cacophony of murmuring voices as those close enough to hear likely spread the tale throughout the ballroom.

"I mean that as a compliment, my dear," Lady Dunston assured her, then winked. "Back in the day I possessed a bit of a wild streak myself." She glanced at Henry. "Ask your mother, my dear boy, to tell you the stories." She winked again, then gestured with her open fan. "I am neglecting my other guests." She met Ren's gaze. "We must have tea together in the near future, my dear. I believe an afternoon spent in your company will be much more titillating than those I must endure in the company of others." To Henry she added, "I do wonder why you wasted a year in a doomed pursuit of that dull Miss Parish when you are acquainted with a glorious creature such as Miss Teague." She flashed a warm smile at Ren, then bid them both a good evening.

"Well," Henry began once Lady Dunston was lost to the crowd. "I would say that was an—"

"Hello, Henry." The cultured, soft, feminine voice halted Henry's words and made him turn. Ren followed suit to find none other than the angelic woman in white who had ignored her greeting moments ago. The woman's bright blue eyes went from icy to warm as they shifted from Ren to Henry. She held out her hand to him.

Henry accepted the gesture and bowed. "You look lovely as usual, Miss Parish."

Ren ground her teeth as she realized she stood face to face with *the* Miss Parish of Henry's rejected proposal. As ashamed as she was to admit it, even silently to herself, Ren had attempted to conjure an image of what Miss Parish might look like. She had guessed blonde and blue-eyed and pretty, but she had not anticipated someone quite so *young*.

"Are you going to introduce me to your friend?" Miss Parish asked, and the ice returned to her gaze as it settled upon Ren.

Ren did not wait for Henry to do the deed. "Morvoren Teague, my lady."

She offered the slightest of curtsies, and Miss Parish trilled like an annoying bird. "Oh, dear, I am not a lady. No, no. I am simply Miss Annabelle Parish."

Until you marry the title you desperately seek.

Ren forced a smile. "It is a pleasure to meet you, Miss Parish."

"Likewise, Miss Teague." Miss Parish's tone said otherwise, but her smile never faltered. "Are you recently come to London?"

"Oh, yes, at the behest of Lady Rowe-Weston." She smiled as Miss Parish's gaze widened. "She and I are *dear* friends." One need not always use a dagger to stab one's opponent.

"I see." Miss Parish, who seemed a bit pale of a sudden, looked to Henry. "It is kind of you to offer escort to your friend's wife's acquaintances."

"Oh, no, no." Ren continued to smile as Miss Parish shifted her attention back in her direction.

"Henry and I have been acquainted for *years*. It's rather a coincidence that one of my dear friends married one of his."

"I see." Miss Parish's fixed smile finally began to falter. "How lovely." She gazed up at Henry. "I will save a set for you if you wish?"

"Of course." His words brought some color back into Miss Parish's cheeks.

Ren scowled. It had been Henry's idea for her to attend this ball in an effort to repair his reputation, and he intended to abandon her to dance with Miss Parish? The fingers of her left hand curled against her skirt, and she felt the outline of the dagger strapped to her thigh. Eirene's eyes had widened at the sight of the weapon while helping her dress, but in lieu of a scold, she had hiked up her dark blue skirts to reveal her own dagger tucked into her garter.

Ren's smile at the memory was short-lived as Miss Parish fluttered her pale eyelashes at Henry. She stroked the outline of the dagger, then froze. Bloody hell, she was jealous. Why? Henry was not *hers*. He could dance with whomever he pleased. She did not care. If he preferred the company of an infant cherub, who was she to interfere? She only needed him in her life for as long as it took to regain her ship's registration. Beyond that—

"Annabelle, my darling," an older woman suddenly appeared beside Miss Parish like a large frigate pulling alongside a skiff. She wore an alarming amount of face powder, a bronze, silk gown with a bodice more suitable to a woman half her age, and a towering turban of matched silk decorated with seed pearls and a large brooch that boasted the worst replicated diamond Ren had ever seen. She also wore an expression of obvious distaste as she looked at Henry.

"Mister Westhaven, how do you do?" The greeting had all the warmth of a frozen lake.

"Mrs. Parish, always a pleasure to see you."

Ren bit her tongue to prevent the laugh that bubbled in her throat at the obvious hostility between Henry and the woman, who must be Miss Parish's mother. Ren felt as if she'd been dropped into a Shakespearean play.

"And who is this…*creature*?" the woman asked as she shifted her attention to Ren. Her watery, blue eyes were not quite as bright or beautiful as her daughter's. They raked over Ren with blatant disapproval. Before Henry could offer an introduction, Mrs. Parish waved a bejeweled hand in the air. "Do not bother with introductions. It hardly matters, and we really mustn't linger any longer. Annabelle is in high demand, you know." She took hold of her daughter's arm and hauled her away.

Ren thought she overheard Miss Parish telling her mother that Ren was dear friends with Lady Rowe-Weston. If the woman replied, the words were lost to distance and the incessant hum of other conversations.

"That woman is a gorgon."

Ren arched a brow. "I assume you mean the mother?"

"Of course, I mean the mother."

"And yet you were going to marry her daughter. Her very young daughter, I might add." She ignored his frown. "Exactly how old is Miss Parish? Sixteen? Seventeen?"

"Nineteen, which is more than old enough to—"

"Yes," she interrupted. "It is quite old enough to do a great many things, but you would never suit with a bride that young."

"You sound like Bram," he growled.

"Bram?"

"Bramley Venton," Henry clarified.

"Venton... Ah, Venton. Yes, of Cragmoor Keep. The witch." Ren recalled Henry speaking about his dearest friend and the adventures they'd had together as young boys.

"Never let him hear you say that."

Ren recalled something else Henry had said. "Venton is the friend you referred to in regards to the card game, is he not?"

"Yes, but I believe there has been a change of plans." He led her to a slightly less crowded corner of the ballroom that displayed a potted palm and stuffed peacock.

She reached down to pet the bird's little blue head—

"I wouldn't do that. Lady Dunston nearly had a guest shot for touching one of her birds."

Ren snatched her hand back and smiled at the image of Lady Dunston defending her precious birds with a loaded pistol.

"Wexler has your registration," Henry announced without preamble, and Ren forgot all about birds and Lady Dunston.

"How do you know this?"

"He told me all about the card game and his new ship and his yearning to have a go at smuggling."

"That popinjay would not last two seconds on a smuggling ship." His crew would toss him overboard.

"Yes," Henry agreed, "but Wexler believes his birthright makes him capable of doing anything he pleases, and it seems to please him at the moment to consider a career in smuggling, but that is beside the point."

"Oh? I must disagree considering it is my ship he plans to use."

"He cannot use what he does not possess."

Ren rolled her eyes and crossed her arms. "A lovely sentiment, Henry, but he does possess my ship."

"For the time being, yes, but knowing he is the one with the papers makes it much easier for us to take them back. There is no need now for the subterfuge of a card game."

"Are you suggesting what I believe you are suggesting?"

"As much as I hate to admit it, yes, I am suggesting we steal the papers from him."

Ren's heartbeat increased. "We should do it now while he is otherwise occupied."

"No, no. If we leave this ball and then he discovers the missing papers, he might put two and two together."

"The man cannot even put together a suit of evening attire, Henry."

"Be that as it may, we will wait for a better opportunity. Wexler has a busy social schedule, so it will not be difficult to find him out of his home for extended periods of time. Trust me."

"Yes, yes, I trust you." And she did, perhaps not with her heart but certainly with— "Oof!" Her thoughts fractured as someone crashed into her from behind. She stumbled, tripped on her hem, and landed in Henry's arms as he extended them to prevent her from falling.

The stuffed peacock was not so lucky. It wobbled, then crashed onto its side to promptly have its beak snapped off.

Ren twisted within Henry's embrace to stare in horror at the damaged bird. "Oh, God, Henry, we broke the bird." She attempted to wiggle free, but he held her tighter, and she shot a frown at him. "Let me go so I can find the beak before someone steps on it and—" She registered the look in his eyes and the fact that he held her in his arms. "Henry?"

He said nothing, but the intensity in his gaze spoke volumes, and it made the vast ballroom vanish and with it the noise of the guests and most likely her common sense.

"Henry?" She whispered his name, and he pressed his index finger to her lips. In that moment, there was nothing she loathed more than the requirement of gloves in polite society.

"You are so beautiful." As he said the words, he moved his finger along her lips, then cupped her cheek with his hand. "Tell me you've missed me as much as I've missed you."

"Henry, I—"

"No lies, Ren." His fingers found her nape and crept up under her hair.

She leaned into the touch and almost moaned out loud. "Yes, I have missed you."

Without warning, he released her, took hold of her hand, and hauled her out of the corner and through a nearby set of doors. She shivered as they stepped onto a large terrace that overlooked a beautiful garden. She barely had time to register the statues Henry had referred to earlier before he gripped her shoulders and spun her to face him.

She looked into his eyes and read his intent. Her inner voice yelled at her to protest, to demand he put a stop to his foolish behavior before things got out of hand. Before he did something neither of them would recover from.

"I want to kiss you, Ren."

"I know."

"Tell me not to."

She put both hands behind his head and pulled him forward for a kiss three years in the making.

Chapter Six

The voice in Henry's head, the one that ruled his intuition and had kept him safe during his ill-advised stint as a smuggler, railed at him for kissing Ren.

Stop touching her.

Get away from her.

For the love of God, you are a fool.

The voice was right, of course. It was always right. He was a bloody fool, but only upon the threat of death, and maybe not even then, would he have released Ren in that moment. Especially given how she melted into his embrace, twisted her hands in his hair, and opened her mouth with unabashed eagerness. It was a blatant invitation and one he could not refuse.

He slipped his tongue into her mouth, and she moaned at the invasion while tightening her grip in his hair and moving her body against his.

God, give him strength...

Without breaking contact with her mouth or body, he managed to walk her backward until the terrace wall stopped their progress rather abruptly. She gave a little "oomph" of surprise, and he mumbled an apology while continuing to kiss her.

The voice in his head spoke up to warn that they weren't private, that there would exist a better time and place, and for the *love of God*, consider the consequences.

Henry ignored it. Nothing existed for him but the taste of Ren's mouth and the feel of her in his arms. He did not give a damn about the risk of discovery or their reputations. He had the woman he loved in his arms, and Society and its opinions could go to hell.

He moved his hand down her body to hook her leg over his hip. As he pressed closer to her, he fought the obstruction of her skirts and recalled her penchant for wearing trousers and how they allowed him to fit himself against the heat of her body in a simulation of lovemaking that had always made them both mad with desire and impatience.

He clawed at her skirts. He wanted—no, he *needed* to feel her heat.

The fabric gave way. Perhaps Ren helped. He did not know, nor did he care. He pressed forward and fitted himself between her legs. Christ, when had she hooked both legs around his waist? She moved with him and gasped his name into his mouth.

"My God, Ren," he begged between kisses. "I can't stop."

"Don't," she breathed. "Don't stop."

He fumbled between their bodies, freed himself from his trousers, tested her readiness, and pushed inside her glorious heat. She ripped her mouth away and buried her face against his neck. He felt the heat of her breath through the infernal layers of cravat and collar. He pushed deeper, and she expelled a muffled sound of pleasure.

"My God, Ren, I—"

A startled feminine shriek split the air behind him.

Ren jerked her head up and their eyes met.

"Bloody hell," was all he could think to say.

Ren clutched Henry's lapels as he began to withdraw from her body. "No, don't move," she ordered in a low whisper. He froze, and she took hold of her skirts, then lowered one leg to the ground. "All right, but slowly."

He eased his body away from hers, and she adjusted her skirts in the hopes of maintaining some semblance of decency.

It seemed to take a lifetime before he stepped a few paces back and she could get both her feet on the ground and shake her skirts out. She looked at his expression, expecting to see a flash of humor in his eyes, but his gaze was hard and deathly serious. Her stomach dropped. She knew that look. It was his "I wish I hadn't done that" look. She'd seen it once before, after she had rejected his proposal.

"Mister Westhaven!" The unmistakable voice of their hostess cut through the air, and Ren saw Henry wince. "I have not been this personally offended since Lord Holt used one of my birds as target practice in a misguided display of his manly abilities that proved to be lacking."

Ren bit her bottom lip to prevent herself from defending Henry's manly abilities, then glanced around Henry's shoulder to see Lady Dunston, red faced and trembling with enough rage to cause her headdress to sway as if the feathers danced to some unheard music. It seemed the woman who had invited Ren to tea had been replaced by a paragon of Society caught in the throes of abject horror.

A crowd had gathered behind Lady Dunston comprised equally, it seemed, of male and female guests. The former seemed nonplussed, but the latter waved their fans and exchanged whispers and eyed Ren as if she'd slithered into their garden party uninvited with the intent to have her way with every man present.

Henry, having arranged his clothing, finally turned to address their hostess. "I do beg your pardon, my lady. It is with great regret that I have caused you any offense." He offered a bow. "We shall take our leave."

Lady Dunston charged forward to smack Henry on the chest with her peacock feather fan. "Of course, you will take your leave, young man!" Another smack. "And you will make an honest woman of Miss Teague, or I will make certain your name is scratched off every invite for the remainder of the Season and those to come. And do not believe my close association with your mother will prevent me from doing so. She would expect nothing less of me." She emphasized her terms with several more smacks of her fan, then cursed like a sailor when she realized her actions had bent a few feathers. "Bloody hellfire and damnation! Look what your behavior has made me do."

Ren continued to bite her bottom lip and tasted blood in her efforts to remain silent. She feared speaking up would only make the horrible moment worse.

"Of course, my lady," Henry agreed, then offered another bow.

Ren shifted her gaze to Henry. Of course, what? What had he agreed to?

"Good, good," Lady Dunston nodded, then folded her damaged fan and clutched it against her bosom. "I expect the deed to be done in no less than a fortnight."

"A fortnight, my lady? Such haste would require a special license, and I fear I lack the proper connections to make such a request."

"Pah! I'll not tolerate your excuses, young man. Nor will your mother once she hears of your behavior. I will see to it that you have your license, and you will see to the matter of making this woman your bride. And that, as they say, is that."

"Very well, my lady."

Ren gaped. Very well? *Very well*? Had Henry just agreed to marry her? She pushed away from the wall and stepped around Henry. Silence be damned.

"I do believe I should have some say in this matter." Her words elicited shocked gasps from the assemblage and an unrelenting stare from Lady Dunston.

"You, my dear," Lady Dunston addressed her, "made your opinion *quite* obvious when you did not stop Mister Westhaven from taking such *public* liberties."

Ren snapped her mouth shut. It did not seem a good time to inform Lady Dunston that she had all but begged Henry to kiss her and that what had followed had been quite mutual.

She glanced down as Henry took her hand and squeezed it as if he knew she longed to shoulder some, if not most of, the blame.

In the face of Ren and Henry's silence, their hostess turned to address her guests. "There, do you see? That is the proper way to deal with such things, unlike Lady Palmer's poor handling of a similar incident."

Ren wondered if Lady Dunston referred to Eirene's failed attempt to get herself ruined by her now husband or some other scandalous incident, but she did not ponder long. Her true concern was to obtain some privacy so Henry could assure her there would be no mar—

Her thoughts ended abruptly as a collective murmur filled the air and people began to turn their attention back toward the ballroom. The unmistakable sound of inconsolable, feminine sobs could be heard.

"Oh, for heaven's sake, now *what*?" Lady Dunston pushed her way through the crowd. "Remove your hand from that bird, or I will personally chew off your fingers, young man! Now who is responsible for that incessant caterwauling?"

Ren grabbed Henry's sleeve the moment they were no longer the center of attention. "Please tell me you are not serious."

He finally looked at her. "Now is not the time or place for this discussion."

"Now is the perfect time for—"

"No." He removed her grip upon his arm only to place her hand on his elbow so he could lead her down the terrace stairs to the back garden.

"I thought we were told to leave?" Ren hiked up her skirts to avoid the moist grass that edged the narrow, gravel path.

"We are, but I would like to avoid the ballroom."

"But my cloak—"

"I'll buy you a new one," he snapped.

Ren shot him a scowl, but of course he did not see it. "Why are you so angry? I can understand embarrassed, yes, but—"

She tripped on loose gravel as he suddenly halted their progress and turned on her. "*Why* am I angry?"

"Yes, that was my question." Ren dropped her

skirts and smoothed out the wrinkles. Really, such high quality fabric was not meant to be so manhandled.

"Never mind the bloody gown!" Henry took hold of her shoulders and gave her a little shake to gain her attention. "I am angry, because when I am with you, I seem incapable of making wise decisions."

"That is not my fault."

He released her and threw his hands in the air. "Just once, Ren, just one time, I would like you to take responsibility for your actions."

"*My* actions? What happened back there"—she gestured toward the terrace—"was not entirely my fault."

"Those were *your* legs around my waist."

"After *you* pinned me to the bloody wall!"

"*You* kissed *me*!"

"You gave me *that* look!"

"Yes, fine, but none of that would have happened if you had chosen a different gown!"

"A different gown? You are blaming all of this on the *gown*? Would you have attacked Eirene had *she* decided to wear this gown this evening?"

He rolled his eyes. "Do not be ridiculous, and I did not attack you. If anyone attacked anyone, you attacked me." His gaze shifted. "Bloody hell."

Before she could look to see what had prompted the curse, he took hold of her arm, and they continued down the path and away from the house.

"Henry—"

"Enough. We will discuss this later. We've generated enough gossip for one night."

"Mission accomplished, it would seem."

He did not reply as he continued to haul her

through the garden as though she were a child discovered where they should not have been. After several moments of being towed about, she'd had enough and dug her heels into the gravel and yanked her hand free.

Henry halted, spun around, and glanced at the long, black glove that dangled from his fingers then at Ren. Whatever he saw on her face made him sigh. "Forgive me for hauling you about in such a fashion, but I have no desire to linger here a moment longer than necessary. Surely, you can understand that?"

She did not know if it was his tone or the look in his blasted, golden-brown eyes, but she simply could not summon any sort of angry retort. "Very well."

In all honesty, she wished to put the entire evening behind her, as well.

Henry held out his arm, and she accepted. Their rather long walk from the garden to the mews was conducted in a companionable silence that was interrupted only when he offered her his jacket. She snuggled into the garment and attempted to ignore the spicy, citrus aroma that clung to the fabric lest she initiate another scandalous display.

Chapter Seven

Dearest Readers,

Well, well, well, Lady D's ball certainly did not disappoint those who hunger for gossip. Under different circumstances, I might use this opportunity to mention the questionable attire of Lord Wx and his interest in the nonexistent niece of Lady D, but I am certain Lord Wx will entertain us at some future event, and it would be remiss of me to speak of anything other than what occurred with Mister H.W. and his mysterious, raven-haired companion. Rumor has it the mysterious woman is a close acquaintance of Lady R-W, a long-time acquaintance of Mister H.W. and none other than the reported young gentleman who was seen in Mister H. W.'s company on the evening of Lady S's floral ball.

Yes, yes, I admit it is quite a lot to take in, but let us focus on what could be considered the *incident of the season. I speak of Lady D's discovery of Mister H.W. and his lovely companion* in flagrante delicto *upon her garden terrace. It is rumored that not since Lord H. attempted to kill one of Lady D's precious, stuffed birds has her ladyship appeared quite so infuriated. She demanded Mister H.W. make an honest woman of his companion, going so far as to remind Mister H.W. of her close acquaintance with his mother.*

For those who may not know, the combination of Lady D and Mister H.W.'s mother could, quite possibly, defeat Napoleon if given the chance.

Ah, I mustn't forget to mention the lovely and innocent Miss A.P., whom you will recall rejected the marriage proposal of Mister H.W. mere days ago. It seems the scandal involving Mister H.W.'s shocking display of affection for his mysterious companion was too much for the young woman to handle. Rumor has it, after an alarming display of hysterics, Miss A.P. had to be carried from the ballroom by none other than Lord Wx...

"They should rename the paper *The Life and Exploits of Mister H.W.*"

Henry glanced up from the paper as Bram strolled into the breakfast room still attired in last evening's clothing. "Is this to be a new habit of yours?"

"What's that?" Bram took a seat and reached for the tea pot.

"Joining me for breakfast," Henry clarified.

"I haven't decided yet, but if you continue to scandalize London, it might have to be." Bram took a sip of the tea he had just poured and nodded in approval. "Good of you to have a fresh pot at the ready."

"I aim to please," Henry mumbled, then looked toward the door as Adrien entered.

"Oh, yes," Bram said, "Adrien is with me."

"Shouldn't you be attending to your pregnant wife?"

Adrien dropped into a chair and scowled at the tea pot. "She all but kicked me out of the house on the pretense of needing to spend the day with Ren. Have you any coffee?"

Henry left the table to ring for Danvers, then returned to his seat and glanced back and forth between his friends. "Why are the two of you looking at me like that?"

"For all of my rumored dark deeds," Bram began, "even I have never publically fornicated at a ball."

"I would hardly classify it as forni—"

"Really, Henry," Adrien interrupted. "What were you thinking? You do realize how this reflects upon Eirene and myself given that Ren is our guest."

Henry raked a hand through his hair, which he'd been doing nonstop since rolling out of bed after a sleepless night full of guilt about what he'd done and regret about having had the deed interrupted. He pinned Bram with a look. "Where were you?"

"Excuse me?"

"You were so anxious to meet 'the infamous Ren' and then you ran off the moment we entered Lady Dunston's home. Where were you?" Henry insisted.

Bram's black gaze narrowed. "I know what you are doing, and it will not work. I will take no responsibility for your actions. I am not now, nor have I ever been, your keeper."

Henry dismissed his friend's words with a sharp flick of his hand, then sighed and raked his hair again. "Bloody hell, that woman makes me lose my mind."

"So now you mean to blame Ren for your behavior?" Bram arched a brow and shook his head. "Sorry, my friend, you have no one to blame but yourself for this mess."

He scowled. "Do you believe I do not know that?"

It wasn't as if Ren would have attacked him like a randy lad. Yes, maybe she had kissed him first, but the rest…well, the rest of it was on him.

"The conversation must have been interesting as you escorted her home," Bram remarked.

"There was no conversation." Nothing. Not a word.

Ren had sat in stoic silence with her gaze fixed out the carriage window. Her behavior had made him want to scream. She was never silent for long periods of time. It was not in her nature. She hadn't even acknowledged his farewell as she stepped out of the carriage. Nothing. Not even a look back over her shoulder.

He looked at Adrien. "Has she said anything?"

"To Eirene, I imagine, she has said plenty, but I've been exiled from their company."

"What do you mean to do?" Bram asked just as Danvers entered the room.

"You rang, sir?" The butler addressed Henry but kept a wary eye upon The Earl of Cragmoor.

"Monsieur Cloutier fancies a pot of strong coffee, Danvers. Have we any?"

"Aye, sir, I believe we do. Will that be all?"

"I could use a rasher of fresh bacon, my good man," Bram added.

Danvers paled as he bowed to acknowledge the earl's request, then all but ran from the room once Henry dismissed him.

"Really, Henry, I do not know why you tolerate such a skittish manservant."

"He is only skittish in your presence, and I thank you for not ordering a raw steak." He'd seen the glint in Bram's eye before he requested the bacon. "To answer the question you asked before we were interrupted, I mean to marry her." Really, with Lady Dunston's threat hanging over his head, what other option did he have? "The real question is how the bloody hell do I convince *her* to marry *me*?"

"Perhaps you could employ the same method of persuasion she did upon rejecting your proposal?"

Henry frowned. "I'll not hold her at gunpoint until she agrees."

"She held you at gunpoint?" Adrien shot a look at Bram. "You left that detail out of the story."

"A story he had no business telling," Henry reminded both of them.

"I suggest you employ a more traditional strategy, *mon ami*."

"Good Lord, Adrien," Bram groaned. "You are beginning to sound like your militant wife. Next, you will tell him to outflank her or how best to ambush her."

Adrien blatantly ignored Bram. "Have you thought about courting—" He broke off as Danvers appeared with the coffee and bacon. "*Merci*, Danvers." He poured a steaming cup of coffee and helped himself to two strips of Bram's bacon before continuing. "As I was saying, have you considered courting her?"

"Ren is not the sort of woman one courts, and we only have a fortnight to be married."

"First," Bram interjected, "all women wish to be courted, and second, if done correctly, you only need a few hours."

"I believe what you are referring to is called seduction, *mon ami*, and Henry has already seen to that."

"Ha! He did not seduce her. He tupped her against the terrace—"

"Bram."

Bram snapped his mouth shut, because even the Dark Lord of the Nobility recognized when he was damn close to overstepping the bounds of friendship. "No offense intended."

Henry acknowledged the apology with a nod, then allowed the matter to drop. "Somehow I will convince Ren to marry me, but I believe it would be easier to accomplish said task if I had a bargaining chip."

"All she wants is her ship, and you are not in possession of it," Bram reminded him.

"No, but Wexler is." Henry's announcement made both of his friends smile. "I see you comprehend the significance of that."

"When do you mean to retrieve the document?"

"I had hoped you would help me decide."

Bram sat back in his chair and crossed his arms. "Let me think for a moment. Wexler is a creature of habit, and he habitually takes his midday meal at his club three days out of the week, and today is one of them."

Henry folded his napkin and placed it alongside the plate bearing his uneaten breakfast. "Bram, can I rely on you to keep an eye on Wexler at the club?"

"Of course."

Henry shifted his gaze to Adrien. "What are your plans for midday?"

"I believe I am standing guard while you burgle Wexler's private residence."

Henry smiled for the first time since Lady Dunston had interrupted his pleasant but ill advised interlude with Ren.

"You do realize," Bram suddenly spoke up, "she

might just shoot you and take the document."

It was a risk Henry would have to take.

****

"Eirene?"

"Yes, my dear?"

"Do you know the location of Lord Wexler's residence?"

Eirene narrowed her amber eyes, then very carefully placed the delicate teacup she'd been sipping from back upon its tray. "Why do you wish to know?"

Ren, who had yet to leave her bed after a night of angry tears, sat against an excessive mound of pillows with crossed arms and sudden determination. "He is in possession of something that belongs to me, and I wish to have it back."

"Your ship's document, I presume?"

"Yes, before Henry and I…well…before *the incident*, he told me Wexler confessed to having the document, and once you tell me where he lives I will retrieve it."

"How?"

"Well, that is entirely up to Lord Wexler." Ideally, she would come upon the document after a quick search of the man's study, but failing that, she would have to persuade Wexler to return it to her.

"Ren, listen to me." Eirene, who sat in a comfortable chair beside the bed, leaned forward. "Being arrested for breaking into Wexler's home and threatening his life will only make your current situation worse."

"Oh, I don't know. If I am in prison, then I cannot be forced to marry." Despite her intention to do so, she had failed to question Henry once alone in his carriage about whether or not he had been serious when agreeing to Lady Dunston's terms. Her gut told her he had been very serious as had the rather stern expression, which had been fixed upon his face throughout the entire, silent, carriage ride.

Emotions had gotten the better of her once she had ensconced herself in her bedchamber and, if not for Eirene's timely arrival, she would have ripped the scarlet gown to shreds and tossed it into the fire. Instead, Eirene had gently helped her disrobe, tucked her into bed, then sat by her side while she cursed Henry and dissolved into tears.

Eirene frowned. "Marriage is not so bad, Ren, and I hear prison is quite horrible."

Ren dropped her head back against the pillows and stared at the bed's canopy. "How did I get here, Eirene?"

"I assume you do not mean that in the literal, so I will answer by saying, you allowed Henry to take liberties he should not have taken in public."

Ren closed her eyes and groaned. "What was I thinking?"

"Based upon my own personal experience, I must assume you were not *thinking* so much as you were feeling."

Ren smiled at Eirene's matter of fact tone. Her new friend had told her all about the circumstances that led to her marriage, the elaborate plan to ruin her reputation, the failed rendezvous, the unexpected feelings, the kidnapping, and countless rejected proposals which had finally led to the realization that life without Adrien would be worse than her preconceived opinion of marriage.

"May I ask you a personal question, Ren?"

She lifted her head and opened her eyes to meet Eirene's gaze. "Of course."

The two of them had shared so much already in their short acquaintance, and the camaraderie had initially shocked Ren. She'd never had a female friend before. Her childhood had been spent by her father's side when he was at home and haunting the pubs when he was at sea. She'd become close with a few of the barmaids, but she had been too young for them to treat her as anything more than a pet. Her current social circle consisted of her ship's crew, other smugglers, pub owners, and merchants. All of them men, not surprisingly.

Perhaps it was Eirene's rather non feminine view of the world that put Ren at ease. Her new friend conducted her life like a military general and possessed an uncanny ability to strategize her next move through the making of lists. Sadly, a list of pros and cons would do nothing for Ren's current situation.

"Do you love him?"

Ren blinked. "Excuse me?"

"It is a simple question, Ren. Do you love Henry?"

"I don't know." She crossed her arms again and slid her gaze away from Eirene's fox-like stare. "I do not see how it matters."

"Ah, well it is simple. If you love him, then I cannot imagine you would wish to have him marry someone else."

"If he loves me, he would not."

Eirene shook her head. "Love and duty are two very different things for a man, and I have yet to encounter a gentleman who does not feel duty bound to marry."

"Marrying me would be a disaster for Henry." She returned her attention to Eirene. "It is the very reason I rejected his original proposal. I told you this."

"Yes, but you are wrong. Lady Dunston invited you to tea. She would not extend such an invite to someone she deemed inappropriate."

"Do you believe that invite still stands after I had a hand in ruining her ball?"

"You did not ruin her ball, Ren. Lady Dunston and all the other Society mavens relish the sort of attention such gossip generates. It is like a strange competition amongst them. Adrien has tried to explain it, but it all seems ridiculous to me." She shrugged a shoulder. "My point is, Lady Dunston will likely thank you for your behavior, unless, of course, you do not marry Henry. That will make her most unhappy, but I suppose it will not matter to you if you are hiding away in Cornwall."

"I do not *hide* in Cornwall. I have a life there."

Eirene made some noncommittal noise.

"Do not make those noises at me. Say what is on your mind."

"I was once known as The Reclusive Lady Rowe-Weston. I recognize hiding when I see it." Before Ren could argue the rather inarguable point, Eirene suddenly turned pale and pressed a hand against her stomach. "Oh dear."

Ren sat up straight. "Are you all right?"

"The tea has turned quite sour in my stomach." She offered a half-hearted smile. "This child seems to dislike the great majority of things I attempt to consume."

Ren relaxed against the pillows again. "When do

you plan to tell your husband he is to be a father?"

"Given his rather cosseting behavior of late, I imagine he has guessed." Eirene's beatific smile suggested she did not mind at all being cosseted by her husband.

"You will make a wonderful mother."

Eirene frowned. "Do you believe so? I never once gave the matter any thought. Babies come with marriage, and I never intended to marry, as you know."

"Yes, I believe you will make a wonderful mother, and Adrien a wonderful father." She mulled over Eirene's words about babies following marriage. Of course, she knew two people did not need to be married to produce a child, and she was also quite aware of the fact she and Henry, despite countless mornings, afternoons, and nights in bed together, had never produced one. She had never given the matter much thought, but now she wondered which of them could not have children. For Henry's sake she hoped it was her problem and not his, because she imagined part of a gentleman's *duty* was to produce an heir.

It was suddenly Ren's turn to press a hand to her stomach as her gut clenched unpleasantly at the thought of Henry marrying and producing children with Miss Parish or the like. He would never be happy with such a woman. Henry craved adventure and a little risk. The Miss Parish's of the world craved only fine gowns and a large circle of friends. Really, were she to be honest with herself, marrying Henry would be doing him a favor by saving him from a life of tedium. Perhaps he would agree to leave London and settle in Cornwall?

It occurred to her she had never asked when first he had proposed. She had merely assumed he would expect her to relocate to London. The realization that she may have thrown away three years of her life based upon a bloody assumption made her feel as ill as Eirene looked.

"I believe you should go lie down, Eirene."

"Yes, I believe I shall. Promise you won't do anything rash while I am resting. I wouldn't like to wake up to the news that you are in Newgate for attempting to burgle Wexler's residence."

"There is no threat of that, seeing as how you conveniently failed to inform me of where Wexler lives."

Eirene halted halfway to the door and turned to give Ren a knowing look. "So I did." A spark shone in her amber eyes. "Allow me to rest for an hour or so, and then I will accompany you to Lord Wexler's."

"I cannot ask you to do that."

"Nor are you. I am insisting, and I imagine prison is more tolerable with a friend."

"What about the baby?" Really, Ren could not approve of Eirene endangering her child.

"Oh, yes, he will come, too." With a cheeky grin, Eirene left before Ren could protest further.

Chapter Eight

"There is absolutely no rhyme or reason to this man's filing system," Eirene announced after she and Ren had been searching Wexler's study for close to thirty minutes. "If he employs a secretary, they should be relieved of their duties, and if he does not employ one, he most certainly should, though I pity the poor creature the task of having to organize this man's life."

Ren smiled at her friend's complaints while remaining focused upon her own task. Eirene had suggested they divide and conquer and had assigned Ren the task of searching through Lord Wexler's books for any loose papers while she searched the desk. Thus far, neither location had yielded anything of interest.

"Have you found anything?" Eirene asked from behind the desk.

"Only a love note." She had discovered it tucked between the pages of a volume of sonnets by Shakespeare and replaced it without reading it. She had no interest in Wexler's romantic entanglements.

"Did you read it?"

Ren glanced over her shoulder toward Eirene. "Only enough to ascertain it was a love note. We are here to find my registration, Eirene, not waste time digging about in Wexler's private affairs."

Eirene sighed and pushed a wayward lock of russet hair from her brow. "If we do not discover your registration, we may require a bit of leverage to obtain it through other means."

"You can only use it as blackmail if it is of value to his lordship."

"He tucked it in a book in his private study. It holds value."

Ren could not argue Eirene's logic, so she located the small volume of sonnets once more and extracted the note.

"Is it signed?" Eirene demanded.

Ren skimmed past the flowery penmanship and her eyes widened. "Yes."

"By whom?"

"Miss Parish." The name seemed to scrape over Ren's tongue.

"Miss Parish? As in Henry's Miss Parish?"

Ren shot a look toward her friend. "I imagine so."

Although, really, she was not Henry's Miss Anything because the angelic little miss with the rosy cheeks had rejected him.

Eirene appeared at Ren's side and took the note. "Hmm. Interesting. I recall now this morning's gossip column mentioning Lord Wexler coming to the aid of Miss Parish after she suffered a fit of vapors at Lady Dunston's ball."

Ren stared at Eirene. "You read the gossip column?"

"I find it diverting." Eirene considered the note. "Well, I am not certain how damning this actually is, but it might prove useful." She tucked the note into her bodice, then returned to the desk. "Continue looking," she ordered.

Ren rolled her eyes. At some point during the

search, her new friend had become General Rowe-Weston and the change was equal parts amusing and infuriating. As a ship's captain, Ren was usually the one barking orders, but they were not on a ship. They were in the London home of a proper London lord, and only a fool would attempt to wrest control while on foreign soil.

"My word!"

Ren spun around at Eirene's sudden exclamation. "What did you find?"

Eirene waved a piece of paper in the air. "You will never believe what Wexler paid for that atrocious suit of clothes he wore to Lady Dunston's."

Nor did Ren care. "Eirene, focus."

"Yes, yes, forgive me, but it pains me to see such a flagrant waste of money, and Wexler is quite guilty of it." She held up another piece of paper. "This is a bill for—"

"Eirene, we haven't got all day."

"Yes, yes, you are right. Forgive me the momentary distraction. I haven't a clue what came over me. If you ask Adrien, he will tell you I am one of the most focused persons he has ever encountered, especially when engaged in a specific task. It is not like me to allow something as trivial as this"—she waved the bill—"to distract me from the importance of our mission." She frowned. "It must be the child."

"Well, you can scold him for his poor influence once he arrives."

"Quite right." Eirene nodded and returned to her task.

Ren pulled another book from Wexler's rather impressive book collection and fanned the pages.

Another note, identical to the first love note, fluttered to the floor. She bent and retrieved it, verified it, too, was from Miss Parish, then folded it and slipped it into her trousers' pocket. Given Wexler's possession of a title, it was not surprising he had captured the attention and obviously amorous affections of Miss Parish.

The sound of a drawer being closed drew Ren's attention to the desk and a dejected looking Eirene. "I found nothing."

"I have more books to search, but I truly do not believe Wexler hid my ship registration in any of them."

"No, he likely did not." Eirene slouched in Wexler's desk chair. "It seems we must search his lordship's private r—"

"You will find nothing there either." Henry's voice was like a taut rope that pulled Ren's focus toward the door. Her entire person reacted to the sight of him with a sudden increase in temperature and *awareness*.

"Hello, Henry," Eirene spoke from her station behind the desk. "Am I to understand you searched Lord Wexler's private rooms?"

Henry shifted his gaze beyond Ren. "We did, yes." As if on cue, Eirene's husband entered the room and brushed by Henry to stop dead at the sight of his wife.

"*Mon Dieu*, Eirene, what are you doing here?"

"The same as you it would seem." She stood up, which elicited a gasp from her husband.

"What are you wearing?!"

"Trousers, courtesy of Ren. I really must commission a few pairs for myself."

Ren felt the weight of Monsieur Cloutier's gaze, met it, and shrugged. "I did not see any harm in allowing her to borrow a pair, and this seemed a task better suited to ease of movement than fashion."

Adrien looked to Henry, as if pleading for assistance, but Henry's gaze never wavered from Ren. "What were you thinking to come here?"

"I was thinking to find my registration, so that I might quit this infernal city and return to Cornwall."

Henry crossed his arms and steadied his already steady gaze. "With or without your registration, you cannot leave London."

"You are wrong, Henry. I will leave the moment I have that paper in my—"

In a flash, he closed the distance between them and caught her arm. His grip was firm but far from aggressive. She could have easily pulled free, but for some reason she did not.

"Are you forgetting about the wedding we must attend in less than a fortnight?"

"There will be no wedding, Henry."

"For God's sake, Ren." He released her to rake his hand through his hair. "I gave my word to Lady Dunston."

"That is your problem, not mine."

"Ren—"

"No, Henry. I said no three years ago, and I am saying no now. I will not marry you for any reason and certainly not because of some ridiculous scandal that will be forgotten by this time next month or sooner."

His jaw tightened, and he glanced toward Adrien. "Perhaps you could give us a few moments of privacy?"

"I do not believe this is the time or the place, *mon ami*."

"Adrien is right. Wexler never arrived at his club." This bit of unwelcome information was delivered in the form of a tall, very dark, very good-looking gentleman who appeared beside Henry. His coal black gaze fixed upon Ren. "Ah, the infamous Ren, I presume?" He held out a hand. "I am Venton. It would break my heart if Henry never mentioned me to you."

Ren smiled and shook the man's hand. "Oh, yes, he mentioned you a time or two."

It was not difficult to surmise why the man was a rumored witch. Not only did he possess dark, fathomless eyes that seemed to stare straight into a person's soul, but there was some unidentifiable allure to his presence that made her reluctant to release his hand.

"Bram, for God's sake, unhand Ren."

Venton did as Henry ordered and stepped back with a devilish wink before turning to Henry. "She is a goddess, Henry, and I am more convinced than ever that you are a fool."

"She rejected me, lest you forget that not so small detail."

Ren looked back and forth between the two men. "*She* is also standing right here and quite capable of hearing you."

"Bram," Adrien spoke up from beside his wife. "What do you mean Wexler never arrived at the club?"

"I mean what I mean. He never appeared at the club, so I thought it best to come here and warn you." Venton surveyed the room once more. "Why are the ladies here, and where are the servants? I did not see or hear a soul as I walked through the house."

"Eirene locked the servants in the kitchen, and our

reason for being here should be obvious."

Henry and Venton looked at Ren as if she'd just announced the servants had been turned into toads and set free in Hyde Park.

"*All* of them?" Henry looked back and forth between Ren and Eirene. "How the devil did you manage to lure all the servants into the kitchen?"

"Today is a half day for all but the butler, cook, and housekeeper," Eirene explained with more than a hint of pride in her tone.

Only Ren knew she had acquired the information by bribing a lad whose task it was to sweep the section of street outside Wexler's home. The boy had possessed a remarkable font of information about the comings and goings of his lordship's household and beamed like the North Star when Eirene informed him he would make an excellent reconnaissance officer some day. The compliment seemed to bring the boy more pleasure than the coins Eirene filled his palm with, and Ren suspected it was because the coins would not be his to keep.

"After the butler answered my knock and confirmed my suspicion Wexler was not at home," Eirene continued, "I simply waited for him to return to his luncheon with the others, then let myself into the house, made my way to the kitchen, and locked the door."

"Beautiful and clever, *mon coeur*."

Eirene smiled in response to her husband's praise in a manner that made Ren feel a tad voyeuristic. She shifted her gaze back to Henry's displeased expression, but before she could say a word, Lord Wexler himself strolled into the room, stopped dead, and gaped like a fish out of water.

The mango-colored attire from Lady Dunston's ball had been replaced by a perfectly tailored, dark gray suit similar to what Wexler had worn during the fateful card game. She recalled the way he had shed his coat, loosened his cravat, and plied her with a seemingly endless supply of whiskey until all of the cards blurred together and she hadn't been able to remember the amount of the standing bet. Her temper flared, and it took every ounce of her willpower not to palm the pistol tucked in the back of her trousers, point it at Wexler's heart, and demand the return of her ship.

"What the devil?" Wexler's gaze darted about and finally landed upon Henry. "What the devil, Westie? What is the meaning of—"

Venton clapped a hand on Wexler's shoulder and forced him to have a seat in the nearest chair.

Wexler gripped the arms of the rather ancient looking wooden chair until his knuckles were visibly white. "Westie, call off your pet witch, for God's sake."

Wexler squeaked like a small child when Venton leaned down and leered into his face. "What did you call me?"

"N-n-nothing. It was nothing, my lord. A joke, what?" Wexler's attempt at laughter sounded like a drowning man catching his last breath before going under. "We all enjoy a good lark, yes?"

"No," Venton countered. "Now listen to me. Recently you acquired a sailing vessel, and this lovely lady"—he nodded toward Ren—"would greatly appreciate its return."

Wexler's gaze flew to Ren and widened as his mouth fell open. "You! I knew you looked familiar when I saw you at the ball." He scanned her person, and the way his attention lingered in certain places made her want to grab her pistol again. "I would have known who you were instantly had you been wearing trousers." His gaze returned to hers. "I don't know too many men who could forget the sight of—"

His words were cut short by the sudden enclosure of Venton's hand around his throat. "Where is the ship's registration?"

"I haven't got it," Wexler rasped, then shot a frantic look toward Henry.

"Leave off, Venton," Henry ordered his friend.

Wexler pulled at his cravat and dragged in great gulps of air once free. "I haven't got it," he said again.

Henry shook his head and crossed his arms, and Ren almost pitied Wexler. "How can you believe for one moment that I might possibly be in the mood for your games?"

"I'm not playing any games, Westie." Wexler attempted to stand, but Venton shoved him back into the chair. "I haven't got what you want."

"You informed me at Lady Dunston's ball that you were in possession of a smuggling ship, yes?"

"Oh, yes, yes, I've got possession of the ship, but I haven't got—"

"For God's sake." Ren pulled her pistol from her waistband, brushed past Henry, cocked the gun, and put the barrel to Wexler's temple. "Where is the bloody document?"

"Put the gun away, Ren."

Ren ignored Henry and gave Wexler a good nudge with the weapon. "I suggest you speak, your lordship."

Wexler's panicked gaze shifted in Henry's direction. "You are actually going to marry this hell—"

He squeaked as Ren gave him another nudge. His gaze met hers. "You cannot possibly be serious about shooting me. I am a lord of the realm, a—"

"I do not care if you are the bloody king. Where is the document?"

Wexler's gaze shifted toward Henry again. "Will she really shoot me?"

"Unfortunately, yes."

Ren stifled a smirk at the sound of Henry's resignation.

"This is ridiculous," Wexler announced, his tone suddenly too calm for comfort. He looked at Ren. "If you shoot me, you will hang, and then what bloody good will your ship do you, hmm?

"There are ways to shoot a man without killing him."

"Oh, yes, indeed there are, and if you employ any of them, you will still hang. You have my word on that."

Ren blinked away tears of rage as she recognized the truth of Wexler's words. With a curse she lowered the gun. "What do you want in exchange?" Men like Wexler always wanted something.

"What could you possibly possess that I would covet?" His gaze scanned her person. "Other than the obvious."

"Another remark like that, and no woman will ever enjoy your intimate attentions," Henry threatened, and Wexler paled and mumbled an apology.

"Perhaps you would be interested in a trade?" Eirene stepped forward with Wexler's love note pinched between her fingers. When she had everyone's attention, she unfolded it, and began to read.

"Dearest Algernon,

How can I possibly express how it feels to lie here in my bed with the memory of your—"

"Enough!" Wexler looked ill of a sudden. "There is no need to sully the reputation of an innocent."

"Given the detailed account in this letter, I would have to conclude Miss Parish is no longer innocent," Eirene said.

"Miss Parish?" Henry asked with more than a hint of shock.

Ren looked at him. "You sound jealous."

"Jealous?" He frowned. "Why the devil would I be jealous?"

"You intended to marry her, you might recall."

"Yes, and I also recall telling you I never loved her, so, I ask again, why would I be jealous of what she does with Wexler or anyone else?"

Ren ended the exchange by giving her attention to Wexler who wore an openly curious expression. "Return my ship's document to me, or the note will be sent to the paper with instructions to publish the contents without the benefit of initials."

"I told you, I haven't got it."

"Then I suggest you tell me where the devil it is." Ren's patience had expired a very long time ago, and she certainly had not forgotten about the gun clutched in her hand. Wexler's threat about hanging for murder was valid, but only if she managed to get caught, and after all her years spent smuggling, she was quite good at avoiding capture.

"It is in Cornwall, and you cannot expect me to abandon the Season to retrieve it."

"Fine," Ren nodded. "Tell me where it is, and I'll

get it myself. Once it is in my hands, I'll send word to Lady Rowe-Weston to return your precious letter to you."

"Ren, you cannot leave London." Henry's calm tone drew her gaze from Wexler.

"Do not throw Lady Dunston's blasted terms in my face again, Henry. As I said, it is your problem, not mine." She turned back to Wexler. "Now, where is the document?"

"I will not allow you to leave London, R—" He fell silent as she turned, raised the pistol, and pointed it at his heart.

"Go on then." Henry held his jacket open. "I believe you said there is no point to threatening a man with a gun if you do not intend to shoot him or something to that effect?" He pulled his jacket wider. "Shoot, and all of our problems will be solved, yes?"

Ren's arm began to shake. Never, ever in the history of her ability to handle a weapon had her arm ever trembled. She prided herself on the fact. Her men praised and envied her. Hammett, her first mate, had a habit of calling, "Steady as she goes!" when she appeared. How shocked they'd be to see her now with her arm shaking like a yardarm in a wind storm.

"I prefer not to have anyone shot upon these carpets," Wexler stated.

She ignored the man and looked into Henry's eyes. He knew she wouldn't pull the trigger. The truth of it was there in his gaze. There was another truth there as well, and it was the one that made her lower the gun, curse under her breath, and storm out of Wexler's study.

Chapter Nine

"Oh yes, the two of you are perfectly suited for one another. Both stubborn as a pair of mules," Venton said into the silence that followed Ren's abrupt departure.

"Not now, Bram." Henry headed for the door only to be cut off by Eirene.

"I shall go after her," she told him with a lethal glare. "*You* are the last person she wants to see right now."

"Perhaps, but I am the one who needs to go after her."

Eirene crossed her arms and continued to glare at him. "I would not put it past her to actually shoot you."

"If she does, it will hurt far less than losing her again." Henry walked away but not before he caught the softening of Eirene's hard glare.

"Has this little drama come to an end then?" Wexler's voice drifted out into the corridor followed by Venton's inaudible, growling response.

Henry ignored both as he came face to face with Ren. She hadn't gone far after her dramatic exit, merely to a small, tufted settee that sat against the wall opposite Wexler's study.

"I expected you to be halfway to Piccadilly." He sat down beside her, though the piece of furniture had been designed to accommodate only one lady and the width of her eighteenth century panniers. The wooden frame creaked as he adjusted his weight in an attempt to locate a comfortable position upon the narrow bench.

Ren gave no indication that she was aware of his presence as she continued to stare at the gun in her lap.

"I believe you are the only person who has ever threatened to shoot me twi—"

"Don't." She looked up suddenly, and the shine of unshed tears glistened in her eyes. "Whatever it is you believe you need to say, please, do not."

"We need to discuss—"

"No, we do not need to discuss anything. I have no intention of marrying you, Henry, no matter what argument you make to the contrary. My only intention is to retrieve my ship from Wexler and go home."

"So just like that, you would ruin me."

She looked away. "I am sorry, but saving your reputation is not my responsibility."

"I am not speaking about my bloody reputation. Look at me, damn you."

She did, and the beauty of her glistening, peridot-colored eyes nearly propelled him off the bench and to his knees to beg.

"I am not asking you to marry me so that I can save my reputation. I am asking because I believe Fate has given us another chance."

She rolled her eyes and looked away. "You know I do not believe in that nonsense."

"But you believe in us." He watched her jaw tighten. "Marry me, Ren."

"Henry." She closed her eyes, sighed, and shook her head. "I cannot."

"Why? Because of some ridiculous notion that you are not good enough?" He took hold of her chin and forced her to meet his gaze. "You are the best person I know."

"You know what I mean when I say I am not good enough, Henry. I am not some polished—"

"You are more honest, intelligent, intriguing, kind-hearted, and graceful than half the ladies in Society. Lady Dunston recognized this after only a few moments in your company. Others will do the same, and before you know it, you will be the toast of every dinner party."

"I do not wish to be the toast of every dinner party."

"Then we will decline the invitations."

She rolled her eyes again but made no attempt to free herself from his hold on her chin. "You have a counter argument for everything I say."

"Of course."

"And your family? Hmm? How will your father feel about welcoming a smuggler into the family? The man is a baron and beholden to the Crown."

"Do you believe he was unaware of my activities?" Henry shook his head. "We never spoke of it, he and I, but I knew he was aware of my smuggling. If he can look the other way for his son, then I imagine he will do the same for the woman his son loves."

"What if you are wrong?"

Henry scoffed and released her. "Do you truly believe my father will have you strung up during our first family meal?"

"No. I believe he will have me strung up to prevent me from marrying into the family."

"You are wrong. My mother would never allow that to happen. Nor would I."

"Is there nothing I can say that will convince you to let this matter go?"

Henry shook his head.

"What if I say I do not love you?" Her words caused a brief stutter in his heartbeat, but he knew them for the lie they were.

"You will have to say it a great many more times and a hell of a lot more convincingly before I believe you."

"What if I confess I am already married?"

"Then I will be forced to fight a duel, so I pray you are not."

She crossed her arms and slouched against the low back of the settee. "Your stubbornness is a horrible character flaw."

"Said the pot to the kettle." Henry caught the slightest hint of a smile, and he reached out, but before he could touch her, a loud noise, like cannon fire, reverberated from the depths of the house. Both he and Ren sprang to their feet, Ren with gun in hand.

The study door flew open to reveal Venton. "What the hell was that?" He stepped into the corridor, followed by Adrien, Eirene, and Wexler.

Another loud noise shook the house and brought dust down onto Henry's nose. He glanced up to see a large chandelier swaying precariously above him, and he moved out of its path.

"Bloody hell," Wexler cursed as he shoved past everyone to step fully into the corridor. "Is someone using a battering ram on my house?!" His wild gaze flew from person to person. "What is the meaning of this?!" He settled upon Ren. "You will have your bloody ship back. I swear it. Now call off your attack."

Ren looked at Wexler as if he'd gone mad.

Another loud noise preceded a more muffled bang, then the sound of rushing footsteps and raised voices led to the sudden appearance of three people at the end of the corridor, one man and two women. The man led the charge with a large cooking pan held aloft. His left flank was protected by a portly woman with a broom and his right by a tall, reed-thin woman brandishing a fire poker. They charged down the corridor like marauders from hell.

Ren stepped in front of Henry and aimed her pistol.

"No!" Wexler jumped in front of Ren. "I will not have you shoot my butler."

"Your butler?" Ren relaxed her finger on the trigger. "Why is your butler attacking?"

Wexler spun around and held up both arms. The three servants halted.

"What is the meaning of this?" Wexler demanded.

"We've come to rescue you, my lord." The butler had yet to lower his frying pan as his gaze swept over the small assemblage. "That one, there!" He pointed, and all eyes turned to Eirene. "She came knocking to ask if you were home, and after we finished our luncheon, I discovered we'd been locked in the kitchen."

Wexler gaped at Eirene. "You locked my servants in the kitchen?"

"It seemed the most prudent course of action so as not to have them underfoot while we searched your home."

Ren ducked her head to hide her smile at Eirene's no-nonsense response.

"We had to use the table to knock down the door,"

the butler went on with his story.

Wexler turned the focus of his gape to his butler. "You knocked down— You used the— My God, why did I get out of bed this morning?"

"I believe it was because you received a message from Miss Parish, my lord, asking that you join her for—"

"Yes, yes." Wexler waved his butler to silence, then turned to face Ren. "I need time to arrange travel to Cornwall to retrieve—"

"That will not be necessary," Venton interrupted. "We will leave this evening."

"We?" The blood drained from Wexler's face as he stared at Venton. "I would rather have this woman shoot me then travel anywhere with a bloody w—"

"Completing that sentence is not in your best interest." Venton's threat made Wexler grow paler. "I will allow you three hours to send round your regrets and what not."

"I cannot pick up and leave in the middle of—"

"It is your choice, Wexler. We can travel like companionable gentlemen, or I can enjoy the comforts of my carriage while you roll about in a sack on the floor. Either way, we leave for Cornwall in three hours." Venton looked at Ren before Wexler could respond. "I will send word the moment I ascertain the well-being of your ship and men."

"Thank you." For unknown reasons, she trusted the Earl of Cragmoor. Perhaps it was simply because Henry had trusted the man for their entire lives.

Venton nodded, then shot a final look at Wexler. "Three hours."

Wexler sputtered but did not voice a protest until

Venton left. "Will all of you *leave* now?" He held a hand out to Eirene. "I believe you have something that belongs to me."

"And I shall keep it until I have word from the earl that Miss Teague's ship is no longer in your possession."

Wexler looked ready to throttle Eirene, but one glance at Adrien turned the expression into reluctant acquiescence.

"Very well. Have it your way." He shooed them toward the door. "Now, please, be gone, and I pray to the heavens I never see any of you ever again."

Eirene and Adrien linked arms and walked out together while Ren brushed past Henry in the hopes she could avoid any further—

"Walk with me," he said as he took hold of her arm.

Ren had two choices. Comply or cause a scene in the middle of the afternoon in one of London's most prestigious neighborhoods. All things considered, Henry would not thank her if she chose the latter option. "You are not worried for your reputation if you are seen strolling with a young gentleman at your side?"

In lieu of an answer, he simply plucked the pins from the bun tightly coiled against her nape. Her hair sprang free and fell about her shoulders like a thick, black curtain.

"I believe that shall deter any such misunderstanding, hmm?"

Ren shook her hair down her back and tucked it behind each ear. The slight afternoon breeze had other ideas, however, and after a few moments of battle, she resigned herself and her hair to Nature's whim.

Henry caught a long coil as it lifted off her shoulder. "I've always believed you to have the most magnificent mane of hair." His own hair blew about in the breeze, then settled over his left eye.

Ren clenched her hands into fists to resist the urge to touch him. "Thank you."

"Venton will see to it that Wexler hands over the registration."

"I never doubted it for a moment." She glanced at him. "It is kind of him to intervene in a matter that has nothing to do with him."

Henry did not return her gaze. "He and I are friends, so he considers my business his business."

"My ship has nothing to do with you."

Henry halted and turned to face her. "You involved me when you accepted my help in Sumner's conservatory. That is enough for Bram. Besides, it was once my ship as well."

Ren gaped. "The Mermaid was never yours. You were merely part of the crew."

He crossed his arms in his oh so vexing, time to go to war stance. "How many other members of your crew have taken her out on a run without you?"

"Are we truly going to argue about this in the middle of the street?"

"Are we arguing? I am merely allowing you the opportunity to correct your statement that I was nothing more than a member of the crew."

Ren rolled her eyes. She loathed when he spoke to her like a bloody member of parliament. "You were a member of the crew who enjoyed the benefits of sleeping in the captain's bed. Satisfied?"

"No." He reached for her without warning and cupped her face in both hands. "I have not been satisfied since you forced me out of your life."

Dear God, he wasn't going to kiss her in the middle of the street?

Why not? He made love to you in the middle of a ball.

She pulled away. "Despite the benefits you enjoyed while on board, the Mermaid was never yours, nor will she be, even if I decide to marry you."

"Lower your hackles, Ren. I do not want your ship. I have my own, you might recall."

"Well, yes, but—" She stopped herself from stating the obvious about his *ship*.

"But what?" He arched a brow. "Were you about to insult my ship?"

"It is hardly a ship." Yes, his little schooner had served him well on his cognac runs, but in comparison to her Mermaid, which had begun life as a sixth-rate ship of the line before being captured by pirates then somehow finding her way to an auction where Ren secured the highest bid, Henry's ship looked like a child's toy.

"To be honest, I always felt the Mermaid was a bit extravagant."

Ren laughed, but it was hard to disagree. The Mermaid, given her size, required a crew larger than most smuggling vessels, and a large crew meant more money to pay them, which meant all of her runs needed to be lucrative and having her current cargo sit idle while other smugglers likely usurped her clients, deposited coin in no one's pocket.

She would have to smuggle Napoleon out of

France and deliver him directly to Wellington in order to make up for lost profits. The entire ordeal made her sick, and Henry wished to delay her further with his insistence that they marry.

"The Mermaid might be extravagant," she said to avoid thoughts of marriage. "But we can agree her guns are a nice bit of security."

When Ren bought the ship, she'd been equipped with twenty-eight cannons on the gun deck and twelve swivel guns on the upper, six of which were mounted on the quarter deck. She had removed half the cannons to allow for more speed but kept the swivel guns, which presumably had been added by the Mermaid's pirate captain.

In the ten years Ren had been smuggling, she'd only employed the canons one time, but the swivel guns had come in handy quite often, mostly to announce to any pursuing ships that the Mermaid would not be taken without a fight.

"Let us hope those guns have not been employed in your absence."

Ren met Henry's gaze. "My men are not foolish, but they will do whatever is necessary to protect the ship and the cargo."

"Yes, I know."

Silence fell between them until she sighed and looked away. "You do realize I cannot linger in London."

She focused on Eirene and her husband who strolled arm in arm several paces ahead. They had their heads together as if plotting a coup of some sort.

"I only ask that you remain long enough for Lady Dunston to secure the special license."

Ren shifted her attention to Henry. "A special license is valid anywhere, yes?"

He shook his head. "I know what you are thinking, and the answer is no. Under different circumstances, it would be fine if we married in Cornwall, but given the gossip, it is best we see to it in London."

"What of your parents? You would have them miss the grand event?" She could not keep the sarcasm from her tone, nor did she really try all that hard.

Henry frowned. "Moments ago, you were worried about my father hanging you, and now, you want them at our wedding?"

She shrugged but said nothing because she knew Henry recognized her question as the poor delaying tactic it was.

"I have no doubt Lady Dunston sent a note to my mother moments after she secured my acceptance of her terms. It was likely why she gave us a fortnight to see to the deed."

"To allow your parents time to arrive," she concluded.

"Yes."

She shook her head. "I do not recall actually agreeing to marry you."

"I am fairly certain you did, or did I imagine our conversation in Wexler's corridor prior to his servants storming the keep?"

"I did not say I will marry you."

Henry, damn his insufferable hide, smiled, then leaned down to brush a kiss across her lips. "You will."

Ren shoved him away. "Is it wise to be seen mauling me in the streets? Think of your precious reputation."

He laughed and offered his arm, which, of course, she accepted. She would likely allow him to escort her straight to the gates of hell if ever the moment arrived.

Chapter Ten

Dearest Readers,

Seven days have gone since the incident *at Lady D's ball. We have it on good authority Lady D submitted a request for a special license the very next day, and with her connections, it should not be long before she has it. As for Mister H.W. and his bride to be… Both have been noticeably absent from all events.*

In other news, Lord Wx has taken his leave of London. Rumor has it he is travelling to Cornwall in the company of none other than The Dark Lord of the Nobility, the Earl of C. I must confess to feeling a bit confused by such a strange pairing, but my confusion cannot begin to compare to my curiosity as I wonder how Miss A.P. accepted the news of Lord Wx's departure. It seemed inevitable she would soon receive the proposal she has rather blatantly been seeking from his lordship, but now that he has departed, I do wonder if she will set her sights elsewhere…

"You have visitors, sir."

Henry glanced up from his breakfast, which he feared he would never again enjoy in peace, as his mother sailed into the room with his father close on her heels. He stood to greet them all the while wondering how the devil there had been time for them to have received Lady Dunston's message and travel to

London.

"Mother. Father. You both look well. What brings you to the city?"

His mother engulfed him in a rose-scented hug, then leaned back within his embrace to give him her best stern expression. Despite his mother's dainty features and kind, blue eyes, it was a look that always made him feel like a naughty seven-year-old boy. "I always visit Elizabeth at this exact time each Season, but perhaps you are too busy creating scandals to recall such mundane details, hmm?"

Elizabeth being none other than Lady Dunston. The two women not only shared an everlasting friendship but also a first name, and it was the only form of address they used when speaking to and of one another. It had a tendency to complicate things at times, but there was no room to misunderstand his mother's censure.

"Imagine my surprise," she went on, "upon hearing of your upcoming wedding."

"You have already been to see Lady Dunston?" Henry fought the urge to tug at his cravat. No matter how old one was, one never wished to have their mother privy to their intimate relations.

"Indeed, I have, and what a tale she had to tell."

"I had every intention of writing you, Mother."

"Oh?" She stepped out of his arms and crossed hers. "When? Hmm? After the wedding? Or perhaps after my first grandchild arrived?"

"Elizabeth," his father intoned. "Can the scolding wait until after we have tea?"

"You consumed a good portion of tea mere hours ago at Elizabeth's, not to mention nearly an entire tray of pastries."

"Yes, well, I suspect I shall require more sustenance to weather the impending discussion." The baron arched a brow at Henry.

Taking the cue from his father, Henry glanced at Danvers who lingered in anticipation of such a request. "A fresh pot of tea, Danvers, and whatever food you can scare up for the baron."

"Very good, sir." Danvers bowed with what seemed to be a bit more deference than normal, then quit the room.

"Such a lovely man, that Danvers," his mother commented as she circled the breakfast table and chose the chair to the right of Henry's.

He beat his father to the task of pulling out said chair. "Yes, Danvers is a good man." Until Venton came to call, but no need to dim his mother's opinion by revealing that tidbit.

"Sit, sit." His mother gestured to both him and his father. "I do not like when people hover over me."

Henry retook his seat, and his father chose the one to his left, opposite his mother.

"Now," his mother said once they were settled. "Who is this woman you intend to marry? Is she of good family? Elizabeth could tell me nothing save you and the woman boast of a long-standing acquaintance and a mutual friendship with Lady Rowe-Weston and her husband. Now, your father has some ridiculous theory about the woman's identity, which I will not waste time repeating, because I am quite certain he is wrong."

He glanced at his father who arched a feathery white brow. He quickly returned his attention to his mother. "That is all Lady Dunston had to say?"

His mother's eyes narrowed. "Oh, no. She had plenty more to say, young man, but I'll not discuss your shocking behavior at the breakfast table." She shook her head in obvious disapproval. "To think *my* son would behave in such a fashion."

"Our son," his father corrected, which earned him a sharp look from his wife.

"Are you insinuating he behaved in such a fashion because he is *your* son?"

The baron paled and mumbled something under his breath that caused his wife to scoff before she returned her attention to Henry. "Well?"

"What do you wish to know, Mother?"

"Why not begin with her name, hmm? Elizabeth insisted she could not recall what it was but believed it had something to do with birds."

"Birds, you say?" the baron asked while once again arching a brow at Henry. "If I am not mistaken—"

The loud rattle of a cart announced Danvers' return. "Will that be all, sir?"

Henry sent Danvers a distracted nod. "Yes, thank you."

"Well?" His mother, clearly impatient for an answer, saw to the task of pouring a cup of tea for his father, light cream, two sugars, then one for herself, no cream, no sugar. She took a small sip and nodded. "Excellent. It makes a mother proud when her son has a ready supply of quality tea."

If only the conversation could stop there.

His mother set down her cup and pinned him with a steady gaze from her blue eyes. "I am waiting, young man."

Henry stared at his tea and wished he could magically transform it into whiskey. He would have to ask Bram if such a thing was possible and if, yes, he would have to insist upon being taught how to perform—

"Must I count to three, Henry?" His mother's warning broke into his thoughts.

"Elizabeth, our son is no longer a—" His father's words ended abruptly as his mother shot a look across the table. He looked to Henry. "Answer the question, my boy. Delaying will only make matters worse."

The latter statement proved his suspicion that his father had understood, precisely, Lady Dunston's bird reference.

Henry met his mother's expectant stare. "Her name is Morvoren Teague." His announcement was met with a slight look of confusion from his mother and a mumbled curse from his father.

His mother looked back and forth between husband and son. "What are the two of you hiding from me?

"Morvoren Teague," his father began before Henry could speak, "is wanted for crimes against the crown."

Henry looked into his father's eyes, which save for the age lines that bracketed them, were identical to his own. "As was I until a few months ago."

His father scoffed. "I'll not have you compare your little lark with what that woman is guilty of."

"My lark, as you call it, was just as illegal as Ren's activities."

"Would you feel better if I arrested you here and now?"

"Eugene!" His mother gasped. "You would not dare."

"Listen to me, Henry," his father went on as if his mother had not spoken. "It is my duty to apprehend that woman if given the opportunity. Not only is she guilty of smuggling, but she is also wanted for firing upon one of his majesty's ships."

"She did so after they nearly blew her out of the wat—"

"From what I know of the situation, she ignored their warning shots, then opened fire. For that act alone she should hang."

"You would hang your daughter-in-law?" The words fell between them like a gauntlet.

"She is not my daughter-in-law yet."

"Eugene!" His mother tried again to inject some semblance of rationale and was rewarded with a not too pleased expression from his father.

"You would welcome a criminal into our family?"

"Perhaps she has changed her ways?" His mother looked to him for confirmation, and when he did not offer any, she frowned. "I see."

"Morvoren Teague will never change her ways," his father explained. "The woman is descended from pirates—"

"That is nothing more than a pub story, Father."

The baron cocked a white brow. "Captain Teague was one of the most elusive and dangerous pirates to sail the seas, and your *intended*"—there was no denying the distaste with which that word was said—"is a direct descendant whether you wish to admit it or not. Hell, Henry, the woman sails a bloody frigate equipped with enough fire power to face off with a ship of the line."

"Is it against the law to own a large ship with a few cannons?"

"Yes, Henry, I believe it is against the law for a civilian to outgun the bloody Navy!"

"Eugene," his mother broke in as his father turned bright red. "Calm yourself, my dear."

The baron shot his wife an exasperated look. "Elizabeth, surely you agree we cannot allow this wedding to take place. Do you wish the mother of your grandchildren to be a notorious pirate?"

"You are over exaggerating, Eugene. The woman is guilty of nothing more than smuggling a few items from France, and you talk as though she has a hold full of Spanish gold."

His father harrumphed and crossed his arms. "If given the opportunity, she would."

"Morvoren is not dangerous, Father." As far as he knew, he and Wexler were the only ones she'd actually ever pulled a gun on, but he could not see how that fact would help his case, so he held his tongue.

"Tell that to the crew of the ship she fired upon."

"Her shot was wide and intended as a warning only."

"If that be the case, she can use that as her defense before the judge."

"Father, you cannot seriously—"

"Yes, Henry, I am very serious. If given the opportunity, I will have that woman in chains."

"Eugene!"

"No, Elizabeth, do not waste your breath attempting to change my mind. The woman is a wanted criminal, and it is my duty to apprehend her." His father pushed his chair back and stood. "For your sake, Henry, I had hoped I was wrong about Morvoren's identity when Lady Dunston made her ridiculous bird reference.

The feelings you harbor for that woman unfortunately change nothing. Come, Elizabeth, we have overstayed our welcome."

His mother hesitated. "Eugene, this is our home. Where do you believe you are going? Now, sit down and allow us to work this out like the adults we are, hmm?"

Henry's father obeyed but none too happily. "There is nothing to work out, Elizabeth. I attempted to warn you of this after we departed Elizabeth's house, but you would not listen to my suspicion as to the identity of Henry's mystery woman."

His mother scoffed and waved away the accusation. "If I listened to every one of your suspicions, Eugene—"

"Our son intends to marry an infamous smuggler," his father went on as if his mother had not spoken and as if Henry were no longer present. "If we sit by and allow that to happen, the family will be ruined. The crown could strip me of my title, for God's sake. Is that what you wish to have happen?"

"What I wish," his mother began as she lifted her tea to take a sip, "is to see our son happy." She flicked her gaze to Henry. "Does this woman make you happy?"

"Honestly? Most of the time I wish to throttle her." His answer brought a smile to his mother's face.

"I imagine your father wishes to do the same to me most of the time."

"Now, Elizabeth, you know that is not true."

His mother arched a brow in his father's direction, then continued to address Henry. "Do you love her?"

"He has loved her for years," his father answered

for him.

His mother frowned at his father's remark but did not shift her gaze away. "Is that true?"

"Yes." He saw no point in being anything but honest.

"Might I ask why you proposed to Miss Parish, or do you expect me to believe you loved that young lady as well?"

"I was under the impression that I loved her, but I did not."

His mother nodded. "Of course, you did not." She took another sip of tea. "I suspect she served as a distraction for you in your efforts to bury your feelings for Miss Teague."

Given the accuracy of the statement, he withheld a reply.

"Odd, I had no idea you harbored feelings for Miss Teague." She shifted her gaze to his father. "Nor was I aware you sailed with her or, as I am now given to believe, that you also engaged in a smuggling career of your own. Why was I not aware of any of this?"

Henry's father busied himself with a flaky pastry, but the weight of his wife's gaze could not be ignored for long. He looked up and across the table. "I was protecting you."

"From what?"

"Elizabeth, really. What mother wishes to know her son is engaged in dangerous, illegal activities or having an affair with a notorious woman?"

"An affair?" She looked at Henry and set down her teacup with alarming delicacy. "Let me see if I understand, hmm? You and Miss Teague were engaged in an intimate relationship?"

"Yes." Henry felt like a seven-year-old again awaiting punishment.

"So, if I understand correctly, the *incident* that occurred at Lady Dunston's ball—"

"Was the result of three years of agony," Henry confessed.

"I see." His mother sipped her tea for a few moments before speaking again. "Might I ask why you did not propose to Miss Teague during your prior relationship?"

"I did. She refused."

"You did what?" his father demanded only to be silenced by his mother's raised hand.

"Might I ask why she refused?"

"Is that not obvious, Elizabeth?" his father interrupted. "The woman's morals are likely as loose as her regard for the law."

"Father," Henry said between clenched teeth. "I would challenge a man for a much lesser insult."

"Good God, boy!" His father looked to his wife. "Do you see? That woman is a horrible influence on our son. First, she lures him into smuggling, and now, she has him so bewitched he is actually threatening to shoot his own father."

"I am currently tempted to shoot you, Eugene."

His father snapped his mouth shut.

"Why did she reject your proposal, Henry?" his mother asked again.

"She believed herself not worthy to join this family. I assured her then, and now, that she is wrong." He shot a look at his father. "I see that was a tad premature of me."

"Son, you know I have duties to the Crown."

"You managed to forget about those duties the entire time I engaged in smuggling."

"You are my son!"

"And Ren will be your daughter if I actually manage to get her to the bloody altar."

His father held his gaze for several moments, then looked to his mother before throwing his hands in the air. "For pity's sake, what chance do I have against the both of you?"

"None, whatsoever, my darling." His mother reached for her tea once more.

"You can honestly say you would happily welcome a criminal into the family?"

His mother ignored the question and settled her gaze upon him. "Did I ever tell you about the time Elizabeth and I entered a dress shop after hours and helped ourselves to a handful of gowns? This was before she was Lady Dunston, of course, and before I met your father. Her coming out season had been delayed due to her family not having the funds to supply a proper wardrobe. It was my idea to simply procure one."

Henry glanced at his father to find the man gaping in shock.

"Elizabeth is quite handy with a needle, and she was able to fashion four new gowns from the six we had *stolen*." She emphasized and directed the last word toward his father.

"A few stolen gowns are hardly the same as firing on one of his majesty's ships, Elizabeth."

"No? I wonder if the Crown would agree seeing as how they incarcerate and transport street urchins for far lesser crimes." She looked to Henry. "Does Ren's smuggling bring her to London?"

"No. She has always preferred to deal with local merchants."

"So, she is truly unknown here in London." His mother held her tea with both hands and adopted a very familiar contemplative expression.

"Elizabeth—"

"Hush, Eugene, I am thinking."

Henry and his father shared a glance. Despite their difference of opinion when it came to Ren, they shared a mutual deference when it came to the woman seated at the table.

"The gossips will wish to know her background," his mother said to no one in particular.

"Flash the right amount of coin back home, and they will soon learn all they wish."

Henry frowned at his father's comment. "I cannot think of a single soul who would sell Ren out."

"Hmph," was his father's only reaction.

"Boys, please," his mother scolded. "Tell me, Henry, has Ren engaged in any respectable activities during her tenure as a smuggler?"

His father snorted, which earned him a dark look from his mother. "Forgive me, Elizabeth, but respectable and smuggling are not words generally used in the same sentence."

"She rescued Lord Pinworth's daughter from France after the treaty expired." The information received an open-mouthed look of shock from his father and a raised brow from his mother.

"Were you involved, as well?" his mother asked.

"Yes."

"How fascinating." His mother glanced at his

father, who shrugged in ignorance of the matter, then she returned her focus to Henry. "Please, tell me the details."

Henry sorted through the Miss Caroline Pinworth incident in his mind. The whole thing had been a bloody ordeal start to finish and culminated with him nearly bleeding to death from a bullet in the back. He very much doubted his mother would want to know about his near-death experience or Ren's role in it. He resisted the urge to rake a hand through his hair, which would alert his mother of his internal distress.

"Henry?"

"Forgive me, Mother, it was several years ago. I am attempting to remember the details." He heard his father snort under his breath at the obvious prevarication. "Lord Pinworth approached Ren and all but begged her to retrieve his daughter. He believed her to be the most capable for the task—"

"Aye," his father interjected, "because she sails a bloody ship of the line."

"Go on, Henry," his mother prompted as she completely ignored his father.

"There's not much more to say. Ren accepted Pinworth's offer, and we retrieved his daughter who I believe is now married to a Scottish earl."

If only it had actually been that cut and dry. He rolled his shoulders in a subtle gesture and felt the pull of his muscle over the gunshot wound. The same wound Wexler had aggravated with enthusiastic thumps upon his back. The damn thing had never healed properly, but given the circumstances aboard ship under which the bullet had been extracted, he was simply grateful to be alive.

"Did Lord Pinworth pay your Ren for this deed?" his mother asked.

"Quite handsomely, yes."

"Hmm, well, sadly"—his mother frowned—"as honorable as her deed was, it could also prove dangerous to have her associated, in any way, with any activity involving a ship and an unauthorized trip to France. We must rely on her activities during her stay in London to make her respectable."

Henry considered Ren's activities since she had arrived in London, including an attempted burglary, public fornication, and threatening to shoot a peer of the realm.

His mother arched a brow. "Elizabeth mentioned that she had invited Ren to tea."

"Yes."

His mother nodded. "Good, good. Being seen in the company of someone of Elizabeth's rank will be very good for your Ren. I shall see that Elizabeth sends the invite soon."

"Elizabeth," his father drew his mother's gaze. "Whether or not Miss Teague gets cozy with your closest friend does not release me from my duties to the Crown."

Henry opened his mouth to respond to his father's not so veiled threat to have Ren arrested, but his mother held up a silencing hand. "You were more than willing to forget your duty in regard to Henry's activities, and you shall do so now in regard to the woman he loves." She glanced at Henry. "Please tell me Ren has never killed anyone."

Not yet. "No, she has not."

"See, Eugene? She has never harmed anyone, and

she certainly would not be the first smuggler in history to evade capture."

The baron looked to Henry. "If you truly mean to marry this woman, I suggest you convince her to leave her smuggling days in the past, for all of our sakes."

"She will never agree to it."

"That is your problem, son, not mine."

"Eugene—"

"No, Elizabeth. No more. We shall allow Miss Teague to show us what is more important to her, our son or smuggling."

Henry feared he knew the answer to that without having to ask.

****

Unaware she was the topic of a heated conversation between Henry and his parents, Ren assessed a bolt of delicate lace that had all the tell-tale signs of being French. Given lace was one of her prime "imports," she considered herself a bit of an expert, and as she turned the lace over in her hand, she narrowed its maker down to two Parisians, one of which had supplied two of the crates that now sat, rotting, in the Mermaid's hold.

"It is lovely," Eirene observed over Ren's shoulder.

"Yes, but the mark up is ridiculous." Ren had often considered the pros and cons of extending her reach all the way to London. Of course, there was more money to be made simply because London merchants required more product to meet a higher demand, but there was also more expense in transporting the goods to London, not to mention more risk. In the end, she always decided it best to keep her operation local.

She released the lace and moved deeper into the

dressmaker's shop. The visit was the result of Eirene's insistence that Ren needed a proper London wardrobe and a blatant refusal to listen to any arguments to the contrary, though Ren had tried.

"I do not need a London wardrobe," she had insisted.

"You cannot meet Henry's family while wearing trousers or a borrowed gown," Eirene had countered.

"I would not have cause to meet Henry's family if not for your initial involvement with my wardrobe."

"Pah! Your behavior at Lady Dunston's ball cannot be blamed on that beautiful scarlet gown."

"Kindly inform Henry of that fact because he believes otherwise."

"Of course, he does, because if he does not blame the gown, he must take responsibility for his actions, and men are horrible at taking responsibility for their actions."

"Says the former, self-proclaimed recluse."

"Marriage has taught me a great deal about men."

"You have only been married for one month."

"I learn fast. Now be quiet and try on every gown I tell you to." And that had been that.

Over the course of an hour, with the help of Eirene and a very non-French Madam Fleur, Ren was slipped in and out of a handful of commissioned but unclaimed dresses until there was a small collection of garments Eirene deemed acceptable. Ren nodded and agreed with whatever Eirene said, because, truthfully, all the gowns began to look the same after awhile and she certainly had no knowledge of what accessories were needed to "complete the ensemble." Back home she made do with a few pair of black trousers, several blouses, some in white and some in black, and two pair of men's riding boots. She did own one gown, but it hung, unused, in her wardrobe.

"You will need a wedding gown," Eirene suddenly announced as she reached past Ren to touch a bolt of ivory silk.

"I certainly do not."

Eirene frowned. "You agreed to marry him, yes?"

Had she? She recalled their conversation in Wexler's corridor. She hadn't exactly said yes as much as she had simply run out of ways to battle Henry's unrelenting determination. "I have stopped saying no."

Eirene rolled her eyes. "Then you will need a wedding dress."

"This will do." Ren plucked a dress from the "to be purchased" pile.

It was a lovely sea-green walking dress with thin, darker green stripes, long sleeves, and a modestly cut, square bodice. Eirene had paired it with a hunter green spencer, matching gloves, and the promise of a coordinating bonnet. Ren had scowled at the idea of a bonnet, so Eirene had promised a lady's top hat instead.

"You cannot get married in a walking dress."

"Trust me, I can get married in the nude and the signatures on the license will be just as valid." Ren's statement caused Madam Fleur to bark with laughter, which she quickly disguised as a sudden coughing attack. Red with embarrassment, the woman excused herself as the bell above the door jingled to announce the arrival of new customers. Curiosity made Ren glance toward the door, and she touched Eirene's arm as she recognized the elder and younger Parish women.

Eirene looked around, frowned, then pushed Ren

deeper into the shop so they could not be seen easily.

"Why are we hiding?" Ren whispered.

"We are avoiding, not hid—"

"Mama, I've told you already that I do not *know* why he has gone to Cornwall." Miss Parish's voice cut across Eirene's whispered reply.

"You've likely scared the man off," Mrs. Parish accused in a tone that would have made the strictest of nannies proud. "I warned you, did I not? You cannot toy with men such as his lordship. You must give them what they wish for or lose them to someone willing to do just that."

Eirene arched a brow and leaned close to Ren to whisper, "Considering the content of those letters, I'd say Miss Parish gave Wexler precisely what he wanted."

"Yes," Ren whispered back. "But we also know his sudden trip to Cornwall has nothing to do with Miss Parish."

Eirene conceded with a nod, and they both fell silent as the Parish drama continued to unfold much to the obvious discomfort of Madam Fleur who seemed unsure if she should continue to hover or return to her other customers.

"My advice to you, young lady, is to do whatever you must to bring Wexler to heel. You wasted far too much time enjoying the pointless pursuit of Mister Westhaven, and now the Season is nearly over. Need I remind you that you are not getting any younger?"

"Pointless? Was it not you, Mama, who told me Henry's interest would benefit me by inciting the interest of other gentlemen within his circle?"

"Henry, is it?" Mrs. Parish harrumphed. "Mister

Westhaven no longer matters. The man has shown himself to be a no good cad, no matter how many titled friends he may claim. Breeding never lies, my dear."

"His father is a baron."

Mrs. Parish harrumphed again. "An honorific only, and for God knows what sort of *service* to the Crown. No, you will forget all about Mister Westhaven. Besides, the man will be married by this time next week to that raven-haired doxy."

Ren took a step forward, but Eirene stopped her with a firm grip upon her arm and a shake of the head.

"He will regret that," Mrs. Parish went on. "A man has no desire to be married to his mistress. It takes away the excitement."

"You truly believe she is his mistress?"

"Of course, I do. You saw her. No gentlewoman would have worn such a gown or allowed such public liberties to be taken with her person."

"Lady Dunston seemed to like her."

"Hmph! Lady Dunston is cut from the same cloth. How someone so common caught the eye of a duke's son I'll never know, but I imagine it had nothing to do with stimulating conversation or refined manners. No, in my opinion, being accepted by Lady Dunston does not enhance a person's standing."

"What of her relationship with Lady Rowe-Weston?"

Eirene's grip on Ren's arm tightened.

"Surely, you cannot have anything bad to say about her ladyship?"

"Hmph! Given the scandal her ladyship was involved in mere months ago, it is no wonder she and Miss Teague are friends. Two of a kind, they are."

"Better our kind than her kind," Eirene whispered in Ren's ear.

"Now then, Annabelle, when did Wexler say he planned to return from his trip?"

"He only said as soon as possible."

"Yes, well, let us hope it is very soon and that, upon his return, you can finally secure a proposal from him, or you will have to move on to someone else."

"But, Mama, I have already allowed Lord Wexler...certain liberties." Miss Parish's voice dropped as she made the admittance.

"Yes, and if necessary, you will allow another gentleman those same liberties until you finally do your duty and secure a title. Is that understood?"

"Yes, Mama." Miss Parish followed her mother and Madam Fleur into the back room.

"Goodness!" Eirene exclaimed as she and Ren came out of hiding. "I do not know if I feel sorrier for Miss Parish because she will likely marry Lord Wexler or because she must call that horrible woman, Mother."

Ren said nothing. Each time she saw or heard about Miss Parish, she was struck anew by the reality that Henry had intended to marry the girl. If things had gone differently in Lord Sumner's conservatory and Miss Parish possessed free will, she might have said yes to Henry's proposal and he would have been lost to her forever.

"Ren? Are you quite all right? You look a tad green all of sudden."

Ren brushed off Eirene's concern with a flick of her hand. "I am fine." But she was not fine. Not at all.

Chapter Eleven

"As torturous as you made it out to be," Eirene announced as she entered Ren's bedroom the following morning, "you will thank me now for our hours spent in the dress shop."

Ren lifted her face from the soft pillows and twisted to glance over her shoulder. Eirene stood at the foot of the bed holding a piece of paper that had obviously once been folded and sealed.

"What time is it?" She glanced toward the windows to see the edges of the thick curtains illuminated by sunlight.

"It is nearly half past nine."

Ren dropped her face back into the pillow. "Why are you waking me up?"

"Because it is nearly half past nine," Eirene said as though Ren had forgotten about some household schedule she had never been informed of. "And also because you have received an invite from Lady Dunston to join her today for tea."

Ren forced her face from the pillows once more and put in a little extra effort to actually roll onto her back and sit up. "Is it acceptable for me to decline?"

"Absolutely not." Eirene tossed the invite onto the bed and crossed the room to open the wardrobe that contained three of the dresses chosen during their shopping excursion. One walking gown, one evening gown, and a house dress. The others, Madam Fleur had promised, would be ready in no more than two days. Eirene extracted the walking dress and returned to the bed. "This will have to do."

Ren looked at the navy blue gown with periwinkle stripes. "I do not recall trying on that gown."

"Oh, you did not. I chose it for you and had Madam alter it while you tried others." Eirene laid the gown across the bed and returned to the wardrobe to withdraw a periwinkle spencer, matching gloves, and a navy blue top hat with a periwinkle ribbon tied around it with the ends left to trail down the back. Ren had to admit it was all quite fetching.

"Now, come, come," Eirene ordered as she clapped her hands. "Lady Dunston expects you at eleven, and it would be horribly rude to be late."

Ren crawled out of the bed and surrendered the next hour of her life to Eirene's fussing, and in the end, the image reflected in the mirror was more shocking than the one she'd seen prior to Lady Dunston's ball. Perhaps it was the conservative nature of the outfit or the restraint of the twisted coif at her nape. Whatever it was, she felt as though a stranger looked back at her.

"What is the matter?" Eirene demanded as she frowned at her expression.

"I do not recognize myself."

"Ah. Well, I can relate. I felt much the same when I attended Lady Palmer's ball. I believe I told you it was my first formal event. Yes, well, I spent nearly an hour staring at my reflection once I had donned my gown. Its gold fabric and low neckline made me feel quite exposed, but I knew I had a duty to perform. I also believe I told you it was Lady Palmer's ball that was to act as the setting for my ruination."

"Oh, yes, you told me." Ren smiled as she recalled Eirene's very detailed explanation of what had transpired at Lady Palmer's ball.

"Yes, well, my point is, all battles require some sort of uniform, and I viewed that gold gown as mine and you shall view the current ensemble as yours."

Ren returned her attention to the mirror. "Do you believe tea with Lady Dunston will be akin to a battle?"

"I certainly hope not." The reply did nothing to ease Ren's concerns.

****

At precisely five minutes before eleven, Ren followed Lady Dunston's butler to a set of glass doors that stood open to reveal an expansive conservatory filled with natural light, a tropical forest worth of greenery, and an abundance of potted and cut flowers that filled the space with an inviting fragrance. She was led to the center of the large space where existed a very cozy arrangement of sofas atop a plush area rug strewn with large, jewel-toned pillows. A low table sat amidst the arrangement, offering a large tea tray, several platters of small sandwiches, and a dish of sugary biscuits.

Lady Dunston, attired in an ivory, floral, robed gown and matching ruffled cap, sat upon one of the sofas. Her guest, a lovely woman of the same age dressed in daffodil yellow, sat opposite. There was something familiar about the woman, but she doubted she had ever seen her before. Her contemplation ended as did the conversation between the two ladies as the butler announced her.

Lady Dunston smiled, set down her tea, and stood.

She extended both hands in welcome. "My, my, aren't you one of the most glorious looking creatures I've ever seen." She clasped Ren's hands and looked her up and down. "What an incredibly fetching ensemble. Do you not agree, Elizabeth?" The last was directed toward Lady Dunston's guest.

"I do, indeed," the woman said with a smile that served to enhance Ren's feeling that she had seen her before.

Lady Dunston returned her attention to Ren. "One ride through the park and you will have every female in London trading in their bonnets for top hats." She shot another look toward her guest. "No offense, my darling Elizabeth, but this creature might be too good for your rapscallion of a son."

Ren snapped her gaze to Lady Dunston's guest. The familiarity she felt came from the shape of the woman's eyes and the line of her nose, both of which had been passed on to Henry. She dropped a curtsy as best she could while Lady Dunston retained possession of her hands. "Lady Westhaven."

"I must say, Miss Teague, you are not at all what I was expecting."

"Dare I ask what you were expecting?" No doubt the question broke no less than a dozen rules of etiquette, but she did not appreciate being lured into an ambush.

Lady Westhaven smiled behind a sip of tea, then set the cup gently upon its saucer. "To hear my husband speak of you, I was expecting a wild woman with a cutlass clutched in her teeth with perhaps a monkey riding upon your shoulder."

"I can place the dagger that is strapped to my thigh

between my teeth, if you wish. In regard to the monkey, however, we will both have to be disappointed by its absence."

Lady Dunston released her hands and clapped with obvious joy. "Oh, Elizabeth, I told you she was a breath a fresh air, did I not?" She clasped Ren's hands again and tugged her toward the cozy seating area. "Sit, sit."

Ren chose the edge of the third and final sofa. As she arranged her skirts over her knees, a large peacock strutted past to vanish into the foliage.

"Oh!" The presence of Henry's mother had made her forget all about the promise of seeing live peacocks.

"There are six, but they are being quite anti-social today," Lady Dunston explained. As if to emphasize her point, there was a loud repetitive call from within the greenery. "That is Harold, the most vocal and precocious of my boys." As if on cue, another call erupted from out of sight. "Oh, do be quiet, Harold," Lady Dunston scolded as if speaking to a child. "I have no idea what has him so out of sorts today."

Ren glanced at Henry's mother and caught the woman's amused expression. They contemplated one another for several moments before Lady Westhaven broke the silence. "Do you love my son?"

Lady Dunston paused in the act of pouring a cup of tea and shot a rather shocked look toward Henry's mother. "A rather blunt way to begin a conversation, is it not, Elizabeth?"

Lady Westhaven's gaze never wavered from Ren. "I find that a great many obstacles can be overcome if two people love one another. Do you agree, Miss Teague?"

"No." The best course of action seemed to be to

meet bluntness with bluntness.

Lady Westhaven arched both of her pale brows. Although the woman had to be nearing sixty years old, she was still strikingly beautiful despite the wrinkling around her blue eyes and the slight thinning of her lips. Hints of blonde shone in her otherwise gray hair, and her hands were steady as she held the dainty cup and saucer above the skirts of her yellow gown. Clearly, Henry had inherited more than the shape of his mother's eyes and her nose. He'd also perfected her steady, penetrating gaze.

She was aware of Lady Dunston taking up a fresh cup of tea and relaxing back against her sofa with the avid attention of a child at their first circus.

"Explain yourself, young lady," Lady Westhaven insisted.

"Love cannot put food on the table or a roof overhead, nor can it erase the lines between classes."

"Ah." Lady Westhaven sipped her tea. "Henry did say you believe yourself unworthy to join our family. Is that true?"

"You professed, based upon your husband's assessment of me, you expected me to arrive with a cutlass in my teeth. I would say that answers your question as to whether or not I am worthy to join your exalted family." Ren refrained from picking up her steaming tea. Unlike Lady Westhaven, who clearly possessed the composure of a saint, she had been known to toss things about in a fit of temper, and she had no desire to arm herself with Lady Dunston's fine china should the moment suddenly warrant a fit of temper.

"And yet, here you sit having tea with one of the

highest ranking ladies of Society."

"Please, Elizabeth," Lady Dunston interrupted. "You speak as though I'm a bleedin' duchess." She looked to Ren. "My late husband was the second son of a duke, but his elder brother produced no less than ten children, eight of which were healthy, hardy sons."

"I see." But, really, she did not, because she had never taken the time to memorize the order in which people ascended through the nobility, though the second son of a duke did sound quite high ranking.

"My *point*," Lady Westhaven continued, "is perhaps you are not as unworthy as you believe."

"I imagine your husband would disagree."

"My husband is my concern not yours."

"Under normal circumstances, perhaps, but your husband has a duty to the Crown, which includes arresting people such as myself, a task he has embarked upon with great determination for many years."

The sound of fabric shifting against fabric drew Ren's gaze to Lady Dunston who now sat ramrod straight upon her sofa. "Elizabeth? Is the girl right?"

"Of course, she is right." Lady Westhaven took a sip of tea, then set the cup and saucer upon the table with much more force than Ren expected. She met Ren's gaze. "The baron can be made to see reason."

"I beg your pardon, Lady Westhaven, but we are not discussing an attempt to convince your husband to accept a new color for your dining room. We are asking him to accept a criminal as his daughter-in-law."

"I am well aware of that," Lady Westhaven snapped. "You have yet to answer my original question. Do you love my son?"

"Yes." Ren saw no advantage in lying, nor did she

believe she could successfully lie to Lady Westhaven. "I love Henry very much." She looked away from his mother's penetrating gaze as her eyes began to burn.

"Do you love him enough to give up smuggling?"

Ren returned her focus to Lady Westhaven. "Ah, is that to be the caveat then? I quit smuggling, and suddenly your husband agrees to call me daughter?"

"Yes and no." Lady Westhaven picked up her tea once more.

Ren narrowed her eyes. "Care to explain, my lady?"

Lady Westhaven sighed softly and set down her cup. She looked at Ren with a great deal of compassion. "My husband believes if you love Henry enough, you will cease smuggling in order to marry him."

"I see."

It was Lady Westhaven's turn to narrow her eyes. "You do not love him enough."

"It is not that simple. Smuggling is not only my way of life, but I have my crew to consider. If I quit, they lose their livelihoods."

"They also lose the threat of a noose about their necks," Lady Westhaven countered.

Ren held her tongue as it was difficult to argue the truth.

"There are legal means of trade in which you and your men could engage."

"While the war continues, there is no profit to be made from legal trade."

Lady Westhaven sighed again. "If you marry my son, you will no longer need to worry about profits."

"Does Henry plan to support my men as well?"

"Knowing my son, if it means making you happy,

he will try." Lady Westhaven looked to Lady Dunston. "Care to help me win this argument?"

"Miss Teague makes valid points, Elizabeth, and it is hardly fair for either of us to tell her how to live her life."

Lady Westhaven got to her feet in a flurry of yellow skirts. She looked ready to lose her temper but, instead, began to pace in obvious agitation. After a few moments, she returned to her seat and sat with a huff of exasperation directed at Ren. "My son loves you."

"Yes, I know."

"And you love him."

"Yes, I do."

"Then, for heaven's sake, stop being so bloody stubborn! My son nearly married that Parish girl because of you. No!" Lady Westhaven held up a silencing hand. "You will listen to me. I cannot tell you what to do, but I can assure you that, if you love my son the way I suspect he loves you and you choose to reject his proposal, again, you will condemn the both of you to a living hell for the rest of your lives."

"I know," Ren said quietly, and the admission seemed to take a bit of wind from Lady Westhaven's sails.

From the depths of the conservatory, one of the peacocks suddenly gave a very loud, honking, cawing call, and Ren wished she could answer in kind. It seemed a most appropriate noise to accommodate the pain in her chest as she considered the past three years without Henry as well as the prospect of a future without him.

"Ren, my dear," Lady Westhaven spoke into the silence, her tone devoid of any earlier frustration or anger, "you must do what you feel is best for you."

She battled against tears as she met Henry's mother's caring eyes. "Why are you being so kind to me?"

Lady Westhaven smiled. "The most obvious reason is because my son loves you to the point of senselessness, but also because I like you."

"You do not know me."

"Elizabeth has always possessed the ability to read people the moment she makes their acquaintance," Lady Dunston explained. "In all the years I have known her, she has never judged a person wrong. It is uncanny."

Lady Westhaven shrugged a shoulder and plucked a powdered biscuit from the tray. "Everyone is good at something."

"Yes, well, unfortunately what I am good at happens to be illegal," Ren commented.

"Did your father engage in smuggling?" The inquiry came from Lady Dunston.

"No. He was the captain of a merchant ship and proud of it." Ren reached for a biscuit. "Considering all the money he lost because of smugglers, he would be mortified to see me as one of them." She ate the biscuit in two bites, then licked the powdered sugar from her fingertips.

"A lady does not lick her fingers, Ren," Lady Westhaven advised.

"No, I imagine they do not." They shared a smile as Lady Dunston chuckled.

After a few moments of shared lightheartedness, Lady Westhaven brought the conversation back to less amusing matters. "What happened to your parents? If you do not mind my asking?"

"My mother died hours after I was born, and my father was killed in a shipwreck ten years ago."

Her statement was met with identical looks of compassion.

"Ten years ago. I assume that is when you embarked upon your smuggling?"

"Yes."

"How old are you, my dear?"

Ren glanced at Lady Dunston. "One and thirty."

Lady Dunston arched a brow. "And you never married?"

"I have never been interested in marriage."

Lady Westhaven helped herself to another biscuit, then wiped her fingers clean on a napkin, which, in Ren's opinion, was a waste of good powdered sugar. "As I said, I like you, Ren. I had no idea if I would or not, but I do, and I believe you are the perfect woman for my son."

"But?"

Lady Westhaven smiled. "But I fear for the turmoil it might cause my family if you continue smuggling."

Ren held Lady Westhaven's steady gaze for several moments, then finally picked up her tea, which at some point Lady Dunston had refreshed. The heat warmed her palms as she cupped the dainty cup and took a sip. The tea was very strong, very delicious, and exactly the fortification she needed to say the words she suspected Lady Westhaven expected to hear. "What is stopping me from saying I will quit without having the intent to do so?"

"Nothing at all, my dear, but I believe you are a tad more honest than that and respect Henry far too much to begin your life with him based upon a lie."

Bloody hell, the woman was sharp. "I shall have to think about it."

"Of course, and while you do that, please consider this war will not last forever, God willing, and once it is over, how lucrative will your adventures continue to be? I would like to say my son will wait as long as he must, but his foolish peccadillo with Miss Parish proves me wrong on that account." She leaned forward and gave Ren a very serious look. "Between you and me, my dear, welcoming a criminal into the family is far less concerning to me than welcoming a nineteen-year-old who is terrified of horses and water."

"She is afraid of horses and water?" And Henry thought to marry this woman?

"Oh, yes, and heights and dogs and probably letter openers, too, for all I know."

"Elizabeth!" Lady Dunston scolded then chuckled.

Lady Westhaven seemed quite unremorseful. "Well, really, the child is afraid of everything."

"She is not afraid of Lord Wexler." Ren's offhanded comment earned her two very curious looks.

"Wexler, you say?" Lady Dunston shook her head. "That man has nothing to recommend him beyond his ancient family title."

"Miss Parish wishes to marry a title, does she not?" They seemed perfect for one another from Ren's point of view.

"Yes, yes." Lady Dunston tapped her chin and adopted a contemplative expression. "I wonder if Lord Wexler is aware of her interest."

"Oh, yes, he knows." Ren went on to explain about the love letters and how she had been in a position to see them.

Lady Westhaven shook her head and laughed with open delight. "And now he is in Cornwall with Venton?" She laughed again. "Well, my dear, rest assured you will have your ship returned to you, because only an absolute fool would double cross Bramley."

"A ship I may have no use for."

Lady Westhaven frowned. "Henry mentioned your rescue of Lord Pinworth's daughter. An honorable use of your ship, I must say."

"But just as illegal, I fear." She had broken the blockade to retrieve Pinworth's daughter, though he had assured her his power would protect her if necessary.

"Yes, well," Lady Dunston spoke into the suddenly heavy, tension filled silence. "First, trust Lord Cragmoor to return your ship to you, because Wexler will have a curse upon his head if he attempts to double cross the earl, and then you can decide how best to move forward."

"Excellent advice," Lady Westhaven concurred. "Now then, assuming you make the right decision," she winked at Ren, "we have a wedding to plan."

Two hours later, as Ren allowed one of Lady Dunston's handsome footmen to help her into Eirene's town carriage, she realized two things. One, Henry had definitely inherited all his stubbornness from his mother, and two, she had somehow agreed to marry him in Lady Dunston's conservatory in three days' time. As for agreeing to give up smuggling, she had promised to strongly consider it, which seemed enough for Lady Westhaven.

Ren settled against the plush carriage cushions and

shook her head. It seemed copious amounts of strong black tea posed as much threat to her decision-making abilities as alcohol.

Chapter Twelve

Dearest Readers,

It seems Mister H.W. will wed the ravishing Miss T tomorrow. The private ceremony will take place within Lady D's home, which is appropriate, yes?

In other news, it seems Miss A.P. is set to become a bride soon, as well. Rumor has it she was shopping for a special wardrobe. It seems safe to assume Lord Wx is the lucky man though he has yet to return from his mysterious trip to Cornwall. As vexing as the man can be, this author does hope he has not been turned into a toad by the E. of C...

Henry paced the length of the parlor and exchanged the occasional silent glance with Adrien who sat before the fire enjoying a glass of brandy. A few months ago, it would have been fine French cognac. He would be lying to himself if he pretended not to miss the thrill of smuggling. It was like an opium high to silently sail past His Majesty's ships and an even bigger thrill to evade Napoleon's fleet.

Ren was an expert at both, no matter the conditions. He had never been able to quite master her skill of maneuvering a ship through thick fog or starless night. She did it as though she had the power of sight that gossips claimed Bram possessed. He would not go so far as to call her a pirate, as his father had, but sailing seemed to be her calling the way some men found their way to the church.

"Eirene will never forgive you if you wear a rut in that new carpet."

Henry halted and leaned against the mantel with his arms crossed. "I have a strange feeling about all of this."

He had come to Adrien and Eirene's home to speak with Ren, with whom he'd had no contact since their conversation outside Wexler's house, only to be informed by his friend that the ladies had gone out shopping for this or that.

"She agreed to marry you, *oui*? The only thing you should feel is relieved." Adrien gestured with his glass. "*Bouger*, you are blocking my heat."

Henry shifted slightly to the left. "*Why* did she agree?"

Adrien put his head back and groaned with a tad more volume than Henry believed necessary.

"My father heavily insinuated that, if she does not cease smuggling, he will uphold his duty and have her arrested, wedding or no." His mother, upon her return from tea with Lady Dunston and Ren, had assured him all was under control and he had no need to worry. A platitude that only made him worry more.

Adrien lifted his head and met Henry's gaze. "The wedding is tomorrow. She must have agreed, *oui*?"

"Ren will agree to anything to get back her ship."

"She does not need to agree to *anything* to get back the ship. I have no doubt Venton has secured the registration and sent Wexler back on his way to London by now."

Henry frowned. "Then why is there a wedding

tomorrow?"

"Perhaps she wishes to marry you, *mon ami*. Is that so very difficult to fathom?"

"Yes." He ignored Adrien's exaggerated eye roll. "You do not know her, Adrien. Ren values her freedom as greatly as her ship, and you've seen evidence of how she feels about that bloody ship. She had the opportunity to marry me, without pressure, three years ago and vehemently declined, but now, suddenly, she is agreeable to the idea after being forced into this situation?" He shook his head. "No. All of this smells like rotten fish to me."

"Do you believe she will leave you waiting at the altar?"

Henry raked a hand through his hair and began to pace again. "That is the problem. I have no idea what she pl—"

"Forgive the intrusion, sir." Adrien's butler stood in the doorway.

Adrien sat up in his chair. "What is it, Hamish?"

"There is a young lady asking to have a word with Miss Teague."

Henry narrowed his gaze at the butler. "Did she offer her name?"

"Aye, sir." Hamish approached Henry to hand him a calling card, and with a single glimpse of the stylized, white rose upon the back, Henry knew to whom it belonged.

He looked at Adrien. "It is Miss Parish."

"Tres interessant."

"I would say it is more curious than interesting." Henry addressed Hamish. "With your master's permission, show her in here."

Hamish glanced at Adrien who nodded his consent, then frowned at Henry. "What's this all about then, hmm?"

"We shall soon find out."

Mere moments later, the rustle of fabric turned Henry's gaze to the door as Hamish led Miss Parish into the large, yet comfortable, parlor. As per usual, she was dressed fetchingly in a white and lime-green striped gown fashioned with a modestly cut bodice and long sleeves. Her golden hair was gathered in a simple, twisted coif that had probably taken hours to create, and her face glowed with youthful vitality that dimmed a bit as she halted in her tracks and gaped at Henry.

Adrien, having stood the moment Miss Parish entered, moved forward to offer a bow. "Good day, Miss Parish."

It seemed an effort to drag her gaze from Henry. "Monsieur Cloutier." She curtsied although Adrien was as common as she.

"Hamish informs me you wish to speak with Miss Teague?"

"Oh, well, yes." Her hands, encased in lime green gloves, twisted into the fabric of her skirt as she looked back and forth between her host and Henry before finally giving Henry her full attention. "It is a pleasant surprise to find you here, Mister Westhaven. Allow me to offer congratulations on your impending wedding."

"Thank you." Henry crossed his arms and leaned back against the mantel. "Might I inquire what it is you wish to speak to Miss Teague about?" He felt Adrien's glance in response to the chill in his tone but ignored it. For reasons he could not explain, Annabelle's desire to seek out Ren raised his hackles. It added to the already fishy smell of the situation, and he did not like it.

"Oh, well, I, that is…I merely wished to extend an offer of friendship." The smile she flashed did not quite reach her eyes. "I imagine she will feel quite out of place and grateful for an ally. Her life in Cornwall and whatever it entailed cannot possibly have prepared her for a life as your w-wife." Her breath hitched around the last word.

Henry exchanged a brief look with Adrien and saw his thoughts reflected in his friend's expression. It seemed they both agreed the offer was rather unexpected.

"Is your mother aware of your intentions to befriend my future bride?" His question drained a bit of blood from Annabelle's rosy cheeks.

"As I am soon to be married myself, I do not require my mother's permission for such things."

"Congratulations," Adrien offered. "Who is the lucky gentleman?"

Miss Parish paled even more. "Oh, well, that is to say, there has been no formal offer yet, but I believe it is only a matter of time before Lord Wexler makes it official."

"Ah, Wexler." Adrien nodded but offered nothing more, and Henry wondered if both of them were thinking of the lurid notes Miss Parish had penned to Wexler. She might believe intimacy would lead to marriage, but it was not uncommon for a gentleman to make promises, take his pleasure, then walk away. According to Bram, Wexler had already done so with one of Lord Worley's daughters.

Annabelle looked to Henry with the wide, bright-eyed expression, which, in the past, had convinced him she would say yes to his ill-advised proposal. "I do hope our marriages do not prevent us from continuing our friendship. That is to say…" She trailed off, then seemed to gather herself. "Is Miss Teague available for company?"

"She is currently out with Lady Rowe-Weston," Henry told her.

"I see." She nodded and released the death grip upon her skirts to twist her hands together. "I do hope you will inform her of my call." She curtsied to Adrien and made a hasty exit.

"Oui, tres interessant," Adrien echoed his sentiment from earlier.

Henry stared at the parlor door through which Annabelle had escaped more than exited. "What the devil do you make of that?"

"Must you look for a conspiracy in everything today, *mon ami*?" Adrien took up his brandy and returned to his chair before the fire. "I admit it does seem strange for Miss Parish to extend an offer of friendship to Ren, but it is what women do, is it not? Besides, cultivating a friendship with Ren puts Miss Parish within my wife's exclusive and rather nonexistent circle of acquaintances. I imagine that prospect keeps Miss Parish and her mother awake at night, vibrating with the promise of untold advantages."

"Yes, I imagine you are exactly right."

"Mais bien sur, mon ami. I am always right. Now, pour yourself a drink and sit down before your pacing and fretting leaves me no choice but to throw you out."

****

Ren stepped down from the carriage and froze as she watched Miss Annabelle Parish exit Eirene's home.

The two women stared at one another for an odd, uncomfortable, rather lengthy moment, but then Miss Parish's face broke into a bright smile, and Ren braced herself in case the girl meant to embrace her.

"Miss Teague! What an advantageous encounter."

"Oh?" Ren saw no advantage in it whatsoever.

"Good day, Miss Parish," Eirene said as she exited the carriage.

Miss Parish curtsied. "Do forgive my accosting you in such a fashion, but I paid a visit in the hopes of speaking with Miss Teague."

"Oh?" Ren knew she must sound like a dunderhead, but she could think of no fathomable cause for Miss Parish to desire a meeting.

"Perhaps we should continue this conversation inside," Eirene suggested. She led the way to the door, which stood open in response to the sound of her return. Hamish dutifully waited inside to collect wraps, gloves, hats, and in Miss Parish's case, a parasol. "I believe we shall take a light refreshment in the library, Hamish."

"Very good, my lady."

Eirene glanced at Miss Parish. "You are alone?"

The girl flushed. "Oh, yes, well…yes. I was shopping with my maid, but she was suddenly overcome with fatigue, so I instructed her to rest for a bit in the park."

Ren wondered what type of shopping Miss Parish did to fatigue her maid. Yes, dress shopping was tedious, but it did not require a sit down afterward.

"Very well." Eirene said nothing more as she led Ren and Miss Parish to the library. The large room overlooked the back terrace, and with its two fireplaces and comfortable furniture, it had quickly become Ren's favorite space in the house. The dark wood paneling and leather-bound books in their glass front cases reminded her of her cabin on the Mermaid.

Ren claimed her favorite seat in the room, a large, cigar-colored leather reading chair though she refrained from tucking her feet under her like she normally did. Eirene took the chair opposite, and Miss Parish perched upon the edge of a tufted sofa. The sound of the fire crackling filled the silence as Miss Parish darted glances back and forth between Ren and Eirene.

The awkward moment was interrupted by Hamish's arrival with a tea cart. "Shall I pour, my lady?"

Eirene waved him away and did the deed herself. "How do you take your tea, Miss Parish?"

"Oh, one sugar and heavy cream, please, my lady. Thank you."

Eirene prepared the concoction, handed it to Miss Parish, then poured two cups of plain, black tea for herself and Ren. "Now then, Miss Parish, I believe you were going to tell us what has brought you here today?"

"Oh, yes, of course, my lady." Miss Parish clutched her tea and looked to Ren. "I wish to offer Miss Teague my congratulations on the upcoming wedding."

"Oh?" Ren mentally kicked herself for echoing the same bloody word for the third time in a row.

"Mister Westhaven is a wonderful man as I'm sure you know, of course," Miss Parish rushed on. "You two are acquainted, after all."

"Intimately." Ren felt the weight of Eirene's gaze but ignored it as Miss Parish turned several shades of pink. She could not put her finger on it, but there was something she did not trust about the young lady, and in her world, being congenial to an untrustworthy person could lead to a knife in the back.

"Yes, well…" Miss Parish sipped her tea, coughed, then cleared her throat. "I imagine London Society is quite different than what you are accustomed to, and I thought you might wish to know that, if you should need one or like one, you will have a friend in me."

"How kind you are, Miss Parish." Eirene responded before Ren could find her tongue.

"Thank you, my lady." She fixed her blue gaze upon Ren. "My offer is most sincere. I believe we could become great friends, Miss Teague."

In that moment, Miss Parish and her angelic smile reminded Ren of Lord Pinworth's daughter, Caroline, whom she had agreed to fetch from France after the treaty had collapsed. Lord Pinworth, while offering Ren a veritable fortune, had assured her his *precious* child would cause no problems whatsoever, so eager was she to return to England and the safety of her family. In reality, the girl had been a bloody nightmare.

Ren's crew had been beside themselves with lust as Lord Pinworth's precious daughter strutted around with pouty lips and vulgar cleavage. Simpson had been the first man to cave to temptation, and Ren had nearly tossed him overboard upon discovering him with his pants down around his ankles while Lord Pinworth's "innocent" daughter serviced him like a dockside whore.

She had ordered the girl locked in her cabin for the duration, but that had not stopped the vixen. A few quiet sobs through the cabin door and Ren's men had lined up to take their turn until Ren made it perfectly clear that any man caught within spitting distance of their "honored" guest would be tossed overboard. Knowing she never issued an idle threat, the men got control of themselves, which forced little Miss Caroline to turn her sights upon the one man not beholden to Ren's warnings and threats. Henry.

Miss Pinworth had attempted to befriend Ren in a blatant ploy to get close to Henry, but Ren had deflected the false offer. She had warned Henry to watch his back, but he had laughed at the notion of Miss Caroline taking him unawares. His amusement ended, however, when Miss Pinworth cornered him in a dark corner of the hold, stripped off her clothing, and offered to do whatever he desired. Henry, always the gentleman, had told the girl to put her clothes on before she caused herself any more embarrassment. Caroline, being the strumpet she was, ignored the suggestion and grew bolder with her intentions.

Ren had come upon the scene just as Miss Pinworth began to paw at Henry who attempted to thwart the girl while also attempting not to touch her naked body. His resistance and Ren's interference had incited Caroline's temper, and the entire ordeal had ended with the girl gaining possession of Ren's pistol. The shot she intended for Ren had gone into Henry's back as he jumped between them. The act of chivalry had saved Ren's life but nearly led to the end of his own.

Ren ended the train of thought and focused upon the young woman across from her. Miss Parish did not have the look of madness in her eyes, nor did Ren suspect she knew how to properly handle a gun, but in hindsight, she would have said the same of Miss

Pinworth.

"I am certain Miss Teague would be honored to have you as a friend. Isn't that right, Morvoren?" Eirene's question forced Ren to respond.

"Of course." She wondered if her smile looked as forced as it felt. "It seems you will soon be Lady Wexler, yes?"

Miss Parish blinked at the question, and her hand shook as she lifted her tea to take a brief sip. "Lord Wexler has not proposed as of yet, and business matters have taken him away from London presently. I have no doubt upon his return he shall make things official."

"Do you love him?" Ren knew it was wrong to ask such questions over afternoon tea, but she also knew if one wished to ferret out the enemy's motives, then one needed to gather as much information as possible.

Miss Parish took another brief sip of tea. "I am quite fond of him."

She recalled the words Miss Parish has written in the notes they had discovered in Wexler's study. There seemed to be more than fondness involved, but perhaps Miss Parish had simply done whatever necessary to secure a title, per her mother's obvious dictates. And people believed London to be more "civilized" than Cornwall? She nearly snorted in her tea at the thought.

"A match with Lord Wexler would be quite advantageous," Eirene observed. "He holds a very old title."

"Yes, and I possess wealth. It is the perfect Society match, is it not?" Miss Parish's smile faltered a bit. "Forgive me. I have no cause to sound so ungrateful. I am quite honored to have gained the attentions and affections of Lord Wexler."

Ren narrowed her eyes at the girl as more warning bells rang in her head. "Forgive my boldness in asking, Miss Parish, but I am curious to know if you regret your decision to turn down Mister Westhaven?"

"Oh! I…that is to say…I… Of course not." She shook her head with such vehemence a few golden tendrils escaped their pins and her teacup rattled upon its saucer. "Mister Westhaven is a most wonderful gentleman, and I admire him greatly, but he and I would never suit, and you seem to suit him perfectly." Her cheeks blazed with color at the implied reference to the scandal. "That is to say…he and I would not suit, and I wish the two of you much happiness with one another."

"Thank you," Ren managed, despite the warning bells that continued to ring within her head. "I wish the same for you and Lord Wexler."

"Ah, yes, well, as I said, he and I will suit just fine, and the match will make me the envy of several of my friends, and it will make my mother proud." She smiled, then giggled in a way that reminded Ren of just how young Miss Parish was. "As you said, my lady"— she nodded at Eirene—"Lord Wexler possesses an old, respectable title and is more than passably handsome. Yes, I am quite lucky to have gained his attentions."

Ren wondered how many more times Miss Parish would have to repeat those words before actually believing them. A blind rat would have had the ability to see the young lady's resignation where Lord Wexler was concerned, and it made two things as clear to Ren as the view out the large picture window. One, Miss Parish had found her title and would do whatever necessary to secure it, and two, if in possession of her own free will, she likely would have accepted Henry's proposal.

It was the latter that made Ren's tea turn sour in her stomach as she wondered how Henry would react to such a realization. He claimed to have never loved Miss Parish, but he had been prepared to marry her. The Henry she knew would never shackle himself to a woman he harbored no feelings for, therefore, he had to have felt *something* for the girl.

She glanced at Miss Parish in all her golden, angelic, rosy-cheeked, wide-eyed perfection and was suddenly very glad she had agreed to marry Henry tomorrow. Perhaps the unease she felt about Miss Parish's offer of friendship would ease once *she* was Mrs. Westhaven. She certainly hoped so, because she did not enjoy feeling threatened by a child.

For God's sake, she was Captain Morvoren Teague. She had stared down the cannon of His Majesty's ships of the line without blinking, and Miss Parish, although in possession of certain charms, was certainly nowhere near as threatening as that.

Chapter Thirteen

Henry sat before the dying fire in his bedroom. The brandy in his glass had long since vanished and the mantel clock had recently chimed three a.m. In a little over twelve hours, he and Ren were to be married. Assuming Ren did not change her mind.

It was that thought that had forced him to pour glass after glass of brandy for the last several hours. If Bram were around, he'd tell Henry not to worry, or perhaps he wouldn't say that at all. Perhaps he would tell Henry he was a bloody fool to love a woman like Ren and to expect her to be satisfied with a quiet life that involved nothing more stimulating than the usual round of social events.

"Good God," he groaned and let his head fall back upon the chair. "She is going to be bloody miserable as my wife."

"Yes, I agree."

Henry jerked upright in his chair so fast he nearly blacked out as the room spun around him. He glanced in the direction of the voice to find Miss Parish standing in the middle of his bedroom. What in the blazes?

"Annabelle?" His parched throat turned her name into a croak.

How the devil could his throat be parched after five, or was it six, glasses of brandy?

He managed to get to his feet and was overcome by

168

the very pressing need to take a piss. Christ.

"If you would excuse me for a moment, Miss Parish, I have need of the— That is to say, I must make use— Please, excuse me." He made a quick exit from the bedroom into the dressing room and felt marginally more focused once he'd seen to nature's call. A glance in his shaving mirror, however, revealed a face in need of a shave and a good night's rest.

He took a few moments to splash room temperature water on his face, then used a little more to slick back his hair. The absolutions did nothing for the dark spots under his eyes, his brandy-laced breath, or the rumpled condition of his shirt. Well, *c'est la vie*, as Adrien would say. If Miss Parish wished to surprise a gentleman in his chambers in the wee hours of the morning, she could not expect said gentleman to be at his best. As he left the dressing room and reentered his bedroom, his head began to pound with one single question.

Why the devil *was* Miss Parish in his chambers in the wee hours of the morning? Not that it mattered. He needed to get rid of her and fast, because the last thing he needed or wanted was another bloody scandal.

Miss Parish had made herself at home in his absence. She'd shed her cloak *and* her shoes and sat curled in the chair Henry had occupied for the past however many hours. She'd also taken the liberty of refilling his brandy glass. The sight of her golden beauty illuminated by the weak fire should have stirred something within him, considering he'd been prepared to marry her, but all he felt was irritation. There was only one woman he wanted in his bedroom, drinking his brandy at three a.m., and it was not Miss Parish.

"You need to leave," he said without an ounce of gentlemanly tact.

She looked over her shoulder with wide, blue eyes. "I know it is incredibly improper of me to be—"

"You need to leave," he said again.

She uncurled herself and stood to face him, which put her back to the fire and rendered the white sheath she wore as transparent as a bloody window. No amount of brandy could blind him to the fact that Miss Parish had seduction in mind, nor did it escape him that the view she presented did nothing to stir his blood. In fact, not once during the year he had pursued her had he ever fantasized about such a moment. In his quiet moments, in his dreams, there had only been Ren. And in twelve hours or so she would be his again. Officially. Forever.

Had he been alone, he might have dropped to his knees to give thanks.

"Is that what you truly want, Henry?"

He blinked and tried to clear his head, knowing he needed to pay attention. "Where is your cloak?"

He glanced about the room but could not locate her cloak or her shoes. She'd been wearing a cloak before he excused himself, so what the devil had she done with it? He blinked several more times to bring the farthest reaches of the room into focus and cursed himself for consuming so much brandy. Though it was not as if he could have predicted Miss Parish's visit, and a man should be able to drink as much brandy in the privacy of his home as he bloody well wished to drink.

A thought struck him, and he focused on Miss Parish once more. "How the hell did you get into my home?" It seemed the visit to the chamber pot had relieved him of his manners as well.

She shrugged a shoulder, which sent the strap of her sheath slithering down her arm. The action pulled the bodice down as well until it caught on the fullness of her breast. "A woman should not reveal all of her secrets, Henry."

Her words sounded like a purr, but the Miss Parish he knew did not purr. She giggled and cooed.

He pressed the heel of both hands to his eyes. Maybe he was hallucinating. It seemed a strange hallucination to have on the eve of his wedding to Ren, but it made more sense to his muddled brain than the reality of Miss Parish's presence.

He dropped his hands. "I have no idea what game you are playing, Miss Parish—"

"I prefer when you call me Annabelle."

"It is not appropriate to do so."

"Henry, darling," she purred again. "I am standing in your bedchamber in my night dress. I do believe we can dispense with some formalities." She moved toward him, seductively, and he found himself wondering when Miss Parish had learned to move in such a fashion.

Before he knew it, she had her arms draped around his neck and her supple curves pressed to his body. He could feel the hardness of her nipples through the thin fabric of her night dress and his shirt, and his only reaction was annoyance.

"Enough is enough, Miss Parish." He took hold of her arms to remove them from around his neck. "I do not wish to summon my butler to have you removed, but I will if you persist in ignoring my request that you go."

"Ooh, yes, you do that." She stepped back and flashed a smile that gave Bram's most demonic a run for its money. "I do wonder how your bride would react to the gossip of me leaving your home just before sunrise. I do not think she would be very happy." She twirled away from him before he could respond, then looked back over her shoulder. "We shared tea together earlier today. Did she tell you?"

"I am aware." Ren hadn't told him, but Adrien had sent round a note to "warn him." At the time, Henry had believed Adrien to be a tad paranoid. When would he learn to pay more attention to his friends?

"Lovely woman," Miss Parish went on. "Not in a traditional way, of course, but I can certainly understand why you fell prey to her wiles. There is something rather…" She propped a hand on one hip and tapped the index finger of the other against her chin. "Loose. Yes, that is the word. I am certain you are not the only man to forgo common sense in her presence."

"And yet, it is you who stands half naked in my bedchamber." Really, he'd had enough. He strolled to the door and pulled it open. "This little visit is over, Miss Parish."

She crossed her arms over her ample bosom and remained where she was. "It seems subtlety is lost on you, my darling. I am offering myself to you." She uncrossed her arms and held them out at her sides. The fire at her back silhouetted her hourglass figure to perfection. "It is my mother's desire that I marry a title, but my desires are much different. I wish to be yours."

"I do not want you to be mine." He had to force the words out as he hadn't quite gotten over her belief that her actions had been subtle.

Her arms fell, and she pouted. "You wanted me as your bride, but you do not want me as your mistress?"

"I do not require a mistress."

"No, I suppose you do not, seeing as how you are marrying a whore."

Henry stalked toward her, grabbed her arm, and hauled her to the door and out into the corridor. "You can leave the way you entered, or I can drag you into the street. Your choice."

"Why are you doing this, Henry? We love one another."

"No, we do not." He looked around the room. "Where are your things?"

"I saw the love in your eyes when you proposed to me," she insisted.

"What you saw was delusion." He spied her cloak draped across his bed and went to fetch it. "Where are your shoes?" He looked over his shoulder and met Miss Parish's rage-filled gaze.

She crossed her arms. "I won't tell you."

"Then I shall toss you out without them." He crossed the room and attempted to hand over her cloak, but she refused to uncross her arms, and the garment fell to the floor. "For God's sake, Miss Parish, pull yourself together and see reason."

"It is you who cannot see reason, Henry darling." She uncrossed her arms and threw them around his neck once more. "Kiss me." She pressed kisses to the underside of his chin and along his jaw line. "Please, Henry." Her mouth found the open collar of his shirt, and she trailed kisses up the side of his neck. "I can make you so incredibly happy."

"No, Miss—"

"Oh, yes," she interrupted. "I can. I've learned things—"

"While in Wexler's bed?" He took hold of her arms and attempted to unhook them from around his neck, but she held fast, and he had no wish to do her harm.

"What I did with Wexler meant nothing. It was a means to an end."

He almost felt sorry for Wexler.

"My mother threatened to disown me if I did not secure a title." Tears glinted in her eyes. "What choice did I have? Do you believe it was easy for me to refuse your proposal then offer myself to Wexler?"

"Honestly? Yes, I do." He made another attempt to extract himself from her embrace, but she merely pressed her body tighter to his. "Annabelle, you are embarrassing yourself."

"Say it again."

He blinked in confusion.

"Say my name again," she clarified.

"Miss Parish."

"No." She stomped a foot and tears streamed down her face. "Call me, Annabelle." She dropped her face against his chest and began to sob.

Bloody hell!

"Annabelle, please, you must calm yourself."

She lifted her face and sniffed loudly. "Do you care for me at all?"

Even drunk, Henry could smell a trap. "Neither of us is in the right frame of mind to have any sort of meaningful conversation." He took hold of her arms, and surprisingly, she allowed him to remove them from around his neck. "Now, be a good girl and gather your things, and we can forget all about this incident."

Instead of doing what he asked, she took hold of the bodice of her nightdress and tore it nearly to her naval. Henry gaped like an idiot at the display of flesh.

"I know you want me, Henry." She parted the fabric to expose her breasts.

Brandy churned in his stomach, and his head exploded with warning bells. He scooped her cloak off the floor and draped it, as best he could without any assistance, over her nakedness. With his hands on her shoulders, he turned her toward the door.

She dug in her bare heels. "You would toss me out in this condition?" Her voice rang with hysteria.

"This is your last chance to tell me where your shoes are."

They stared at one another for several moments until she finally told him they were under his bed. He retrieved them and dropped them before her. "Put them on and leave."

To his surprise, she put on the shoes, then slipped into the cloak.

He opened the door, and she brushed past him to step into the corridor.

She turned back before he could close the door behind her. "You will regret this," she warned.

"Goodbye, Miss Parish." Henry closed the door and leaned his pounding head against the paneling. He heard Miss Parish's curses, then the soft tread of her slippered feet as she retreated. He made a mental note to inform Danvers to have all the locks changed and perhaps purchase a very large dog. The sort of hell hound Bram always seemed to have at his side while in Cornwall. Miss Parish was terrified of dogs, or so she had claimed.

At the moment, he was not certain if anything he knew about her was true.

He pushed himself away from the door, checked the lock, then stumbled across the room to fall face first on the bed. It did not take long for the brandy to drag him into the arms of Morpheus, but there were no dreams to be had, merely the blackness of sleep.

Chapter Fourteen

Once, when Ren had been about thirteen years old or so, she fantasized about her wedding day. The fleeting moment had come after she'd witnessed a local wedding procession passing the cottage. Her father had remarked upon the bride's beauty, and Ren had stared after the procession and imagined herself in the bride's place with a handsome groom by her side. The day would be bright and sunny, and the sea calm enough for an evening sail along the coast. The fairy tale had not lasted long, for there had been chores to do, but she could recall it as though it had happened yesterday, and it most certainly had *not* included the threat of arrest or the presence of peacocks.

Harold, or so she assumed, stared at her from several meters away, then let out one of his obnoxious screech honks before he shook his majestic tail in what she took to be a display of vexation over the influx of people into his territory. Another peacock suddenly appeared at his side from within the foliage and joined Harold in his noise making.

Ren battled the urge to screech in reply. The novelty of live peacocks had worn off relatively fast upon exposure to the creatures, and she hadn't a clue how, or why, Lady Dunston tolerated the racket. However, the peacocks were not the main cause of her frustration. That honor fell to Baron Westhaven and his son.

The former glowered at her from across the conservatory, no doubt prevented from arresting her by the expression of obvious displeasure upon his wife's face. It bothered Ren to think she was the cause of discord between the couple. She liked Lady Westhaven a great deal and suspected she might even like the baron if given half a chance. However, she did not feel a great deal of favor toward Henry at the moment, given his suspicious absence from his own wedding. The wedding he had stubbornly insisted upon.

At first, she had merely assumed he was late, perhaps delayed by an overly stubborn cravat, but her willingness to give him the benefit of the doubt had expired an hour after the agreed upon time of the wedding.

"Adrien has gone to check on Henry," Eirene said as she appeared at Ren's side.

Ren frowned and looked away from the peacocks. "I had expected him to be here at the crack of dawn, so eager is he for this wedding."

Eirene offered a weak smile. "I am certain there is a logical explanation for his delay."

"Oh? Such as?" Her question made Eirene frown.

"Well, I do not know. Perhaps he encountered a problem in the streets."

"One that would prevent him from walking here?" She did not have the layout of London's fancy neighborhoods memorized as she did every inlet of the Cornish coast, but it seemed safe to assume Henry could walk from his home to Lady Dunston's with ease.

"No, Eirene, he likely realized what a bad idea this is and changed his—"

A spectacularly loud peacock call interrupted her words. She clapped her hands over her ears and exchanged a look with Eirene, who seemed to share her opinion of the creatures. Before either of them could comment on the noise, Henry appeared.

Ren dropped her hands and stared at him. He looked awful. Truly awful. As though he had been set upon by ruffians. His hair was a tangled mess, his features looked as if he hadn't slept in days, his clothing was all out of sorts, and he lacked a cravat, gloves, and a hat.

He caught her eye and marched toward her, but before he could reach her, his mother flew across the conservatory with the speed of a launched cannon ball.

"Henry, darling! What happened to you?" Lady Westhaven embraced her son, then ran both hands over his person as if checking for broken bones.

He took possession of his mother's hands to halt her examination. "I am fine, Mother. Poseidon threw a shoe."

"Where? In Scotland?" the baron asked as he appeared alongside his wife.

Ren glanced at the baron, and he caught her eye and scowled. The exchange did not bode well for a future of family dinners.

"Forgive my appearance and tardiness," Henry said to no one in particular. "Poseidon can have a bit of a temper." He focused on Ren. "Might I have a word with you in private?"

"Of course." Good Lord, did he mean to call off the wedding? Her heart raced as Henry excused himself from his parents and led her to a quiet corner.

"Someone took a shot at Poseidon," he announced

without preamble.

"Excuse me?" Ren's heart ceased altogether. "My God, is he—"

"He is fine." He raked a hand through his hair. "The bullet merely grazed his shoulder, but it scared the devil out of him, and he bolted right into an oncoming phaeton, which resulted in much chaos, splintered wood, and several lacerations on his forelegs. Thankfully, the driver of the phaeton suffered no injuries, though, after an endless amount of arguing, I was ready to alter that outcome." His gaze shifted past her. "I see you and my father have not killed one another yet."

Ren ignored the comment. "Who would shoot at Poseidon and why?"

"No, no," Henry shook his head. "I did not mean to insinuate it was intentional. Merely a wild shot."

"In the middle of London?" She crossed her arms. "If you believed that, you would not have concocted that ridiculous story for your parents about Poseidon throwing a shoe and a tantrum."

"I gave it no thought, to be honest. I was more concerned with ensuring Poseidon's well-being."

She believed him, of course. Poseidon was like a child to Henry. "Where is he now?"

"Feasting like a king in Lady Dunston's mews."

"Eirene sent Adrien to find you."

Henry nodded. "And he did. As I was arguing with the owner of the phaeton."

"And?" She knew there was more.

"Despite my insistence that it was too late and unnecessary, he rode off in the hopes of apprehending the person responsible for the shot."

"So he believes it was no accident either." Who the devil would take a shot at Henry? "Do you have enemies?"

"None I was aware of." He raked a hand through his hair, which did not improve it at all, then shook his head. "Look, now is not the time to discuss this. I believe we have a wedding to attend." He offered his arm. "By the by, you look beautiful."

Ren smoothed her hands down the bodice of the emerald-green gown Eirene had decided would be perfect. "Thank you." She looked him up and down. "I imagine, when you left your home, you looked quite handsome." To be honest, a little blood and dirt and mussed hair did not diminish his handsomeness one bit.

He laughed at her rather backward compliment but had no time to reply as Lady Dunston appeared. She shook her head and clucked her tongue. "You cannot possibly get married in such a state, Mister Westhaven. I have prepared a room and a bath for you—"

"Really," Henry interrupted. "You should not have gone to the trouble. I cannot think it matters to anyone that my clothing is a little wrinkled."

Ren frowned at Henry's assumption. It obviously mattered to Lady Dunston, and it likely mattered to Henry's mother, and why the devil did he assume it did not matter to his future wife?

Lady Dunston clucked her tongue again. "You will do as I say, young man."

"I have delayed the proceedings enough as—"

"No more." Lady Dunston held up a hand and shook her head. "James"—she indicated the footman who hovered behind her—"will show you to your room, and do not worry about the delay. Vicar Collins will wait if he wishes to be paid."

If Lady Dunston had possessed a peacock tail, Ren imagined she would have rustled it in vexation.

Harold chose that moment to let out another of his alarming calls. Lady Dunston cursed. "What the devil has gotten into him of late?" She stalked off in the direction of the call.

"Sir?" James, the footman stepped forward.

Henry glanced at Ren. "Do forgive me. This is not at all how I imagined our wedding day would be."

"You imagined our wedding day?"

"Of course."

"And?" Curiosity consumed her.

"And," he said with a smile, "I shall tell you later."

She frowned after him as he followed the footman from the conservatory, but there was not much time to feed her curiosity as the conservatory erupted with a chorus of peacock calls coupled with Lady Dunston's failed attempts to soothe the birds, followed by the appearance of Adrien who looked only a tad less unkempt than had Henry.

He stalked toward Ren. "Where is Henry?"

"You just missed him. Lady Dunston ordered him into a bath, and she might do the same for you."

Adrien waved away her warning with a flick of his wrist. "I need to speak with him."

"What is going on here?" The Baron Westhaven materialized beside Adrien. "And I shall have the truth, thank you very much. No more poppycock about thrown shoes."

Adrien bowed toward the baron. "Perhaps we could speak somewhere private, my lord."

"A fine idea." Baron Westhaven's gaze flicked to

Ren. "I imagine you will join us whether I wish it or not."

"You know me so well and on such a short acquaintance, my lord."

"Marriage to Lady Westhaven has honed my abilities to recognize a stubborn woman when I see one."

She dipped her head to hide a smile and recalled her earlier assessment that she could like the baron if only he would give up his desire to arrest her. Henry had inherited his father's golden-brown eyes, unruly hair, sensual mouth, and she suspected, his wit and charm, though the baron had displayed neither of those attributes in her presence.

"Adrien?" Eirene joined them as did Henry's mother.

Adrien kissed his wife on the cheek and bowed to Lady Westhaven. "Forgive my appearance, ladies."

"What is going on?" Lady Westhaven demanded. "I did not believe one word of Henry's story about Poseidon. That horse, despite his size, is one of the most docile creatures I have ever encountered. Elizabeth's peacocks throw temper tantrums. Poseidon does not."

Confusion marred Adrien's expression. "I haven't a clue what you are talking about, my lady."

Ren touched Adrien's arm to gain his attention. "Henry excused his delay with a story about Poseidon throwing a shoe and a bit of a tantrum."

"I see."

"As you can also see," she continued, "no one believed the story."

"Oui." Adrien sighed. "It is not my story to tell—"

"You shall tell it regardless," Lady Westhaven interrupted.

"D'accord, d'accord," Adrien acquiesced with a nod. "Henry was shot at."

"Shot at?"

"My God!"

Lady and Baron Westhaven reacted in unison, then the baron looked at Ren with a gaze that held a bit too much accusation.

"Who is responsible for this?" he demanded.

"What are you implying, my lord?"

"Eugene—"

"Do not interfere, Elizabeth," the baron said to his wife without taking his eyes off Ren. "Answer me, Miss Teague. Which of your enemies has cause to shoot at my son?"

Ren crossed her arms and glared right back at Henry's father. "I apologize for having to disappoint you, my lord, but I haven't any enemies."

"Hmph! Other smugglers? Old crew members? *Think*, Miss Teague."

"As I said, I do not possess any enemies."

"Then explain to me why my son is being shot at on the very day he is meant to marry *you*?"

"Why must the two be related?" she countered.

Adrien cleared his throat. "The baron is correct."

Ren gaped at Adrien. "Excuse me?"

"I'm sorry, Ren, but the baron's assumption is correct."

"How do you know this? Did you catch the person responsible? Did they *tell* you their connection to me?"

"Yes and no." He sighed again. "I ran the shooter down, and after a bit of *persuasion*, the ruffian admitted he'd been hired to 'put a stop to the wedding.' "

"By whom?" she demanded as her heart began to pound painfully.

"He did not know. Claimed he was hired through contacts and says he knows better than to ask too many questions. I pressed for more, but there was nothing more to learn."

"Why would I hire someone to stop the—" She looked at the baron.

"If that looks insinuates what I believe it does..." Baron Westhaven put up both hands and vehemently shook his head. "You cannot possibly believe I would hire someone to shoot at my own son."

"No, but nor can I think of anyone else more opposed to this wedding."

"A former lover of yours, perhaps?" the baron suggested, which caused his wife to scoff in displeasure.

"Eugene, you have no right to accuse Miss Teague in such a fashion."

Ren did not take her eyes off Henry's father. "I feel it would be a waste of my breath to tell you I only possess one former lover and he happens to be the man who was shot at. Now, if you will excuse me. I suddenly have a headache."

Not caring if she was rude or not, Ren stalked from the conservatory before she said something to the baron that could not be forgiven.

****

Henry had to admit as he submerged himself in hot water, a bath had been a bloody good idea. He reemerged and swiped water and hair from his eyes to find Ren perched on the edge of the copper tub. The vision of her was so surreal he blinked several times to make certain she was not a hallucination.

"This is highly improper of you," he scolded.

She rolled her eyes. "Improper would be if I joined you."

His body stirred at the suggestion. "I'll not say no if that is what you wish to do." He leaned back and placed his arms on the sides of the tub. The clear water did nothing to hide his reaction to her presence, nor did she make any attempt not to notice. "If you continue to look at me that way, you will find yourself very wet," he warned.

She flicked her gaze to his. "You assume I am not already?"

"Jesus Christ, Ren." He groaned. "Have mercy on a man. Lady Dunston will have us both strung up if we delay this wedding any further."

The playfulness ebbed from her gaze as she shifted it away. "Adrien ascertained the shooter was hired to stop the wedding."

Henry sat up with a violent slosh of water. "Who in the blazes—"

"Your father believes it is one of my former lovers," she said as she looked at him once more.

Despite the heat of the water, his blood ran cold. "And? Is he correct?"

"Bloody hell, Henry!" She shot to her feet to glare down at him. "How could you even ask that?"

"We have not seen one another in three years."

"Your point is?"

"That is a long time for a woman with your level of passion to be—"

"Say one more word, and I swear to God *I* will

shoot you." She stalked away to the other side of the room and halted before the fire.

Henry took the opportunity to leave the bath and secure a towel about his waist. It seemed arguing with Ren about marriage, while naked, was to be a bit of a habit. At least she did not have a pistol in her hand.

"Ren."

She spun around, and he took a step back at the green fire in her eyes. "Did it not occur to you," she began in a tone that matched the heat of her gaze, "that the passion you refer to was because of you? Do you truly believe I would give myself to another man after what we shared?" Her voice cracked, and she blinked as though she had something in her eyes.

Dear God, her obvious attempt not to cry made him want to get back in the tub and drown himself. "Forgive me." He had no idea what more to say.

She shook her head and turned her back once more. "If we are to be married, it is good that I know what you think of me."

Her words struck like a bullet, and Henry raked both hands through his wet hair, attempting to find the right thing to say to undo the damage his senseless words had obviously caused, but as he had observed upon occasion with his parents, silence was sometimes the best course of action.

"I accused your father of hiring the shooter," Ren said after several excruciating moments.

"I am sorry I was not there to see his reaction."

She looked over her shoulder, and he saw that some of the fire had left her gaze. "He was quite offended."

"Well, you accused him of hiring a man to shoot at

his son."

The fire returned. "*After* he accused *me* of having a harem of jealous, former lovers. An accusation you obviously believe."

"I do not believe such a thing."

"You did."

"Perhaps for a split second." He regretted the words instantly. "And I have a feeling you will never allow me to forget that split second for the rest of our lives."

"Assuming I marry you."

"You do not mean that." God, he prayed she did not.

She turned fully to face him. "Someone shot at you, Henry, and according to Adrien, they did so to prevent our wedding. I confess that does not make me very anxious to return to Vicar Collins until we discover who and why."

"Then it seems we have a bit of a mystery to solve."

Chapter Fifteen

Dearest Readers,

In a most shocking turn of events, the wedding between Mister H.W. and Miss T. did not take place for reasons this author is sadly unaware of. Nor can I say if the wedding has merely been postponed or cancelled altogether.

In other news, which may or may not be related, Monsieur A.C. was seen riding at breakneck speed across Hyde Park in what appeared to be pursuit, but alas, I haven't any further details on that incident either. There were also several reports of a supposed gunshot being heard near the park prior to the monsieur's wild ride, and I should also mention Lord B was seen in a fit of theatrical rage after his gaudy, new phaeton was turned into a pile of firewood due to a collision with Mister H.W.'s horse. All parties seemed uninjured, the horse included. Perhaps Mister H.W. was too overcome with angst after his run in with Lord B. to attend his scheduled wedding?

Lord B. does have a way of making people wish to retire from polite society...

"Really, we could do this all day and never arrive at any useful information." Henry threw down his pen and rose from his place behind Eirene's massive, antique desk. He, Ren, Adrien, and Eirene were gathered in the latter's office with the intent to put their minds together and solve the mystery of the "unknown assailant", so named by Eirene as she wrote the large words across the top of the paper that Henry had been tasked to use to make a list of possible suspects. In true Lady Rowe-Weston fashion, the paper had been divided into two columns, one for highly likely suspects and the other for unlikely but in need of consideration.

Ren leaned forward in her chair to better see the list and frowned at the absence of names in the first column. She glanced at the second column. "Maybe we should move Wexler to the first column."

"In my opinion," Henry began as he rounded the desk and headed for the brandy cart, "we should remove his name altogether." He held up the carafe. "Anyone else?" Upon receiving three negatives, he poured himself a glass and returned to the desk to stand over the list. "What cause does Wexler have to halt our wedding?" He directed the question at Ren.

"Maybe he wishes to remove you from the picture in an attempt to maintain possession of my ship—"

"How the devil does killing me impact his possession of your ship, which, I might add, he likely no longer has."

Ren scowled at him. "I do not know, but at least it's a name on the bloody list. That is more than the rest of you have offered during this futile gathering."

"It will sound mad, but I believe we should add Miss Parish's name to the list," Henry suggested as he took a sip of brandy then scowled and looked at the drink as if it tasted foul.

"Miss Parish? I doubt she even knows of the existence of ruffians let alone how to hire one, *mon ami*."

Henry sat down and acknowledged Adrien's observation with a nod. "I would agree with you if not for a recent incident that has made me question everything I thought I knew about Miss Parish."

Ren stared hard at Henry as the warning bells, which had plagued her during her tea with Miss Parish, began to ring again. "Care to elaborate?"

"Honestly? No." He lifted his glass but seemed to change his mind and set it down.

"Allow me to rephrase the question," Ren began only to be silenced when Henry lifted a hand and shook his head.

"No need. I will explain." He picked up the pen and wrote Miss Parish in the *Highly Likely* column.

Ren arched a brow but held her tongue. Patience had never been one of her strongest attributes, but Henry's demeanor suggested she forgo her usual tendency to fire off a barrage of questions.

"Miss Parish paid me a visit the evening before our wedding." He looked up from the paper and directly at Ren. "At three in the morning, to be precise."

"I see. And let me guess The purpose of that visit was to inform you that she has no desire to marry Wexler and wished she was free to marry you."

"There was a bit more to it than that." Henry sat back in the chair and raked a hand through his hair. "Perhaps I should preface all of this by admitting I had consumed a great deal of brandy prior to Miss Parish's arrival."

Ren's blood ran cold, and she looked at Eirene and Adrien. "Could we have a few moments of privacy, please?" She waited for their host and hostess to leave, then pinned Henry with a steady gaze. "What did you do?"

"For Heaven's sake, Ren, I did not *do* anything. Miss Parish appeared in my bedroom—"

"Your *bedroom*? How the hell did she *suddenly* appear in your bedroom?"

"I do not know. When I asked, she played coy about it."

"Coy? Miss Parish? Are we speaking of the same woman?" Ren considered herself fairly good at reading people, and although she did not exactly trust Miss Parish's intentions behind her offer of friendship, she could not equate the word coy with her. Coy suggested a level of worldliness that Miss Parish simply did not seem to possess.

"You are no more shocked than I was, believe me."

"Henry, tell me what happened."

He sighed. "As I said, she suddenly appeared in my room, dressed in naught but a nightdress, and proceeded to offer herself to me despite her impending engagement to Wexler."

"I see." Ren had to give Miss Parish some credit for possessing a sizable pair of ballocks.

"I told her to leave, of course, which, predictably, made her a tad angry. She reiterated her offer to become my mistress, in case I missed the point of her visit, and when I assured her I had no need of a mistress, she proceeded to slander you. At that point, I physically removed her from my room, and that was that."

"What did she say about me?"

Henry frowned. "Does it matter?"

"In a petty sort of way, yes."

"She called you a whore."

"Let me see if I understand correctly. Miss Parish arrives *uninvited* to your bedroom at three in the morning wearing a nightdress and offering to become your mistress, but *I* am a whore?"

"Which is precisely what I said to her."

"Did you really?" She enjoyed the thought of it but could not imagine Henry being quite *that* rude to—

"Oh, yes, I did. As I said, I'd had quite a bit to drink and it was difficult to recall my gentlemanly manners."

"And this unexpected display of irrational behavior from Miss Parish, you believe, warrants adding her name to the list of suspects?" She sensed there was more he hadn't told her about the visit.

Henry shrugged. "Jealousy can certainly motivate people to violence. You and I have witnessed it."

"You speak of Miss Caroline Pinworth."

"Indeed, I do." He rolled his shoulder and winced. "Her jealousy has left a permanent reminder."

"It still pains you?" Ren did not like to recall the aftermath of Henry being shot. The conditions aboard ship had not been ideal to extract the bullet, which had lodged itself between muscle and bone. The procedure had nearly killed him, and she died a little death each time she thought of it.

"Aye, it pains me, but I've learned to ignore it for the most part."

"I should have tossed that vixen overboard at the first sign of trouble."

"Then you would have had Lord Pinworth to deal with, and that would have ended far worse for both of us than a mere gunshot wound."

She waved her hand to dismiss the unpleasant topic. "You truly believe Miss Parish would hire someone to shoot at you?"

"I believe we should not entirely discount the possibility."

"Do you mean to confront her?"

"Directly? No. But I do believe we should reschedule the wedding and see if we can lure the guilty party out into the open."

"Are you suggesting a public wedding?" Ren did not care for the idea of a big wedding attended by people she did not know. Peacocks were bad enough.

"No, no," Henry assured her with a shake of his head. "I see no reason for that. I shall speak to Lady Dunston and arrange something similar to what should have taken place yesterday." He arched a brow. "If that is agreeable to you?"

Ren hesitated. "Are you asking if I am agreeable to getting married in Lady Dunston's conservatory or to you?"

"Both." His golden-brown eyes narrowed, and his brows furrowed in doubt. "Perhaps this delay has given you the opportunity to change your mind."

"You assume I wish to change my mind?"

He sighed. "Honestly? I never know with you, Ren."

She was tempted to make him suffer a little as retribution for proposing to Miss Parish, but she could not bring herself to cause him even a little bit of pain. "I have every intention of marrying you, Henry, if for no other reason than to eternally vex your father."

"Oh, is that the reason?" He sat back in the chair and crossed his arms. About twenty minutes into their meeting with Adrien and Eirene, he had shed his jacket and loosened his cravat with an apology toward Eirene. Eirene had waved away the breach of etiquette with a laugh and a reminder that she considered Henry and Ren family, and if one could not loosen one's cravat in the presence of family, it was indeed a sad world.

"Would your grandfather approve of such a sentiment?" Adrien had inquired.

Ren had learned in her time with Eirene that Eirene's grandfather had been more than a tad militant in his actions, opinions, and attitude.

"Grandfather approved of nothing." Eirene had stated, and that had been that.

Ren's gaze settled upon Henry's exposed throat. Their heated, hurried, scandalous, and unfinished moment at Lady Dunston's ball had done nothing to ease her three-year-long ache for his touch. In fact, the moment had only served to enhance said ache.

"Ren?"

"Hmm?" she answered without taking her eyes off his throat.

"Are you aware you are looking at me as though I am a prime cut of beef?"

"Am I?" She could recall the exact flavor of his skin, and it made her lick her lips in anticipa— An unwelcome thought intruded, and she lifted her gaze to look Henry in the eyes. "What were you wearing?"

He frowned in confusion. "Come again?"

"What were you wearing?" She made a little sound of exasperation as she saw his confusion deepen. "When Miss Parish appeared in your bedroom."

"Ah. I don't recall."

Ren almost growled in frustration. "I am not asking

you to recall the exact articles of clothing. I merely wish to know *which* articles you were wearing."

He smiled. Slowly. "It was three in the morning, Ren. Do you believe I was fully clothed?"

Vivid images of scratching Miss Parish's eyes out formed in Ren's mind, but she quickly dismissed them as not only petty but futile. Removing the girl's eyes would not remove the memory of seeing Henry in a state of undress. In Ren's experience, nothing removed the memory. Alcohol and near death run-ins with the French and British Navy certainly hadn't done the trick. She had still crawled into bed and dreamt of Henry.

She forced herself to refocus on the matter at hand. "Your suspicions about Miss Parish may have more merit than you believe."

"I am listening."

"Eirene and I overheard a conversation between Miss Parish and her mother the other day in the dress shop. It was rather enlightening, especially when taken with Miss Parish's offer of friendship, should I require one." She shifted forward in her seat as little details began to click into place. "Mrs. Parish all but ordered her daughter to stay well away from you and your acquaintances, and that included Eirene, who Mrs. Parish believes to be scandalous and bad company."

"Interesting. Adrien believed Miss Parish offered friendship to you for no other reason than to gain access to Eirene's inner circle."

"It seems Adrien was wrong about that, and I think we can all agree, despite the amorous notes found in Wexler's study, that Miss Parish does not love him and is marrying him only out of duty." Ren hesitated but then forged on. "It is you she wants, Henry, and now that you have rejected her, she is a woman scorned."

"Forgive me for pointing out the obvious, but would it not have made more sense to hire someone to shoot *you*?"

"Yes, well"—Ren settled back into the chair—"that part is a bit confusing, and it is also the one detail that has prevented me from mentioning your father as a serious suspect."

"My father? I believed you accused him merely in retaliation for him accusing you."

"At the time, yes, but you cannot ignore how opposed he is to our marriage."

"I am well aware of his disapproval, but if he truly wished to prevent the wedding, he need only arrest you."

"Yes, true." She sighed. "So we are left with Wexler and Miss Parish, and I must admit, that is not a very promising list of suspects."

"Especially considering Wexler is not even in London at the moment." Henry cursed and picked up the pen to draw a line through Wexler's name and met Ren's gaze. "That leaves us with Miss Parish, and as difficult as it is to fathom…"

"She seems guiltier by the moment," Ren finished for him. "Perhaps Eirene and I should invite her to tea again. If she is eager to be my friend, just imagine how excited she will be when I invite her to our wedding."

"Be careful, Ren. If Miss Parish is guilty of hiring a man to shoot at me, there is no telling what she is capable of."

"I hardly believe Miss Parish will make an attempt upon my life while in Eirene's sitting room, but in the event that she does, you know I can take care of myself."

"Against the French and British Navy, yes, but when it comes to dealing with a woman who may be blinded by jealousy…" He shook his head. "Promise you will be cautious."

"Oh, Henry." She stood and circled the desk to stand beside his chair. She reached out and tucked the wayward locks of his hair behind his ear and allowed her fingers to linger as he turned to look up at her. "Of course, I will be careful."

He caught her hand and kissed the underside of her wrist. The contact turned her blood to lava. "You are looking at me in *that* way again."

"Am I?" Ren arranged herself upon Henry's lap, grateful that she had chosen to don trousers in lieu of a gown that morning. Gowns had their advantages of course. She hadn't been blind to the way Henry reacted to the sight of her trussed up like a proper lady, but a gown did not allow for her to easily fit herself against Henry's body quite the way trousers did. She shifted closer, and Henry caught her hips and cursed.

"Bloody hell, Ren, we are in Eirene's office."

She ignored the obviousness of his statement and leaned down to finally kiss the swath of skin that had been tormenting her from within the edges of his open collar.

He dropped his head back and tightened his grip upon her hips. "Ren…"

"Hmm?" She hummed the question against his throat, then licked him.

He took hold of the braid that hung down her back and used it to disengage her mouth from his throat. Their gazes met and he shook his head. "No." He shook his head some more. "We will not engage in another unsatisfying romp in a highly inappropriate place."

She looked around, then back at Henry. "The door is closed, and I am quite certain Eirene and Adrien would knock before ent—"

He laughed but continued to shake his head. "No. I will not take advantage of our friends' hospitality by making love to you on Eirene's desk."

"There is always the rug in front of the fireplace," she suggested.

"You are incorrigible."

"Only with you." She shifted her weight against the evidence of his arousal.

He groaned, then took hold of her hips once more and quite easily lifted her from his lap. He stood as well, likely to prevent her from straddling him again. "After we are married, I may decide to keep you in bed for a full week."

"And I may decide to keep *you* in bed for two."

Henry tugged her close. He dipped his head and brushed his lips to hers. "Consider me your willing prisoner," he teased before kissing her.

After several breathless moments that only added fuel to the fire in Ren's blood, Henry ended the kiss and stepped back. "I suggest we speak to Lady Dunston about rescheduling the wedding as soon as possible."

Chapter Sixteen

Two days after becoming the number one suspect in *the mystery of the "unknown assailant"*, Miss Parish was shown into Eirene's library by Hamish. Per usual, the young lady looked as fresh and dewy as a spring flower in her white dress flocked with tiny, multi-colored flowers. A Spencer of pale green with matching gloves and bonnet completed the ensemble.

"You look fetching as always, Miss Parish," Eirene commented from the edge of the sofa upon which she perched.

Miss Parish blushed and curtsied. "You are too kind, my lady, but I fear I could never aspire to be as fashionable as you."

Ren silently agreed. Eirene wore a modestly cut, dark green gown adorned with delicate gold braiding at the high waist. Ren had chosen a dove gray gown with charcoal trim. A bit somber perhaps, but she could not quite develop a taste for the favored pastels. With each passing day, she loathed more and more the necessity for skirts, stays, and stockings, and if she'd had her way in the dress shop, she would have purchased everything in black. Eirene had balked in horror at the notion Ren would wish to "go about London looking like a widow or a witch." Ren had seen no point arguing it was a matter of practicality not appearance.

Soon enough, God willing, she would be home and

back in the comfort of her trousers and blouses.

Miss Parish glanced at Ren and offered a friendly nod and smile. "Good day, Miss Teague."

"Miss Parish." Try as she might, Ren simply could not imagine the cherubic Miss Parish attempting to seduce Henry in his private chambers at three in the morning. Despite the letters she'd penned to Wexler and their passionate nature, the girl seemed more the type to close her eyes and think of England.

"Please, join us." Eirene gestured for Miss Parish to sit and dismissed Hamish with a nod. "Has Lord Wexler returned yet?"

"Oh, no, he has not." Miss Parish removed her bonnet and set it on the sofa beside her. "Nor have I received word from him."

"I do hope he did not encounter any trouble during his trip," Ren offered, though she rather hoped Venton had ordered her men to toss Wexler into the sea.

"I am sure all is fine." Miss Parish looked back and forth between Ren and Eirene. "I must admit I was rather surprised by this invitation, my lady."

"Is that so?" Eirene smiled slightly, because of course, Ren had told her all the details Henry had imparted concerning Miss Parish's early morning attempt at seduction. "Well, Miss Teague has something she wishes to ask you."

Alarm flashed in Miss Parish's blue eyes as she shifted her gaze to Ren. "I only hope I can supply a helpful response, Miss Teague, but please, ask me anything."

It was on the tip of Ren's tongue to ask what the bloody hell the girl had been thinking to throw herself at Henry on the eve of his wedding, but instead, she took a sip of tea to burn the words away and offered Miss Parish what she hoped was a friendly smile. "You are aware that unforeseen circumstances forced Mister Westhaven and I to postpone our wedding?"

Miss Parish's gaze faltered. "Oh, yes, of course. I read about it in the paper. You must be so disappointed."

"Quite, but not for long." Ren took another sip of tea to give Miss Parish time to wonder at her words. When the girl's lovely blue eyes narrowed, Ren continued, "We have rescheduled the wedding."

The button that adorned Miss Parish's glove and that she had been blindly fidgeting with for the past several moments, popped off and fell to the floor. "Oh!"

Ren could not be certain if the exclamation was a reaction to the button or the news that the wedding had been rescheduled. Either way, Miss Parish seemed quite off balance, which gave Ren the perfect moment to fire a broadside. "As one of my only friends in London, I do hope you will attend."

All of the fetching, rosy coloring leeched from Miss Parish's face as she gaped. "Excuse me? You are inviting me to your wedding?" The girl made it sound as if she'd been invited to watch a public hanging.

"Of course. We are friends, yes?"

"Oh…yes. Friends. Of course."

"Here," Eirene said as she handed a freshly prepared cup of tea to Miss Parish. "You seem in need of a little fortification."

Miss Parish accepted the tea and quickly rested it upon her lap in a failed attempt to hide the very visible fact that her hands trembled. "Thank you, my lady. I do not know what has come over me all of a sudden."

I do, Ren thought as she sipped her own tea. *You are watching your devious little plan to ensnare Henry slip through your pampered little hands.*

"Perhaps it is merely the weather," Eirene offered. "It does seem unseasonably warm today."

"Yes, that must be it, exactly." Miss Parish looked to Ren. "When is the wedding to be?"

"The day after tomorrow."

"I see."

Silence fell, punctuated only by the occasional clink of china against china as they all sipped their tea, until Miss Parish finally spoke again. "I am honored you wish to include me in your special day, but I must decline."

Ren waited, quite certain Miss Parish had more to say.

"I wish you well, of course," the young woman said hurriedly, then pinched her lips together and darted her gaze away from Ren.

"Is there something you wish to say, Miss Parish?" Eirene asked, though the answer was written all over Miss Parish's face.

The latter shot fleeting glances at both Eirene and Ren for several moments, then set down her tea and twisted her hands together. "Forgive me," she said to Ren.

"What, precisely, am I to forgive you for?" Ren could certainly think of a few things, but she was quite curious to hear Miss Parish's answer.

"Please understand I have no wish to distress you—"

"Miss Parish, please, I am quite difficult to

distress." In fact, she could think of only two times when that term had been applicable to the situation. The first when Henry had nearly died from Miss Pinworth's gunshot and the second when he had walked out of the captain's cabin after she had rejected his proposal. She highly doubted anything Miss Parish had to say could come within range of those two moments.

"Very well." More silence and hand twisting followed those two words, and Ren was ready to take hold of Miss Parish, shake her, and demand she say whatever the bloody hell was on her mind, because, although feeling distress was rare, impatience was not.

Somehow, she resisted and managed to sit quietly, though the effort likely shed years from her life.

Finally, Miss Parish broke the silence. "Mister Westhaven paid me a rather unexpected visit the night before your wedding." It was said in a rush, though, to her credit, Miss Parish never broke eye contact with Ren.

"Is that so?" Eirene asked, which gained Miss Parish's attention. "What sort of visit?"

Miss Parish looked down at her lap. "Indecent," she said softly.

Ren glanced at Eirene who rolled her eyes and mouthed, "Say nothing."

She nodded, though she had intended to do just that. She was rather interested to hear Miss Parish's account of the "indecent" visit.

Miss Parish looked up from her lap, her eyes moist with unshed tears. "If we are to be friends, then I feel it is my duty to inform you of Mister Westhaven's true nature." She blinked, and a single tear ran down her left cheek.

Ren admired the young woman's talent.

"He came to me to confess he was still in love with me." She blinked, sniffed, and more tears streamed down her face. "Of course, I told him he should not say such things to me, but…" She looked away.

Ren held back a sigh at the dramatics and played her part.

"But what?" she prompted.

"Oh, Miss Teague, I beg you to forgive me for what I am about to tell you." Miss Parish flew off her chair and crumpled at Ren's feet to gaze up at her with imploring, wide, wet eyes.

Ren chanced a glance at Eirene, who shook her head and sipped her tea, obviously quite unimpressed by Miss Parish's display.

Miss Parish grabbed Ren's hands and her attention. "You must believe me when I say I did all that I could to stop him, to make him leave." She gasped for air as more tears streaked down her face. "But he was so determined to have me."

As if she could no longer continue, Miss Parish covered her mouth and sobbed behind her hand.

"Are you insinuating what I believe you are insinuating?" Ren did not have to pretend to be shocked. How dare the girl accuse Henry of such a deplorable act.

"Do you see?" Miss Parish looked up at Ren. "You cannot possibly marry him."

"If what you say is true, I fear what will happen if I refuse to marry him." Two could play this game.

"Oh, no, no. You can simply return to Cornwall. I can help you—"

"I assure you, Miss Parish, I do not require

anyone's help in returning to Cornwall." What the devil did Miss Parish think to offer? Traveling expenses? The use of her fine carriage? Ren nearly shook her head at the implied insult.

"Then you should leave immediately." Miss Parish's teary gaze had been replaced, quite quickly, with steely determination.

"Your concern is touching." *If not a tad nauseating.* "Perhaps I should speak to Henry first before making any—"

"Oh, no, no, you mustn't!"

Ren glanced at Eirene as her friend coughed around a sip of tea. They shared an amused look, then Ren returned her attention to Miss Parish. "Do not distress yourself, Miss Parish. I thank you for telling me of the incident, but I will not be able to allow the matter to rest until I confront Henry. I do not take being made a fool of lightly."

"Do what you must," Miss Parish said quietly as she climbed to her feet and swiped away one stray tear. With an abbreviated curtsy in Eirene's direction, she gathered her things and left without another word.

"Well, that was interesting," Eirene said as soon as they were alone.

Ren collapsed back into her chair with a loud sigh. "That was bloody grueling."

"Yes, but what do we make of it? Are we convinced Miss Parish is the guilty party?"

Ren sighed again. "I have no idea."

"She is near mad with envy. That much was quite obvious."

"Of me?"

Eirene nodded.

"I have nothing she could possibly covet."

"You have Henry."

"Need I remind you, it was Henry who was shot at? If Miss Parish wants him so badly, why the devil would she hire someone to shoot him?"

"They shot the horse."

Ren sat up straight. "You believe that was intentional?"

"Think about it, Ren. A crowded London street and the bullet grazes Henry's horse just enough to cause a great deal of chaos, confusion, and ultimately the cancellation of your wedding? Yes," Eirene nodded. "As difficult a shot as it might have been, I believe the man did precisely as he was ordered to do."

"And you believe Miss Parish orchestrated the entire thing?"

"Quite frankly, yes, I do. After her little performance today, it is very obvious she is quite desperate to prevent this wedding."

"How do we prove it?"

Now it was Eirene's turn to sigh. "I have no idea."

Ren said nothing as she leaned her head back and studied the paneled ceiling of Eirene's library. "What if we are wrong about Miss Parish?" She lifted her head to look at Eirene. "That would mean there is someone else determined to halt our wedding."

"And you can think of no one?"

"Not a soul." Beyond frustrated, Ren stood and wandered toward the garden doors. It was a beautiful day despite the heat Eirene had mentioned to Miss Parish. She reached for the latch to throw the doors open just as glass shattered all around her. She glanced down as a lancing pain seared her side.

"Ren!" Eirene's voice sounded far away, and as Ren turned toward the call, the world went black.

****

Henry leaned over the billiard table to line up his shot.

"You will never make that angle," Adrien observed as he had before nearly every ball Henry had sunk.

"I will, and you know it." Henry drew back the stick, but before he could strike the ball, the unmistakable sound of a gunshot rang out. He looked at Adrien. "Did that sound a little too close for comfort to—"

His words were cut short by the sound of Eirene screaming Ren's name.

Adrien dropped his whiskey and rushed for the door, Henry fast on his heels.

They arrived at the library to find Eirene collapsed on the floor with Ren lying across her lap. She looked up. "She was shot. Someone shot her through the garden door." Her words sent Adrien racing toward the door, but they all knew the shooter would be long gone.

Henry dropped down opposite Eirene. "Adrien, go for the doctor."

"I sent Hamish," Eirene told him.

"Good, good. Let me see the wound." He held his breath as Eirene exposed the wound. She had used the hem of her gown to apply pressure, and the fabric clung a bit before letting go. The bullet had struck Ren in the side, directly above her right hip. He looked at Eirene. "I need to see if the bullet exited, but you need to maintain pressure."

"Yes, yes, I know."

Henry ignored Eirene's clipped tone, very gently

208

gripped Ren's hip, and shifted her body toward him. "Adrien, I need your eyes."

"No exit wound, *mon ami*."

Henry cursed, though he was not surprised by Adrien's words. "We shouldn't move her until the doctor arrives."

He fetched a pillow from one of the sofas, and with Adrien's help, they managed to replace Eirene's lap with the pillow so Ren could lie in a more natural position. Eirene remained by her side with her hands pressed to the wound.

"Tell me exactly what happened," he said to her.

"There is nothing to tell. She went to the door and reached for the latch, and a gunshot shattered the glass and struck her. I managed to catch her before she could hit the floor and possibly do more damage by striking her head."

"Did you see anything?" He knew the question was futile.

"I glanced out the doors but only for a moment. My concern was Ren's wound."

He covered her hands with his and squeezed to show his gratitude for her fast thinking. Adrien liked to tease his wife for her militant upbringing, but Henry was damn grateful for it. Not too many women would have remained as calm in such a situation. Miss Parish, for example, likely would have fainted upon the sight of blood. Or would she have?

The doubt brought several other questions to mind, but now was not the time to interrogate Eirene. His only priority was assuring Ren would live.

"Where the devil is Hamish with that doctor?" he snapped, then felt both Eirene and Adrien's gazes upon him, but he refused to meet them lest they project sympathy. Ren needed him to keep a level head. There would be time enough to go mad if he lost her.

****

Ren opened her eyes to find her vision filled with Henry's handsome, albeit somber, face. His expression became a bit less somber when their gazes met.

"Why do you look as though someone died?" she asked.

"Because you almost did."

"Me?" Ren shifted and sucked in a sharp breath as an excruciating pain shot through her right side. The shock made her realize she might be very wrong about the reasons why she lay in bed with Henry by her side. "What happened?"

He raked his hair back, closed his eyes, and exhaled slowly before answering. "You were shot."

"Excuse me?" A person would surely remember being shot, and she had no such recollection.

"Someone took a shot at you through the library's garden door."

She slid a hand beneath the weight of the blanket and gingerly pressed it to her throbbing side. A wad of thick bandages met her fingers. "Is the bullet—"

"The doctor was able to remove it without too much trouble, and he stitched you up with the skill of a Parisian seamstress. I doubt you will have much of a scar to boast about."

"All good news to be sure, and yet you sound and look like hell."

"I thought I was going to lose you." He shoved both hands through his hair again with an aggression she'd only witnessed a few times.

"It would seem we are even now."

"No." He shook his head, and his hair slid forward again. "Do not make light of this."

"Henry?" She reached for him, but the movement made her side protest, so she dropped her arm back onto the bed with a huff of frustration.

He put his hand over hers. "What do you need? Are you in pain? Should I allow you to—"

"Kiss me."

"I am not certain that is a—"

"Please."

He leaned down and pressed his lips to hers in what could only be described as the most platonic kiss Ren had ever experienced. As he made to draw back, she risked the pain and hooked her left arm behind his neck. Then she kissed him the way she wanted to be kissed. He resisted for a few seconds, then angled his mouth, and she surrendered control.

For her, kissing Henry was a sensation unlike any other. She'd attempted to explain it to him once, but he had laughed and called her silly, though she had seen the look in his eyes and knew he understood and felt the same. Would it have been nice to hear him say it? Of course, but sometimes simply *knowing* had to be enough.

After a few more moments of pleasuring her mouth, he ended the kiss and rested his forehead on hers. "I was so damned scared when I walked into the library and saw you—" He inhaled a shuddering breath. "I thought I had lost you."

Ren tightened her arm around his neck. She wished she could give him a real embrace, but moving her right arm and aggravating her wound seemed like a bad idea.

"I am here." She kissed his nose. "I am beginning to believe it will take more than bullets to separate us."

He suddenly removed her arm from around his neck and sat up. "We will leave London as soon as you are fit to travel."

"And the wedding?"

"We can get married in Cornwall. Privately. In my study if we wish. All we need is a vicar, the license, and a few witnesses."

As heavenly as that sounded, she could not help but be suspicious of why, all of sudden, he would suggest such a thing. "And your parents?"

"I will inform them of our plans to leave London. What they do with that information is their choice."

"Why?"

He frowned down at her. "Why what?"

"Why are we leaving London? Do not say it is because of a few stray bullets."

"That is precisely the reason, and I would not call them stray." He left the bed and began to pace about the spacious room. "We know for a fact the bullet that grazed Poseidon was meant to halt our wedding, and I believe it is safe to assume the one Doctor Grayson removed from your side was meant to do the same."

"If we leave, we will never know who is responsible."

He halted and turned to look at her. "I'll not put your life at risk merely to satisfy a curiosity."

She attempted to sit up, but the pain was too much. With an aggravated sigh, she gave up and craned her head to meet Henry's gaze. "You would be content never knowing who is responsible?"

"I believe it is safe to assume Miss Parish is the

guilty party."

"And you arrived at this conclusion when and how?"

"I spoke to Eirene, who confirmed the gunshot occurred mere moments after Miss Parish left your tea party. Adrien and I were in the billiard room and never heard a carriage, which means she departed in her carriage *after* we left the billiard room."

Ren stared at the ceiling in contemplation. "Based on what you are saying, you believe whoever shot me accompanied Miss Parish in the carriage?"

"Or they are one in the same person."

She lifted her head from the pillow. "You believe Miss Parish shot me?" That was truly outside of what she was willing to consider. Miss Parish might be the mastermind behind the attempts, but she could not imagine the girl actually pulling the trigger.

"If it was not her, then it was her coachman, because, according to Eirene's groom, no one else arrived in the carriage."

"Henry, listen to what you are saying. You are implying Miss Parish said her farewells, called for her carriage, then ordered her coachman to go around back and shoot me? How would either of them have known I would be standing at the garden door?"

"Miss Parish knew your location in the room and likely assumed you would linger for a time after her departure. The coachman, assuming he was the shooter, likely intended to approach the door and fire into the room while you sat in your chair, but upon entering the garden he saw you at the door and—" He raked a hand through his hair.

She shook her head, then laid it on the pillow

again. Her eyes had begun to grow heavy, and her side throbbed like the devil. "Why would Miss Parish risk everything merely to halt our wedding?"

"She must deem me worth the risk."

"Mmm. Maybe." Ren could barely keep her eyes open or her thoughts straight.

Henry appeared beside the bed. "You need to rest." He stroked his fingers across her brow. "No matter who was responsible, you need not worry that it will happen again. Eirene has gone into full combat mode and has the place locked down tighter than Napoleon's headquarters."

Ren smiled at that as her eyes drifted closed. "Kiss me again," she whispered.

"You are incorrigible." Despite the scold, his lips brushed across hers.

"Forgive me for interrupting."

Ren forced her eyes open at the sound of Eirene's voice. Eirene smiled at her, then looked to Henry and extended a letter. "Danvers had this sent over. He believed it might be important."

The letter boasted an impressive, though somewhat ominous, black seal.

"It is from Venton," Henry explained as he broke the seal. He was silent for a few moments as he read the contents, then he read it out loud.

"Tell Ren her ship is secured, and I have the registration in my possession. I intended to send it to her via Wexler, but the chap decided to remain in Cornwall. Seems he's not keen to tie himself to Miss Parish, or so I gleaned from his unending monologue during our journey. Remind me to never again lock myself in a carriage with that man. I, too, intend to

remain here a while longer. My solicitor decided to inform me of a hidden codicil in my father's will. Amazing how the bastard continues to plague me from the depths of hell. ~V"

"Wexler's absence will not sit well with the Parish women," Eirene commented.

Ren nodded in agreement, then glanced at Henry. "Thank you."

He frowned. "For what?"

"For seeing that my ship was returned to me."

"Save your thanks for Venton when next we see him. It was his doing."

She let the matter drop, knowing Venton had only involved himself because of his loyalty to Henry, but she also knew Henry had never been comfortable in the face of excessive gratitude. He knew what part he had played in the matter, as did she, and that would be that.

Her eyes began to feel heavy once more. "The sooner I heal, the sooner we can leave London."

"Aye." Henry dropped a kiss on her forehead. "Rest well, my mermaid."

Chapter Seventeen

A fortnight later…

Dearest Readers,
It seems a mass exodus is in progress. Not only have we lost the alluring, if not intimidating, presence of the E. of C and the entertaining presence of Lord Wx to the wilds of Cornwall, but I must now report that several days ago Mister H.W. and his bride to be, Miss T., quit London, as did Lady R-W and her husband Monsieur C. The former couple is rumored to be on their way to Cornwall, and the latter is said to be returning to their country estate. Miss A.P. has also left London for the wilds of Cornwall, leaving this author to wonder if Cornwall is soon to become the "new London…"

Ren glanced up from the three-day-old London paper as Henry set a cup of coffee next to her empty breakfast plate. They had stopped at a delightfully comfortable inn the previous evening, and she felt loath to climb back into the carriage despite her anxiousness to return to her ship.

"Marry me."

She jerked her gaze from the coffee to clash with Henry's golden-brown one. "Yes, that is the plan."

"No. Marry me today."

"Today?"

"Yes." He pulled out the other chair of the small, round table and sat opposite her. "Why should we wait? I'm sure the local vicar will be agreeable to marrying us." He crossed his forearms atop the table and leaned toward her, his eyes bright with excitement. "Think about it, Ren, a quaint village wedding, just the two of us, a beautiful, sunny day. What could be better?"

Nothing. It was her dream wedding come true. Suddenly, she recalled his promise to tell her what he had envisioned for their wedding. "You never told me how you imagined our wedding day."

"Ah, yes." He sat back, and his smile widened. "Initially, I imagined marrying you on board a ship, miles off the coast, while the sun set."

Ren smiled at that.

"But," Henry continued, "I realized you would not wish to be aboard someone else's ship other than your own, and you could not have performed the wedding ceremony as captain and taken part in it as well, so I scrapped that idea and imagined a small wedding in a little village, far away from everything, on a day when the sun shines as bright as your eyes do when I am inside you."

She barked out a laugh at his shocking words and tossed her napkin at him.

He caught it before it could hit him in the face. "What? Was it something I said?" His eyes shone with devilment.

"What of your family? Your mother will be terribly disappointed." His parents had left London ahead of them. To prepare things at the house, his mother had said, so Ren would be comfortable and want for nothing. Ren had tried to summon annoyance at Lady Westhaven's mothering but simply could not. Even Henry's father had thawed toward her. He still threatened to arrest her, but he had a tendency to wink at her afterward, and in those moments, she caught glimpses of the Henry she would grow old with.

"My mother will recover, and it will give my father one less opportunity to pout."

"I believe your father actually likes me."

"Of course, he does, but you'll not hear him admit it."

"As stubborn as his son," she murmured.

"What was that?"

"Oh, nothing." She smiled and reached for her coffee. "Have you been to check on Poseidon this morning?" The horse had seemed less than thrilled to spend days tethered to the back of a carriage, but Henry had refused to leave Ren's side lest the movement of the well sprung carriage suddenly aggravate her healed wound. She still experienced a few sudden twinges of pain now and again, but nothing to alarm and certainly nothing to warrant an overbearing, male nanny.

"Of course, I have seen him this morning, and he is in a temper and desperate to be ridden, but he is fine. Now, cease stalling and agree to marry me today."

Ren suspected Poseidon was not the only one "in a temper and desperate to be ridden," and it made her smile as she sipped her coffee. Henry only had himself to blame for his current state. She had made her willingness to share a bed quite clear at each inn they had stopped at, and he had been equally clear about his intent to wait until they were married. She had pointed out the ridiculousness of that, but he had remained firm on the matter. She'd been tempted to sneak into his room, crawl into his bed, and test just how firm was his resolve, among other parts of him, but she had resisted.

"Why so anxious?" she asked as she set down the coffee. "Are you worried I will change my mind once we reach Cornwall and I am back onboard my ship?"

"Yes."

She looked into his eyes for some sign of humor but saw none. He was serious, and for some reason, that made her love him even more, though she had had no idea she *could* love him more. "I have no intention of changing my mind, but, yes, I will marry you today."

She was rewarded with a smile that nearly had her crawling across the table and into his lap, and to hell with marriage and waiting and resisting and all that other moralistic nonsense.

"I will pay a visit to the vicar while you finish your breakfast." He stood, still smiling like a lad who had just been gifted his first real horse.

She hated to diminish his joy or watch that smile vanish, but she'd read something in the paper that seemed rather important. "One thing before you go."

He rounded the table, took hold of her chin, lifted her face, kissed her lips, and continued to smile. "Anything. Name it."

"It is not a request. It is something you may wish to know." Her tone got through to him, and he regained his seat, his expression now serious. "According to gossip, Miss Parish left London several days ago for Cornwall. One can only assume she is on her way to—"

"Wexler," Henry finished for her. "She may already be in Cornwall, and that gives us an even greater incentive to marry before we arrive."

"You believe she will continue to be a threat to us?"

"I have no idea what to believe where she is concerned, but better safe than sorry as Venton is fond of saying." He stood. "I'll return in an hour or so."

"Or I could accompany you now if you are willing to wait for me to change." She could only imagine Eirene's horror once she discovered Ren had gotten married in one of her traveling gowns, but she had seen no point in packing her entire London wardrobe when she could simply fetch all that she needed from her cottage.

Henry agreed with a nod, and Ren gave him a kiss on her way from the dining room. "I will not be long," she promised.

****

The vicarage was the very definition of lovely with its low roof, arched door, paned windows, and flourishing rose garden. A black spaniel appeared from behind the house and raced toward them with an enthusiastic bark and wagging tail.

Henry sawed on Poseidon's reins as the horse protested the sudden appearance of the excited dog. "Easy, boy."

The gunshot had made Poseidon skittish, and Henry prayed it was a phase that would pass with time.

"Lucy! Heel!" The yell came from somewhere in the vicinity of the rose garden and was followed by the appearance of a white head and wide, toothy smile. "Can I help you folks?"

"We've come to see the vicar," Henry called over the dog's continued barking, which resulted in him yelling directly in Ren's ear, given she sat before him.

"Sorry about that," he said, in a much lower tone.

"Lucy! Enough!" The man's harder tone got through, and the dog slinked to his side. The man stepped from the rose patch and shoved a pair of gloves into the front pocket of his grass-stained apron. He studied Henry for several moments, then flicked his gaze toward Ren who looked like the most proper high born lady in her charcoal gray traveling gown with matching jacket and top hat. "Come to get married, have ye?"

How the man had deduced such a thing with such accuracy gave Henry pause and the perfect opportunity for Ren to speak. "If it is not too much bother, yes."

"No bother at all." The man's smile widened. "By the by, I am Vicar Connelly. You'll have to forgive my appearance, but I do enjoy spending my mornings with my roses."

"I do not blame you," Ren said with an answering smile. "They are very beautiful."

The vicar smiled at the compliment, then busied himself with his shears. He approached Poseidon to offer Ren a large, blood-red rose with black veins. Henry had never seen anything like it.

"A rare beauty for a rare beauty," the vicar pronounced.

Ren accepted the rose, smelled it, then sighed as if she had just caught the fragrance of Heaven. "It is glorious."

The vicar cocked his head. "My wife believes the fragrance is too heady. Says a bouquet of them would overwhelm a room."

"Yes, I agree. A rose this extraordinary should stand alone in a vase and coax a person closer to enjoy its aroma."

The vicar's smile nearly dimmed the sun. "My thoughts exactly." He looked to Henry. "I would not want to wait either, young man." He winked, then gestured. "See to your horse and come inside. I'll put a pot on."

Man and dog strolled toward the vicarage and disappeared through the arched doorway.

"I suppose a dog is more conventional than peacocks," Ren commented as Henry jumped off Poseidon and turned to lift her down. She placed her hands on his shoulders and allowed her body to slide down the length of his. She held his gaze the entire time, and he snarled at her as her feet finally touched the ground.

"Behave, Ren."

She blinked up at him with feigned innocence. "What did I do?"

He took her hand and showed her exactly what she had done, which, in hindsight, was a bloody mistake, because she curled her fingers around the front of his breeches and made his predicament much worse.

"Bloody hell, Ren," he hissed as she caressed him. "Keep that up and I'll drag you into that garden and have my way with you amongst the vicar's glorious roses."

She tightened her grip. "Promise?"

"Jesus." Henry yanked her hand away and took a few steps back for good measure. "Why don't you go inside and visit with the nice vicar while I see to Poseidon."

"Aye, aye, my lord." She dropped a curtsy and yelped as he smacked her on the bottom. "What was that for?"

"For being a cheeky vixen."

She rounded on him and closed the distance between them. She did not touch him, but she was close enough to blend her body heat with his, and he imagined the two of them surrounded by a ball of invisible fire. She lifted her chin to look him dead in the eyes.

"Ren," he warned though he hadn't a clue what she intended.

"Spank me like that again, when we are alone, and I will not be responsible for what happens."

His blood heated to a nearly unbearable degree. "Is that so?"

A voice in his head tried to remind him that they were in the vicarage's courtyard, but all he could hear was the echo of Ren's naughty little threat.

"Oh, yes." She nodded and slowly dragged her tongue along her bottom lip.

"Ren."

"Hmm?"

"Please go inside before I lose all self-control." He prayed she would do as he asked, because God help both of them if she laid so much as a single finger on him.

He sighed with relief as she smiled and walked away. She dipped her head to smell the large rose, and the picture she presented imprinted in his mind. He hadn't grown accustomed yet to seeing her dressed like a proper lady, but he liked it. The way the riding habit complemented her lithe figure stoked a fire in his veins, and as he watched the short train drag across the grass behind her, he nearly gave chase.

"Uf! Got yourself a handful with that one, you do."

Henry snapped into focus and turned to find a man leaning in the doorway of the small stable. He was younger by at least two decades than the vicar but possessed the same toothy grin.

He came forward and thrust his hand out. "Colin Connolly. The vicar's my father if you hadn't surmised as much already."

Henry shook the lad's hand. "Henry Westhaven."

"As in Baron Westhaven?"

"That would be my father." Though why a small vicarage, two days' ride outside Cornwall would know of his father, he hadn't a clue.

Colin nodded. "I see the resemblance now. Good man, the baron." He must have seen Henry's confusion, because he nodded and explained. "A bit of carriage trouble forced him and his wife to stop here on their way to London recently. We shared a pot of tea and then my father gave your mother the grand tour of his rose garden. I warn him about eternal damnation each time he boasts about those flowers." The lad winked and shared a laugh with Henry. "Though I've never seen him cut one until today." Before Henry could respond to that, Colin approached Poseidon and spoke softly before stroking his nose. "It seems an appreciation for beautiful women and fine horseflesh runs in the Westhaven veins, eh? Though, this fellow is much too fine to pull a carriage."

"Poseidon would agree with you."

The horse responded to the sound of his name with a shake of his large white head.

Colin gave him a final stroke and looked to Henry. "I'll see he's comfortable while you join your lady."

"Thank you." Henry reached into his pocket, but Colin refused the coin he produced.

"No, no. It's all part of what you pay to have my father perform the wedding, but I do appreciate the gesture. It's more than some folk think to do." He shook his head. "Your lady might be a vixen, but I can see she possesses manners, unlike the hellion we were forced to accommodate a handful of days ago."

Colin took the reins from Henry and calmed Poseidon with a few quiet words before returning to his tale. "From London she was. Mad as a cornered fox over the necessity to stop, but her coachman insisted the horses needed a break, and he mistook us for an inn. My father, being who he is, invited them in, but the lady wasn't having it. She demanded I do whatever needed to be done to the horses so they could be on their way."

Colin shook his head. "As if a few oats and a rubdown was all they needed after days on the road. I told her they should rest over night, and she stomped her foot and demanded I find two more horses to carry them the rest of the way to Cornwall. It was like facing down an avenging angel."

"An angel, you say?" He presumed Colin had encountered Miss Parish on her way to Cornwall.

"Oh, aye. Golden hair, rosy cheeks, bright blue eyes. Dressed all in white, she was, right down to a white ribbon threaded through her hair. Not exactly a practical traveling costume, but I got the impression she had left London in a bit of a hurry. At any rate, I did as she asked and hitched our horses to her carriage." He thumbed a gesture toward the stable. "Hers are still here, but I don't think they will bother your boy."

Henry brushed by Colin to enter the stable. It boasted only three stalls, two of which were occupied by a pair of perfectly matched grays. He recognized them instantly as belonging to Annabelle and recalled how he had thought it a horrible waste for someone deathly afraid of horses to possess such beauty.

"Recognize them, do you?" Colin appeared at his side, and Poseidon stretched his nose out to acknowledge the gray gelding as it did the same. "See there? I told you they wouldn't give your boy any trouble. Not sure I've ever seen two horses with such calm temperaments."

"They are indeed fine." Henry patted the nose of the gray nearest him and glanced at Colin. "Were you paid for their keeping?"

"As a matter of fact, no, but Father insists people like that will settle their fees when they meet God." Colin's tone indicated he would prefer such fees be settled in the here and now.

"I'll see to it, and I'll not hear a word of protest."

"So you do recognize them, eh?"

"I do, yes, and I am acquainted with the young lady you described."

Colin shook his head. "And here I always thought London ladies were as serene as those little figurines people like to display on their mantles."

Henry clapped a hand on Colin's shoulder. "There are angels and hellions everywhere, my friend."

"I shall remember that." Colin nodded at the gray, which had turned its attention to a bucket of fresh oats. "Any idea where the young lady was headed in such a hurry?"

"Unfortunately, the same place we are headed."

Colin narrowed his eyes. "You sound a bit concerned about that."

"Merely cautious, my friend." He left Colin with another clap on the shoulder and headed for the house. He attempted to keep his thoughts focused on his imminent wedding, but he could not help but wonder if, perhaps, it would be best to return to London and forego Cornwall and whatever threat Miss Parish might pose. Though, such a suggestion would likely make Ren more dangerous than one hundred Miss Parishes, given it would mean denying her the longed-for reunion with her ship.

Henry sighed. In all honesty, he would rather face whatever Miss Parish had in mind than to see even a hint of disappointment in Ren's eyes.

****

The inside of the vicar's home was a welcome reprieve from the warmth of the sun. The low roof, small windows, and thick walls made for a dim interior but they also kept the place cool. Still, Ren sighed quietly as she removed her hat and jacket.

In a matter of days, she'd be able to shed all of London's trappings and once again enjoy the freedom and comfort of an open-necked blouse and trousers. Not to mention the cooling sea breeze. More than once, she'd been tempted to inform Henry that they could travel faster, that it was not necessary for them to stop quite so often, but then her side would begin to ache and the temptation would pass.

She pressed her hand to her side and winced as the pressure aggravated the wound. It had healed fine, but the doctor said it would take some time for the bruising to go away, and until then, it would cause her pain if she did not take care.

"Are you all right, dear?"

Ren turned to find a woman entering the main room from one of the four doors that led deeper into the house. Given the fine quality of her simple dress, it seemed safe to assume she was the vicar's wife.

"Hello," Ren offered. "The vicar said I should make myself comfortable."

The woman smiled. "Forgive me for saying so, but you do not look as though you heeded his advice. Is there something I can do for you?"

The woman's gaze drifted toward the hand Ren still held pressed to her wound.

"Oh, no, no, I am fine. I recently sustained an injury, and it has not fully healed."

"Well, you can at least sit down and allow me to fetch you some tea. By the by, I am Mrs. Connolly." She dropped a quick curtsy.

"Oh, no, no," Ren protested with a wave of her hand. "No need for that. I'm as common as they come." Ren thrust out her hand. "My name is Morvoren."

Mrs. Connolly shook Ren's hand and surveyed her person at the same time. "I do not know of many common folk who can afford such a grand riding habit, but I shall take your word for it." The woman smiled. "Is it safe to assume you have a wee one on the way?"

Ren frowned in confusion until she realized what the woman implied. "Oh! No, no. It is not like that. We simply do not wish to wait any longer to be married."

"And have you been waiting long?" Mrs. Connolly asked as she moved across the room to throw open one of the window sashes. A meager amount of light flooded the room.

"Three years."

Mrs. Connolly paused in the act of reaching for the next sash and glanced over her shoulder at Ren. "The war?"

Ren considered lying simply to prevent any more questions, but lying to a vicar's wife within a vicarage felt incredibly wrong. "No. He proposed three years ago, and I turned him down, and now circumstances have brought us into one another's lives again—"

"And you believe that is a sign you should be together?"

"The only thing I believe is, I have no wish to repeat the hell of being without him, pardon my language."

"No harm done, dear." Mrs. Connolly patted Ren's arm as she brushed by. "I will fetch the tea."

She vanished into the kitchen, and Ren wandered to one of the windows that faced the stable. She looked out just as Henry emerged from the small outbuilding. His strides were long and determined as he moved toward the house, and there was a visible tension in his posture that hadn't been there before. She left the window and met him at the door.

"What is it? What has happened?"

He removed his hat and moved past her to enter the house. "We are alone?"

"The vicar is in the chapel, and his wife is in the kitchen. Now, tell me what has you wound tighter than a sail."

He took a moment to brush his hat against his thigh, then laid it on a nearby side table. He did the same with his gloves, and the delay made Ren want to scream, but she held her tongue and waited.

Finally, Henry met her gaze. "Miss Parish came through here a few days ago on her way to Cornwall."

"To get married?"

Henry shook his head. "No. Her coachman mistook the place for an inn and put in to rest the horses. According to the vicar's son, Miss Parish was in quite a hurry to get to Cornwall."

"I almost feel sorry for Wexler."

"Better him than me," Henry said.

Ren crossed her arms. "Not for want of trying on your part."

"Do you mean to remind me every day for the rest of our lives that I proposed to that woman?"

"Maybe."

Henry laughed at her. "Come here."

She closed the distance between them, wrapped her arms around him, and laid her cheek against his shoulder. "The possibility that she might have said yes to your proposal haunts me."

Henry slid a hand under her chin to get her to look at him. "If it makes you feel any better, it haunts me, too." He dropped a kiss on her lips, but it was brief. "Now, enough about Miss Parish. This is our wedding day."

"Aye, and I think you can do better than that brotherly kiss you just gave me."

He lowered his head to comply, but before his lips could touch hers, Mrs. Connolly's voice rang out. "Save it for after the ceremony, my dears."

Ren and Henry parted and turned as one to face the vicar's wife. The woman smiled and bobbed a curtsy.

"Anne Connolly, my lord." She glanced at Ren. "I see now why you grew tired of waiting."

Henry offered the woman a nod and a warm smile. "I am merely Mister Westhaven, and forgive us for invading your lovely home with no notice."

Mrs. Connolly waved away his words. "No bother. It isn't as if we are Gretna Green with a queue of runaways waiting outside. Now follow me and have some tea while it is hot."

She led them into the kitchen, which boasted a large window that allowed the space to be bright with natural light. The tea was indeed hot and a delicious blend of herbs that Ren did not recognize but certainly enjoyed. The plate of small, fluffy, buttery pastries was enjoyable as well, and Ren had to stop herself from consuming more than her fair share.

Mrs. Connolly smiled at Ren's restraint. "I'll see that you have a basket to take with you, my dear."

"You are too kind."

"Nonsense." Mrs. Connolly waved her hand in the air and looked back and forth between Ren and Henry. "If it is none of my business, I expect you to tell me, but did I hear you say you are acquainted with the young woman who came through here a few days ago?"

Ren and Henry nodded in unison.

"Being a vicar's wife and all, I do not like to speak ill of folks, but that woman set off warning bells in me head, she did. I invited her in for tea while Colin—" She looked to Ren. "Colin is our son," she explained, then continued. "As I was saying, I invited her in while Colin saw to her horses, and there was a wildness in her eyes that made me uneasy."

"Uneasy, how?" Henry asked.

The woman puckered her brow and shook her head. "You'll think me off in the head if I try to explain."

Ren covered the woman's hand with her own to gain her attention. "We know better than to think such a foolish thing."

Mrs. Connolly patted Ren's hand and smiled. "You're a good girl, you are. Remind me of my Colin's Elizabeth, you do. Sweet girl with a bit of steel in her spine." She glanced at Henry. "A lucky star was shining on you the day you found this one, my boy."

"I agree."

After a few moments, Mrs. Connolly returned to the subject of Miss Parish. "We had a horse once, most beautiful creature ever. Pure white it was." The woman frowned. "The devil was in that horse. I warned Connor, but he wouldn't listen. Stubborn man, my Connor, but he saw I was right, he did. Nearly died in the process, too."

Ren realized she'd been holding her breath and let it out quietly. "What happened?"

"The devil horse threw him is what happened. My Connor says they were trotting along lovely as you please, and suddenly the beast's eyes rolled back, its ears went flat, and it let out the most unholy shriek and reared and pawed at the heavens until Connor couldn't hold on any longer. The moment my Connor was on the ground, the beast ran off never to be seen again and good riddance, I say. Possessed by the devil, that beast was," she concluded.

Ren glanced at Henry and back to Mrs. Connolly. "You believe the young woman that passed through here is possessed by the devil?" She tried but failed to keep the skepticism from her tone.

"I believe there is something not right about her, is

all I will say." Mrs. Connolly stood. "Now then, finish your tea while I see if Connor is ready for you in the chapel."

She left them, and it was several moments before Ren broke the silence.

"I do not know what disturbs me more, Mrs. Connolly's opinion of Miss Parish or the fact that you do not seem the least bit surprised by it."

Henry furrowed his brow and shook his head. "Growing up with Venton has taught me not to dismiss things simply because they sound implausible."

"Care to explain exactly what *that* means?"

"There is more to Venton than meets the eye."

Ren recalled the moment Wexler referred to Venton as a witch. "Are you implying Miss Parish is a witch?"

A chill swept into the room and covered Ren like a thick mist.

"No, but when she paid a visit to my room, I saw a glimpse of something in her eyes that makes it very difficult to dismiss Mrs. Connolly's comparison to Vicar Connolly's wild horse."

She shivered at the implication in his words. "I do not know if she is possessed by the devil, but I do know she is possessed by an unhealthy amount of jealousy and perhaps obsession."

Henry reached across the table to cover Ren's hand with his own. Their gazes met and locked.

"Miss Parish will fetch Wexler and drag him back to London as quickly as she can, if she has not already, and she has no idea that we have left London." He squeezed her hand. "Now then enough about that. We have a wedding to attend, Miss Teague."

Chapter Eighteen

Ren stared at the ring on her finger, which Henry had placed there moments before the vicar pronounced them man and wife. The wide, silver band was a deep carving of two entwined serpents, or maybe they were dragons? She could not ascertain for certain, but their sinewy bodies coiled around one another and the ring, though they did not form a complete circle. In the space between tails and faces the letters H and R had been intertwined to create a decorative insignia. The ring was thick and heavy and most likely more suited for a man, but she loved it, and obviously Henry had known she would.

She looked up at him. "How long have you had this?"

"I had it made one week before I asked you to marry me, three years ago."

What a fool she'd been then. She blinked back the sudden sting of tears as she looked at the ring again. "We've lost so much time because of me."

Henry's fingers lightly grasped her chin, and he tilted her face up. "Do you mean to waste more by thinking about it?"

"No." She threw her arms around his neck and kissed him with all the fire and regret and love she possessed. It was a far cry from the chaste kiss they had shared at the end of the ceremony, and Henry held her tight and surrendered to her need to show him exactly how much he meant to her, how much she had missed him, and how desperately she wanted him.

The vicar had given them the key to a small cottage near the edge of his property and told them they could remain as long as they wished but to please excuse the lack of comforts as the place hadn't been lived in for quite some time. If there was a lack of comforts, Ren certainly had not noticed, nor did she care.

Ending the kiss, she took Henry's hand and led him from the main room into a small but homey bedroom. A colorful quilt topped the moderately sized bed, and the late afternoon sunshine streamed through the open window. Not a speck of dust danced in the rays, and she suspected Mrs. Connolly kept the place neat and tidy on a regular basis.

"The low ceiling and cramped quarters remind me of your cabin," Henry said with a wink. "Without the infernal swaying motion, of course."

Ren arched a brow as she moved to the window to close the shutters. "After all these years are you admitting you never fancied the motion of the sea?" She loved it. In fact, it was one of the things she missed most while on dry land. She always slept better on the ship with the sound of water lapping at the hull.

"At the risk of offending my new bride, I will admit I do sleep better without a cacophony of creaks and groans brought on by a rocking ship."

"Is that so?" Turning her back to the window, she crossed her arms. "You never seemed to have any trouble sleeping aboard the Mermaid." She could easily recall the sound of his snores.

"Ah, that is because you were in my arms." He

closed the short distance between them, took her in his arms, and smiled. The gold in his eyes caught the light as the sun streaked through the shutter slats. "With you by my side, I could sleep soundly anywhere under any conditions."

"How ridiculously romantic of you to say, but it isn't sleep I have in mind at the moment."

"Nor I, my feisty mermaid." He pushed her jacket off her shoulders and peeled it from her arms to let it drop on the floor. Before she could protest the treatment of the garment, he began to blindly undo the buttons down the back of her bodice. All the while, he rained kisses on her mouth, nose, cheeks, then mouth once more before finding her ear.

"I confess I fantasized about peeling that scandalous scarlet gown from your body on our wedding night, but divesting you of a charcoal gray riding habit in the middle of the day will serve just fine."

Her blood heated. Eirene had insisted Ren keep the gown, and she made a mental note to surprise Henry with it some evening when their lives were a bit more settled.

Her bodice sagged, and Henry pushed the gown to the floor. It pooled at her feet, and she kicked it away. In deference to the warmth of the day, she had foregone all undergarments save for a thin chemise, and it stopped just shy of mid-thigh. Since being forced to go about in skirts, she had asked Eirene's lady's maid to shorten all of her chemise hems to allow for ease of access to the dagger she'd worn strapped to her thigh. The ingenious maid had also cut a discreet slit in all of her gowns, so she need not hike up her skirts to retrieve the weapon.

Henry held her at arm's length and, quite literally, consumed her with his gaze. "Did you anticipate having to fight off ruffians on the way to the chapel?" He nodded toward the dagger.

"One never knows." She reached down to remove it, but he stayed her hand.

"Leave it." The heat in his gaze matched the fire in her blood.

Ren licked her lips and swallowed past the sudden dryness in her throat. "Kiss me."

He leaned toward her, and his breath danced across her lips, but he did not kiss her.

"Henry—"

"Shh." He kissed the edge of her mouth, then bold as he pleased, cupped her breasts through the chemise. He lifted his head and smiled like a hungry tiger when her nipples hardened in response. "No stays. How scandalous."

He moved his hands to abrade her nipples with his palms. His touch was neither soft nor rough, but there was a sureness to it that sent wave after wave of heated anticipation through her.

"Do you mean to fondle me until I beg?"

His smile became even more predatory. "The thought of you on your knees does hold a great deal of appeal."

"If I go down on my knees before you, it won't be to beg."

His nostrils flared, and he slid his hands beneath her breasts. "The feel of you has haunted me."

She met his gaze. "Likewise."

"I want you to know there has been no one else."

"Henry—"

"It is true."

"Three years is a long time," she said, though she desperately wanted to believe him.

"Oh, yes, it is a devilishly long time." He suddenly picked her up and carried her the short distance to the bed. "Too long." He laid her down gently, then pulled away.

She reached for him, but he evaded her touch and began to remove his clothing. Piece by piece, layer by layer until he stood as naked and glorious as the day she had rejected his proposal at gunpoint. She allowed herself several moments to drink in the sight of him, to take note of the changes three years had brought. He was as lean as ever, but he had acquired a bit more muscle here and there and a few scars. A rather vivid one sliced across the top of his right hip.

She crawled to the edge of the bed and traced it with her index finger. "This must have hurt. How did it happen?"

"Venton decided to train me in—" His words abruptly ended as she kissed the scar.

She smiled against his skin and looked up. "You were saying?"

"Venton decided to train me in the finer points of sword play."

"Why? As I recall, you are quite adept with a sword." The skin was rough beneath her touch and gave way to the smooth, hard expanse of his stomach. She spread her fingers open to touch as much of him as possible. His muscles tightened in response.

"Yes, sword, cutlass, and rapier, but not a Scottish broadsword. I am lucky all I sustained was a few scars, because Venton fights like a man possessed, and those bloody swords can easily slice a man in half."

At the casual mention of possession, Ren recalled the vicar's wife's insinuation about Miss Parish.

"No, no, no," Henry suddenly scolded.

Ren caught his gaze. "What? What did I do?"

"You are thinking, and now is not the time for thinking." He gave her shoulders a playful shove. "Lie down, wench."

Ren laughed. "I am the captain, and therefore, I give the orders." She rose to her knees, pulled her chemise over her head and tossed it away. Holding Henry's avid gaze, she reached to free her hair from its multitude of pins and shook it loose to allow it to cascade over her shoulders and down her back. "Now then—"

Before she could issue a single order, she found herself flat on her back with Henry kissing his way up her body. He lingered over her wound, then continued on until his mouth was at her ear. "Would it be horribly insensitive of me to admit I haven't the patience for foreplay?"

Ren grabbed a fistful of his hair and tugged until he got the hint and lifted his head to look her in the eyes. "No."

"Thank God." He pushed her a little ways up the mattress and groaned when she opened her legs. "Jesus, Ren, you'll finish me before I'm even inside."

She smiled at that. "Then perhaps you should stop wasting time and—"

He thrust into her, and she caught her breath and closed her eyes as her body accepted his with the same ease and elation one felt when placing the last piece of a puzzle into place. She felt his hair skim her face then his breath against her ear.

"I was a bloody fool to walk out of that cabin three years ago." He punctuated the statement with a shift of his hips that buried him deeper within her.

Ren gasped again, opened her legs wider, and canted her pelvis up, which Henry took as an invitation to push even deeper. She clawed at his shoulders with the wild need for him to move.

"What's wrong, love?" His voice teased her ear. "Hmm?" He shifted within her, then chuckled at her sharp intake of breath. "Tell me what you want."

Did he truly expect her to be able to speak?

He shifted within her again at the same time he placed a hot, open-mouthed kiss on the side of her neck.

Every muscle in her body contracted in response, and she heard and felt Henry catch his breath. She opened her eyes to find him looking down at her. His hair hung in his face, and she reached up to tuck it behind both ears so she could see his eyes.

Without a word, he began to move, slowly at first, then a little faster, all the while holding her gaze. She could not look away from his eyes. She gripped his shoulders, found his rhythm, and moved with him.

Time stopped. She was aware of nothing but the feel of Henry moving with her, the sound of their bodies and their breathing, and the intensity of his steady gaze. His rhythm changed, his jaw clenched, and she knew...

"Ren," he breathed.

She tightened her hold on his shoulders but said nothing. His hair slid out from behind his left ear, and she shifted her gaze from his, momentarily distracted by the rhythmic sway of his hair against his jaw line.

"Look at me," he growled.

She returned her gaze to his.

"I want to see your eyes when I make you mine."

She smiled at that. "I have always been yours."

He shook his head but said nothing. His movements intensified. He thrust hard and deep, showing no mercy, but she did not want or need any. Her body tightened around him, and he blew out a breath and pushed harder.

The impact of his body against hers caused a dull ache to her wound, but no force in Heaven or on Earth could have compelled her to give a damn about it. It did not matter. Nothing mattered beyond the fast approaching end to the longest three years of her life.

Her inner muscles tightened which caused a slight hitch in Henry's movements.

"Henry…" She clawed at his shoulders again and fought against the urge to close her eyes as the first wave of her orgasm rolled through her.

"Say it again."

She did not need to ask what he meant. "Henry."

His lips met hers and he breathed her name into her mouth then caught her small scream as she climaxed fully.

"Ren," he said again as he finished with her.

After several moments, he collapsed on top of her and she gave a little "oof" as his weight pinned her to the bed. He buried his face against her neck and panted. Her wound throbbed, her left hip started to cramp, and several strands of Henry's hair were caught in her mouth, but she wrapped her arms around him and ignored all of it.

"That was nice," she finally said into the silence.

He barked out a laugh against her neck and pushed himself onto his elbows to meet her gaze. "I love you."

"Women are warned never to believe those words while a man is inside them."

"Is that so?"

Ren nodded. "I remember a barmaid telling me that when I was ten."

"Ten? That is a little young to be speaking of such things with a barmaid, is it not?"

She shrugged as best she could. "Penny seemed determined to teach me all that she knew about men, and believe me, her knowledge was vast."

"An authority, eh?"

"She believed so."

"Well, in that case." Henry shifted his weight onto his hands and withdrew from her body, but he stayed close enough to tease her sensitized flesh with the tip of his cock. "I love you," he said again.

Her eyes suddenly burned. "I love you, t—"

He was back inside her before she could fully return the sentiment. He moved against her, and she felt him harden again.

"Henry."

He shook his head then lowered it to brush his mouth against hers. "I want you again."

He parted her lips with his own and kissed her for several blissful moments. By the time the kiss ended and their bodies moved in tandem, she could no longer fight the tears that had been threatening. They leaked from the corners of her eyes, and she could not hide them as he levered up on his hands to look down at her.

He lowered his head to kiss a few of them away.

"Tell me these are tears of happiness."

Ren tightened her arms around him and hooked her legs around his hips. "Of course, I am happy." And she was. Terrifyingly so.

Henry kissed a few more tears away, then moved his lips to hers. He kissed her breathless while coaxing her body to another powerful climax.

****

Henry had no idea what time it was when he opened his eyes to find the room pitched in total darkness. Ren lay pressed to his side with her head on his shoulder, her hand splayed atop his chest, and her breath steady and even against his throat. At some point, they had decided to actually get *in* the bed, and she had crawled on top of him to make love to him. The sight and feel of her moving over him had brought him to a quick end, and he had apologized and promised to make it up to her once they caught their breath.

She had smiled, kissed him, and told him he had the rest of his life to do so. Then she had snuggled at his side and promptly fell asleep.

He stared into the darkness and smiled. He was so damned happy, but the feeling could not blind him to the reality of what might await them when they stepped out of the idyllic sanctuary of the vicar's cottage and back into the real world. It had been on his mind to speak to her about her intentions once she regained her ship, but a part of him knew the answer, so he had avoided the conversation. Removing her from the sea would be akin to capturing a mermaid and expecting it to be happy and fulfilled in a bathtub. Some things were simply meant to be together, and Ren and her ship were two of those things.

Unfortunately, his father, despite his recent thawing toward Ren, would feel compelled to do his duty if she returned to smuggling. Such a circumstance would tear the family apart, and although Henry knew Ren loved him, he did not know if she loved him enough to turn her back on the life she'd lived for the past decade. Nor did he know if it was even right to ask her to do so. What he did know, if he wished to be honest with himself, was that he longed to return to the sea, to join Ren and her crew aboard the Mermaid, to feel free and alive once more in a way no amount of London Society could ever provide.

Christ. He laughed without a drop of humor as he thought of his father's reaction to having a son and a daughter-in-law engaged in smuggling.

And there was the matter of Miss Parish to consider. Smuggling might not be an issue at all if Miss Parish continued in her attempts to remove Ren from his life. He would like to think their marriage might put an end to Annabelle's obsession, but he recalled the look in her eyes the night she had visited his rooms. What he had seen in those blue depths made him believe the woman would not give up until she had what she wanted.

He held Ren a little tighter and vowed to protect her from Miss Parish, from his father, and from any other force that might think to take her away from him, because there was one thing he knew with absolute certainty.

He did not want to live without her ever again.

Chapter Nineteen

Henry and Ren arrived in Cornwall well after sunset and decided to have the carriage drop them and Poseidon at the Golden Pilchard Inn, if for no other reason than to have an excuse to stretch their legs and escape the monotonous sound of carriage wheels that had plagued them for the past six days. The journey had been prolonged by Henry's continued concern for her comfort, which she had insisted was not necessary, as well as a few extra hours spent in various posting inn beds. The latter had seemed quite necessary though still not sufficient to make up for three very long years of abstinence.

As Ren waited for Henry to see to Poseidon's well-being, she wondered if they could forgo a meal and simply rent a room.

"What is on your mind?" Henry asked as he joined her at the inn's pub entrance.

"What makes you believe anything is on my mind?" She batted her lashes, and he laughed.

"If you mean to ravish me for hours on end, we need to eat first." After giving her a quick kiss, he opened the door, and they stepped inside.

Several of the tables were occupied, and the space hummed with the drone of multiple conversations and the occasional cracks and hisses from the two large fireplaces blazing from opposite walls. Ren took a deep breath, grateful to be home. The Pilchard had, since childhood, always been one of her favorite haunts, though, unlike several other smugglers, she'd never been foolish enough to use the expanse of tunnels that ran underneath the old building. For her, it was simply a good place to eat, relax, and catch up with friends.

"I will choose a table while you fetch us something to eat and drink," she said and headed for a small round table situated close to one of the hearths.

"Captain?"

Ren halted and looked toward the nearest table to find five of her men gaping at her like freshly caught fish. Hammett, her first mate, was the first to spring to his feet. His handsome, weathered face crinkled into a smile that lit the depths of his dark eyes.

"Bloody hell, look at you!" he bellowed. "Never thought I'd see you done up like a fancy lady. Captain," he amended.

Ren returned Hammett's smile as she weaved her way to the table to join her crew.

Hammett held out a chair for her. "My lady," he teased.

"I'm no more a lady now than when I left for London, Hammett."

"'Tis a relief to hear it, Captain."

She took the seat and gestured for her men to retake theirs. Once each of them had welcomed her back, she looked to Hammett. "How is the Mermaid?"

"Oh, she's safe and sound now, but I ain't gonna lie to you, Captain. We were getting a mite worried that she'd be lost forever until that devil showed up with a fancy lord in tow."

"That devil is a friend."

"Oh, aye, aye, I read the letter you sent along with him, but still I wasn't expectin' him to stroll aboard as though he bloody owned the ship."

"I hope you did not give him any trouble, Hammett."

Hammett shook his head of long corkscrew, seal-brown curls. "No, no, but I'd be lying if I didn't say he gave me and the rest of the crew the shivers with that black stare of his."

"There's rumors about that particular earl," Simpson commented. "The Demon Earl, they call him."

"Among other things," Hammett added.

"Yes, well, the only thing that matters is that the earl accomplished his task, and the Mermaid is back in my possession." Ren knew from past experience her men would gossip amongst themselves like a knitting circle of old maids if given half the chance. "And what of the cargo?"

As she asked, she peeled off her gloves and removed her top hat. Her question went unanswered as a heavy silence fell about the table.

"Is that a wedding ring, Captain?"

Ren followed Hammett's gaze to the wide ring on her left hand. "Yes."

Hammett scowled. "Pardon me for sayin' so, but you took the time to get married while we were here risking our lives to keep that London lord from taking the cargo?"

The anger in his tone shocked her a bit.

"Explain yourself." To her recollection, Wexler had told Henry there had been very little time, if any, to assess the cargo.

"The moment you left for London that popinjay

boarded us and threatened to see all of us hanged if a single crate was removed from the ship in his absence. Waved a pistol around to make his point, he did." Hammett glanced around the table at the other men before continuing. "Well, it didn't sit right with any of us to take orders from one such as that, so we decided to offload the cargo. We're smugglers, aye? Should have had no problem emptying the ship with Lord Fancy Pants none the wiser."

"And?"

"And damn near got our heads blown off, we did, before we could even lower the boat into the water. Seems his lordship set some of his own men to watch our activities, and they'd been ordered to use any means necessary to see that none of the cargo left the ship."

"Was anyone hurt?" She'd have Wexler's head if any of his men had injured hers.

"No, but I imagine we would have been had we ignored the warning shots."

She glanced around the table. The other men seemed content, as usual, to allow Hammett to speak for them. They trusted him, and it was one of the main reasons she had assigned him to first mate.

She returned her gaze to Hammett. "I apologize for lingering so long in London. There were circumstances beyond my control that needed to be dealt with."

"That being one of them?" Hammett gestured toward her ring.

Ren twisted the ring, unsure if the answer to that was yes or no. She no longer thought of her marriage to Henry as the result of their scandalous interlude at Lady Dunston's. At some point during the hours after their wedding, while they enjoyed the solitude of the vicar's cottage, she had realized marriage to Henry was as inevitable as the changing of the seasons.

"Who is the lucky man, Captain?" Simpson's question broke the prolonged silence.

Hammett harrumphed. "Seeing as how our captain is trussed up like a proper lady, it seems likely the bloke is a proper London lord."

Ren shook her head at Hammett. "As a matter of fact—"

"Are the lot of you taking my name in vain?" Henry's voice boomed over Ren's head followed by the sound of multiple chairs scratching the floor as Hammett and the others jumped to their feet and took turns shaking Henry's hand and thumping him on the back.

Hammett looked to Ren, who remained seated. "You finally made an honest man of this one, eh, Captain?" He snatched up his drink. "A toast, men, to the captain and Mister Westhaven." He raised his tankard high. "May the seas ahead always be calm and the stars bright."

"Aye! Aye!" the rest of the men shouted then threw back their drinks.

Ren glanced up at Henry. "It seems they approve."

He leaned down and placed his mouth close to her ear. "Of course, they do. Your men always liked me a bit more than they like you, because I don't order them about like a bunch of wayward lads."

She shifted in her seat to stomp hard on his foot. A hiss of pain filled her ear followed by a husky laugh that stoked the fire of their rekindled intimacy. She shifted again, for a much different reason.

"I want you, too," Henry all but purred in her ear,

and she cursed his ability to read her like a book.

She shoved at his chest. "Sit down and behave."

He obeyed with another laugh. "Our drinks will be here shortly, and I took the liberty of ordering another round for the men."

His words were met with a chorus of gratitude and a few hard thumps upon the back from those nearest him.

Ren could only shake her head at the display. Her men *did* like Henry. Not for the reason he teased about, but simply because he was a damned likeable fellow. However, despite the camaraderie, her men never forgot who their captain was.

She caught Hammett's gaze. "I assume the rest of the crew is on board?"

"Aye, Captain. We take shifts and send daily reports to the earl, though I suspect, now that you have returned, we won't be needing to continue on with those reports."

She acknowledged the last assumption with a nod. "I shall come aboard first thing in the morning, and we will begin preparations to offload the cargo."

She glanced toward one of the pub's deep set, rather useless windows. It was full dark outside, but she'd seen the moon high in the sky when they'd stepped from the carriage. It was half full and bright as an unshuttered lantern, and in the coming nights, it would only get brighter. Not the most ideal conditions to move smuggled goods, but the thought of precious lace spending any more time in a damp ship's hold made her feel a little ill.

One of the pub's serving girls arrived with a tray bearing a small pot of tea for Ren, a frothy tankard of ale for Henry, and, as promised, another round for the men.

"Anything else, my lord?" the girl asked Henry as she tucked the large empty tray under her arm in a manner that served to enhance her already impressive bosom.

"This is fine for now, thank you."

Ren did not miss the wink or the meaning behind it as the girl sashayed away.

"Pity you're married," Simpson mumbled into his drink and received a solid smack on the back of the head from Hammett. "What the hell?" he sputtered.

"Mind your tongue, you bloody fool."

Ren rolled her eyes and poured herself a steaming cup of black tea. She'd grown numb to the seemingly endless bickering between Hammett and Simpson. The two had grown up together, their fathers likewise before them, and she knew the bickering would never escalate into anything close to actual animosity.

"In all the excitement," Hammett began. "I failed to mention that fancy lord hasn't left Cornwall."

"Yes, I am aware," Ren answered.

"Aye, maybe you are, but are you aware of the fact he's bunking in this very inn?"

Ren exchanged a look with Henry, then refocused on her first mate. Given the Pilchard's high standards and excellent accommodations, the news did not surprise her. "Is he alone?"

"As a matter of fact, no." Hammett set down his ale and leaned forward. "He was up till a day or so ago, but then this little lady showed up and he's been a bit scarce ever since." He winked with not so subtle implications.

"A blonde?" Henry asked.

Hammett shifted his gaze to Henry. "Oh, aye. She looks like one of them Italian marble angel statues."

Simpson snorted. "When the hell you ever seen an Italian angel statue?"

"In books, you illiterate idiot."

Simpson snorted again but let the matter drop.

"Speak of the devil," Henry said under his breath and directed Ren's attention toward the staircase at the back of the pub.

Wexler descended into their midst with all the arrogance of lord of the manor. Miss Parish followed at his heels, looking as ethereal as ever in a white gown with her golden hair plaited over one shoulder. Her expression was one of a very satisfied cat.

"By the look on Miss Parish's face, I'd say Wexler proposed despite any hesitations he might have confessed to Venton."

Ren nodded as Henry echoed her thoughts, and she shifted her attention from Miss Parish to meet his gaze. "I would think an upcoming wedding will keep her too occupied to plague us."

"It is *after* the wedding that has me worried."

Ren frowned at that, and Henry leaned closer to speak directly in her ear. "She has already informed me marriage will not hinder a relationship between us."

She did not necessarily care for the reminder of Miss Parish's scandalous visit to Henry's bedroom.

"In fact," Henry went on, "with a ring on her finger, she will have more freedom."

"Perhaps, but if there is one thing I do know about the nobility, it is how important heirs are, and Wexler will wish to secure one before allowing his wife to run wild."

Henry's gaze shifted beyond Ren. "True, but I would still feel less concern if she were in London and not— Bloody hell," he suddenly growled. "Wexler has spotted us."

"Westie!" Wexler bellowed from across the pub with a level of enthusiasm that belied his wish to never lay eyes on either of them ever again. He dodged and weaved his way in their direction, and Ren could not help but observe that, even in buff trousers, a burgundy jacket, and subdued cravat, the man looked like a strutting peacock.

"How has someone not shot that obnoxious popinjay?" Hammett muttered under his breath.

"I had a gun pointed at his heart," Ren informed her first mate.

"And you didn't pull the damn trigger?"

"I convinced her Wexler is hardly worth hanging for," Henry interjected just as the man himself reached the table and thumped Henry hard on the shoulder.

"Westie, by God, what are *you* doing here?" Wexler's gaze scanned the table and landed upon Ren. He paled. "Look here, I no longer have your registration. That business was taken care of, and the earl assured me—"

"Yes," Ren interrupted. "I know."

Wexler gave a little laugh. "So, you aren't here to shoot me, eh?"

"Not yet."

Wexler looked ready to choke as he whipped his gaze back to Henry. "Scandal or no, I told you before, I'd think twice before tying yourself to this one in eternal matrimony, Westie. She's likely to stab you in your sleep and steal the family fortune."

"I appreciate your advice, but the deed is already done. Allow me to introduce you to the new Mrs. Westhaven."

Wexler slid his attention back to Ren and opened his mouth to speak, but the voice that came out was not his.

"Mrs. Westhaven?" Miss Parish appeared alongside Wexler and gaped at Ren with undisguised loathing and perhaps a bit of shock to find her alive? Then she looked at Henry. "How could you?"

Her arrival had brought Henry to his feet, but Ren's crew did not seem inclined to show such respect. The lot of them remained seated with drinks in hand and avid gazes fixed upon the unexpected entertainment.

"Annabelle, darling, you should return to the room and lie down." Wexler's words and gentle tone had no visible impact upon Miss Parish as she continued to stare at Henry.

"How could you marry *her* if you love me?"

"Annabelle."

"Miss Parish."

Wexler and Henry spoke in unison, but neither had the opportunity to say more as Miss Parish let out a gasping sob, then balled her hands into fists and pummeled at Henry's chest. "How could you?!"

Henry grabbed her hands and held them to put a stop to the little attack. "Calm yourself, Miss Parish."

"Miss Parish, this. Miss Parish, that." Annabelle snatched her hands away and turned her focus to Ren. The vitriol in the blue gaze nearly stole Ren's breath. "This is your fault, you whore. You stole him from me, but he will not be yours for long."

"Annabelle, darling." Wexler took hold of Miss Parish's shoulders as his face contorted with shock and embarrassment. "You are speaking nonsense, because you are in need of rest. Think of your condition."

Miss Parish did not seem to hear a word Wexler said to her as she continued to glare at Ren. "You may have his ring on your finger, but I've got his babe in my belly." The announcement caused Wexler to snatch his comforting hands from her shoulders.

Ren slid a glance toward Henry to gauge his reaction, though she knew the accusation to be as false as the innocent front Miss Parish displayed to the world.

Henry, however, kept his attention upon Miss Parish. "Perhaps you should escort Miss Parish back to her room, Wexler."

Before his lordship could see to the task, Annabelle darted away to run through the pub and up the stairs in a show of dramatics that reminded Ren of the silly heroine in a gothic novel she had once read.

Wexler looked to Henry, then pulled a glove from inside his waistcoat. He dropped it on the table, and Henry quickly snatched it up and shoved it against Wexler's chest.

"Have you gone mad, Wexler?" Henry growled. "The girl is lying."

"No, she is not."

Ren frowned as Henry seemed to pale a little.

"She *is* with child," Wexler said as he took possession of his glove and once more tossed it onto the table.

"Likely yours, you fool," Henry countered.

"I know for a fact it is not mine, and I vowed to avenge Miss Parish's honor if ever I discovered who was responsible for defiling her and leaving her."

"You cannot be s—"

"Choose the time, place, your second, and weapon of choice, Westhaven."

"I'll not fight you, you fool. The child is no more mine than the king's. The letters Lady Rowe-Weston still holds in her possession certainly argue the child is, indeed, yours."

"What occurred between Miss Parish and myself did not involve…" He broke off and cleared his throat. "Suffice to say, I know the child cannot be mine, and I saw her ruined nightdress."

"Which she tore herself." Henry shook his head. "She is lying to you, Wexler. Open your bloody eyes, and you will see it."

Wexler raised his chin a notch. "Now then, I have issued a challenge, and honor dictates you accept or publicly take responsibility for what you have done. You have until noon tomorrow to decide." With that, his lordship turned and strolled away with his head high.

Henry looked at Ren. "For Christ's sake, they are both mad. I never touched the girl."

"Miss Parish tells a much different story."

Henry sat down hard. "Care to elaborate?"

As succinctly as possible, Ren told Henry about Miss Parish's dramatic display in Eirene's library and the implication Henry had forced himself upon her.

"Why the devil are you only telling me this now?"

Ren arched a brow at his tone. "I was rather preoccupied with a gunshot wound."

Henry cursed under his breath. "Forgive me."

Beneath the table, Ren laid her hand atop Henry's knee and squeezed.

"I would choose a sword, Mister Westhaven," Hammett suggested. "That gent is likely to be a crack shot."

Henry gaped at Hammett, then looked to Ren once more. "I refuse to fight Wexler."

"Then it seems you will be publicly acknowledging a child that is not yours."

"Bloody hell," Henry echoed. "Why the devil did I ever look twice at that woman?"

"That is certainly a question I've asked a time or two," Ren confessed.

Chapter Twenty

Henry rode Poseidon into the courtyard of Cragmoor Keep early the next morning. Following Wexler's absurd, yet unavoidable, challenge, Hammett had graciously offered to act as Henry's second, and Henry had just as graciously declined on the grounds Bram would never forgive him if he fought a duel without him.

He dismounted and handed the reins off to the waiting stable lad, a boy with devilishly dark hair and eyes and a rather familiar jaw line.

"What's your name?" he asked before the lad could hurry off with Poseidon in tow.

"George, my lord."

"You can call me, sir, George. That's a fine name. Have you worked in the earl's stables for long?" Henry assumed not since he'd never laid eyes on the boy before.

"No, sir. Maybe a week or so."

"Does your father work for the earl as well?"

"Oh, no, sir. I don't have a father." Poseidon chose that moment to stomp restlessly, and Henry waved the boy away to see to his duties. He suspected the lad was Bram's, of course, but he knew not to pry too deep into his friend's private doings. When Bram wished it, Henry would learn all he needed to about young George.

"Good day, sir." Fish, Cragmoor Keep's loyal, ancient butler, stood at the open front door with one of Bram's three hell hounds by his side.

Henry strolled forward with a smile for the butler and a pat on the head for the enormous black Irish wolfhound. "Which one is this, Fish?"

"I haven't a clue, sir, nor does it matter. The beasts only listen to their master, as you well know."

Henry played with the hound's ears until the dog decided it had endured enough attention. With a low whoof, it turned tail and trotted down the corridor to disappear into the bowels of the massive house.

"Speaking of the master, is he, by chance, awake this early?"

"I cannot say if he is awake or not, but you will find him in his study." Fish stepped aside to allow Henry entrance, then closed the door with a loud squeal of hinges. The bolt fell into place with an equally loud sound. "Shall I announce you, or do you feel brave today?"

Henry chuckled and patted the man on the back. To his knowledge, he and Fish were the only two souls not afraid of Bram. "I shall enter the devil's den alone, my good man."

"Suit yourself, sir." Fish took possession of Henry's hat and gloves before he shuffled away.

Despite the poorly lit interior of the keep, the multiple closed doors, and the maze-like corridors, Henry had no trouble making his way to Bram's study. He'd spent countless hours haunting the place at his friend's side and knew every stone as if he'd placed it himself. It saddened him to see the ancient keep in such a state of disrepair, but Bram's father had loathed the place with a passion and hoarded his wealth while neglecting the needs of Cragmoor Keep. As a result, the earl had died with a sizable cache of wealth to his name. None of which his son could touch until he produced a virginal, noble wife.

Thinking about his friend's situation made Henry's current predicament with Wexler seem even more ridiculous. He had considered making another attempt to have Wexler see reason, but the man's pride would blind him.

He knocked on the study door.

"Go away!"

"It's me," he said as he opened the door and walked in only to be stopped from further advancement by the three hounds of hell. He hadn't a clue which one he'd been petting at the front door, because all three stared at him as if they'd been denied food for a fortnight. "Call off your beasts, Bram."

"Cerberus! Heel!" Bram's command was obeyed without hesitation, and the dogs retreated to sit, shoulder to shoulder, before the blazing hearth as if guarding the gates to the underworld.

"I wonder, Bram, do *you* know which one is which?"

"Of course, I do." Bram glanced up from whatever task he seemed absorbed in and pointed toward the fire. "Cer is on the left, Rus is in the center, and Ber is on the right."

"You don't have them trained to line up in order?"

"Rus is stubborn." Bram set down his pen and settled back in his chair. "Why are you here, Henry?"

"I can't visit a friend and thank him for a task well—"

"Cut through the shit, and tell me what has happened."

Henry dropped into the chair positioned before his friend's large desk. "Wexler challenged me to a duel."

"Interesting." Bram stood and pulled the heavy curtains open that covered the window behind his desk. The action let in a dismal amount of light, given the thickness of the window casing and the quantity of clouds in the sky. "Do you want a drink?" he asked as he helped himself to one from the decanter that sat on the edge of the desk.

Henry stared at the blood red liquid as it splashed into Bram's glass. "Dare I ask what it is?"

"It is merely a new concoction from Bordeaux, or so I am told." Bram held the glass toward the window, but the weak light barely penetrated the thick, red liquid. "One can never be certain if smugglers are telling the truth."

"Which ship brought it in?"

Bram shrugged and sipped the drink. "I do not ask, nor do I care." He gestured toward the decanter. "Help yourself if you wish." Then he retook his seat. "Why does Wexler wish to kill you?"

"He believes I got Miss Parish with child."

Bram choked and sputtered, then lowered his glass. "Is she with child?"

"She claims to be."

"Is it—"

"No, it is bloody *not* mine, you fiend."

Bram smiled. "Me thinks thou doth protest too—"

"Are you through?" Henry set aside his misgivings and poured himself a drink. He took a sip then gaped at his friend. "Bloody hell, this is good. Dry as a desert

261

but good."

"And cheap. The bloke hasn't a clue what he has if you ask me. Had I the money, I would purchase the vineyard without delay."

"Adrien has the money." Henry sipped his drink again. The wine deserved to be served exclusively to royalty not smuggled into Cornish pubs.

"Aye, Adrien has the money, and I do not."

"Stuff your pride and suggest a partnership."

"I shall consider it."

Henry rolled his eyes but let the matter drop. "Will you act as my second?"

"You actually mean to meet him?"

"What choice do I have? I refuse to publicly claim a child that is not mine." Henry hesitated, and the silence stretched long enough to cause Bram to arch a brow.

"Whatever it is you wish to ask, ask," Bram prompted.

"Is the stable lad yours?"

"Ah, you met George. He is a good lad, but no, he is not my son. The resemblance you no doubt detected is inherited from our dearly departed father."

"The boy can't be more than eight years old." Henry did some quick calculations in his head, but Bram did not allow him the chance to voice his shock.

"Aye, my father was a randy devil well into his dotage, it would seem."

"And the boy's mother?"

"Currently employed in my kitchen, though I haven't the coin to pay either of them."

"At least they have a roof over their heads."

"Oh, aye, one that leaks." Bram shook his head and

gestured with his glass. "Back to Wexler. If you mean to go through with this, I suggest swords. Wexler is a crack shot, but he wields a sword like a drunkard. You will skewer him in no time."

"I do not plan to skewer him."

Bram shrugged. "Suit yourself. Name the time and place, and I shall be there."

"Thank you."

Another shrug. "What are friends for, eh?"

Henry glanced at the papers spread across his friend's desk. "What are you working on?"

Bram flipped the top paper over. "Nothing." He finished his drink and reached for the decanter. "By and by, what brings you to Cornwall?"

"Ren was shot."

Crystal knocked against crystal as Bram halted his task to gape at Henry. "Care to elaborate?"

Henry extended his glass. "We will both need quite a bit more of this if you mean to hear all that you missed after leaving London."

Several glasses of fine, red, dry, Bordeaux wine later, Bram left the desk and prowled to the fireplace. The hounds, which at some point during Henry's visit had fallen asleep, jumped to their feet to greet their master. Bram patted each on the head, spoke a few soft words that settled them back onto their rug, then propped an elbow against the mantel and glanced to Henry. "Where is Ren now?"

"I suggested she remain at the inn with Hammett and the others until I return." Not an easy task, given how desperate she was to see her ship. He had threatened to chain her to the bed if she did not obey him just this one time. She had acquiesced, but he could vividly recall the irritation in her gaze. "God willing, she is still there," he added more to himself than to his friend.

"Aside from you, she is one of the most stubborn individuals I've ever encountered," Bram observed, then shifted his gaze to consider the fire. "Do you recall our first conversation about Miss Parish?"

Henry frowned and searched his memory. "I believe you told me she was too young."

"Aye." Bram looked to Henry again. "But what else did I say to you?"

"Christ, Bram, that was over a year ago—" He snapped his mouth shut as the memory surfaced. "You warned me not to toy with her."

He had scoffed at the warning but had gone on to inform Bram his only intention toward Miss Parish was marriage.

"And here we are." Bram set his wine glass on the mantel then turned and crossed his arms. He leaned back and settled his unnerving, black gaze upon Henry. "The girl is not right in the head, Henry. I sensed it the moment I met her, and I warned y—"

"In the vaguest way imaginable, I might add." Henry stood up, which caused the hounds to lift their heads, rumble in unison, then glance at their master for the kill order.

"Easy, Cerberus," Bram intoned.

Henry rolled his eyes and crossed to join his friend at the fireplace. "How many people have these mongrels killed?"

"None, yet, but that might change if you refer to them as mongrels again."

Henry held up his hands in surrender, then dropped

into one of the leather chairs. The hound nearest to him laid its giant head across his right boot and proceeded to drool.

"As I was saying," Bram continued. "Miss Parish possesses a sort of darkness about her, disguised, of course, by her ethereal appearance."

"And you are insinuating this darkness, which *you* took note of instantly, has turned her into a jealous, murderous lunatic?"

"I am merely reminding you of my warning not to toy with her affections."

"*She* rejected *my* proposal, Bram."

"Yes, because you are not what she was instructed to marry by that harridan mother of hers, but then *you* rejected *her*."

"Yes, I rejected her offer to be my bloody mistress."

Bram arched a brow as if to say, "Yes, exactly."

Henry scoffed. "I am hardly worth killing over, Bram."

"Perhaps, but in Miss Parish's mind you are, and it only further incites her to witness your obvious affection for Ren."

"Christ." He raked both hands through his hair and stared into the fire. "You make it sound as if she won't stop until Ren is dead." The silence that followed his statement made him glance toward his friend. "That is exactly what you believe."

Bram nodded.

"My God, I refuse to have Ren spend the rest of her life looking over her shoulder because of Miss Parish's misguided obsessions."

"She needs to be locked away." Bram looked away

as he made the suggestion, one that Henry knew could not have been easy for him to make. "Sometimes it is the only solution."

"We have no proof that she is behind the shootings."

Bram's gaze was black as night when he looked at Henry again. "There are several institutions that do not require proof."

"Yes, maybe there are, but only a family member or guardian can have someone locked away, and Miss Parish's mother is her only family."

"Wexler could do it, once they are married."

"Wexler is willing to fight a duel over the girl."

Bram frowned. "Then you must catch her in the act, with witnesses."

"How in the bloody blazes do you propose we do that?"

"Invite her into your home."

Henry gaped at Bram. "Are you mad?"

"It is not my madness in question here, Henry. Invite the girl into your home, and I assure you the temptation will be too much for her to resist."

"What temptation?"

"The temptation to eliminate your beloved Ren, once and for all."

****

"I'm beginning to wonder if you are as crazy as Miss Parish," Ren told Henry after he informed her of Venton's suggestion to invite the woman into their home.

"It is a good idea, and we will be perfectly safe."

"Oh, yes, until she pulls out a gun and shoots us."

"Danvers will not allow her to come armed into our

home."

Ren arched a brow at that. She liked Danvers a great deal and believed him to be an exemplary butler, not that she had a great many other butlers to compare him to, but she could not envision the man searching Miss Parish for weapons.

"I know what you are thinking," Henry said.

"I am thinking you are a fool to allow that woman anywhere near us." Ren turned to fully face Henry. They stood on the shoreline of a rather secluded cove waiting for her men to bring in the boat so she could *finally* board the Mermaid after what seemed a lifetime away from her. Having to wait for Henry to return from Venton's had been torturous enough, but then Hammett had suggested they wait till nightfall to avoid any watchdogs that might have been alerted by her return to Cornwall.

She glanced up at the night sky. The moon, still a few days shy of full, hung bright and fat amidst thick clouds that warned of foul weather. Given the way the waves crashed against the nearby rocks and the biting chill of the wind as it tore at Ren's braid and cut through the fabric of her clothing, they were in for one hell of storm before dawn.

She pulled the edges of her cloak together and continued to regard Henry, who, thanks to his hat, seemed nonplussed by the wind. "Unless Danvers means to search every nook and cranny of Miss Parish's person, there is no way to guarantee our safety."

Henry shook his head. "She is not you." He reached out and tapped her on the nose. "She would never think to hide a pistol in her bodice or have it strapped to her thigh."

"It astounds to me that you believe you know what she would or would not think to do." Ren crossed her arms. "Tell me, did you know she would attempt to seduce you or shoot at you to stop our wedding or accuse you of getting her with child?"

"Of course not." He had the good grace to look a bit regretful.

"But you are confident she will not stuff a pistol down her gown." Ren shook her head and looked back out to sea. "If necessary, the woman would likely shove it up her own ar—"

"Ren."

She snapped her mouth shut. "I do not like the idea," she finally admitted into the silence.

"I know, but Venton is correct that we need to catch her in the act to have any hope of having her institutionalized, and I cannot think of a better way."

He was right, and she knew it, but she still did not like it. The thought of being anywhere near Miss Parish sent chills down her spine. She had underestimated the girl and been rewarded with a bullet. And now Henry wanted to invite the creature into their home for the sole reason to provoke her into making another attempt on one, if not both, of their lives. Did it not occur to him that Miss Parish might actually succeed? Aye, she'd be locked up nice and tight afterward, but one of them would be dead.

Ren blinked.

"Are you crying?" the ever-observant Henry asked.

"It is the wind." She blinked again and sent a little prayer toward the heavens that, if they failed to thwart Miss Parish, God willing, she would kill both of them, because either alternative could not be borne.

"I know what you are thinking," Henry said again as he gathered her into his embrace.

"No, you do not," she mumbled against his chest and snuggled deeper into the warmth of his body. He was always warm. There had been nights she had cried herself to sleep simply because she missed his heat.

"Yes, I do." He stroked her hair. "You are worried she will succeed, and that one of us will lose the other."

She said nothing.

Henry eased her away from his body and tipped her chin up. "That will not happen."

"You cannot guarantee such a—"

"It will not happen," he interrupted. "Understand?"

Ren tucked herself against his body again, inhaled his scent, absorbed his heat, and listened to the sound of their hearts beating in tandem. "If you are wrong, I shall kill you."

His laughter echoed across the expanse of the cove, and he tightened his arms around her. "I love you, my troublesome mermaid."

Ren looked up. "Troublesome?"

"Oh, yes. Nothing but trouble." He dipped his head and kissed her while smiling.

When the delicious kiss ended, Ren snuggled against Henry once more. "When is the duel?"

She felt Henry sigh. "Venton is arranging it, but it is my hope that it will never occur."

"Because we are to host the viper in our home beforehand."

Henry chuckled. "Yes."

"Who knew that marrying you would prove more dangerous than smuggling?"

"I believe it is the other way around."

Ren lifted her head. "Oh? You believe all of this is *my* fault? You are the one who thought to marry Miss Parish. Not I."

"Yes, yes, do not remind me."

"What *were* you thinking?"

He looked at her for a moment before answering. "I was only thinking I needed to forget you somehow. I needed to move on and live my life and pretend to be happy."

"It would have been a disaster."

"Oh, yes, you and everyone else has said so numerous times, thank you."

Ren gazed out toward the sea and gnawed on her bottom lip. "I am sorry, Henry."

"For what?"

She met his gaze. "For reacting so horribly when you first proposed to me."

"Ah, we are baring it all this evening, it seems."

Ren shrugged. "Seems as good a time as any." After all, they were alone with nothing but the wind and the waves to hear them.

"There is no need to apologize for rejecting my proposal."

"I wasted so much time. It was my fault we were apart for three years." She'd beaten herself up almost nightly over the fact.

Henry once more tipped her chin up. "I told you before I'll not have you waste more time worrying about the past. What is done is done. Let it go before it destroys our future."

He had a point, but before she could inflate his ego by telling him he was right, something caught her attention in the distance. "Do you see that?" She stepped from his embrace and pointed. "There." She squinted, then held out her hand. "Do you have your spyglass?"

Cold metal slapped into her palm, and she extended it, then raised it to her right eye. It took a moment for her to locate what she'd seen, but soon she was fixed on the bobbing, orange glow.

"What is it?" he asked.

Ren moved the spyglass down a notch and made out the silhouette of a rowboat. "It is a boat but moving in the wrong direction." She focused on the orange dot again as the clouds overhead parted. Moonlight streaked down just long enough for her to identify the source of the orange glow. "Oh my God." Her blood chilled. "It's a torch."

"A torch?" Henry nudged her and requested the spyglass, but she ignored him.

Blood roared in her ears, and her heart banged painfully in her chest as she watched the boat drift out of sight behind the high outcropping of rocks where the tallest of the Mermaid's masts was just barely visible. She lowered the spyglass and dropped to her knees in the sand.

"Ren!" Henry knelt beside her and took hold of her shoulders. "Ren, what is it?"

He shook her, then snatched the spyglass from her hand.

****

Henry scanned the horizon but could not see a bloody damn thing. Certainly nothing that would have caused Ren to collapse as if the air had suddenly gone out of her sails. He shifted the spyglass to pick out the faint silhouette of the Mermaid's mast. Ren's men should have already launched a boat to make their way to shore, but he saw no sign of it. Time seemed to stand still as he scanned the horizon again and again for some sign of something.

There!

A boat but not the Mermaid's skiff from the looks of it, and it was headed away from the beach.

Henry tracked the direction of the small boat and determined it was likely headed toward a smaller cove farther north. Fishermen perhaps? He had noticed the increase in the number of pilchard close to shore and knew the fishermen would be out in droves, day and night, to take advantage of the surplus, but his gut told him the boat in the distance was not out trolling for fish.

A flash off to the left shone in his peripheral, and he swung the glass over and watched the night sky slowly turn orange. "What the devil?"

"She is on fire," Ren said.

Henry lowered the glass to stare at her, but her gaze was fixed on the horizon.

"Whoever was in that boat set her on fire." Her tone lacked any inflection at all, and each dry word scraped at his heart.

He lifted the glass to his eye again just as the Mermaid's skiff cleared the concealing rock outcropping. He could clearly see six men on board. Knowing Hammett and five others were still ashore, those six men accounted for the rest of Ren's entire crew, which meant the Mermaid had been abandoned. He watched the skiff as it pursued the smaller craft he'd noticed earlier.

"Your crew is chasing after a small boat," he

informed Ren.

"All of them?"

"Yes."

She finally looked at him. "They would not have abandoned her unless they believed the fire was imposs—"

An explosion lit up the night.

****

After an hour spent convincing Ren to remain at home because that was where her men would think to find her, he headed for the Pilchard. The barmaid did not seem inclined to give him the information he sought until there was a pile of coin between them. With a gruff thank you, he headed up the stairs, located room 11A, and barged in without knocking.

Wexler, who had been sitting before the fire, lunged to his feet, and gaped at Henry. "Westie! What the devil are you doing here at this hour?"

Henry stalked across the room, grabbed the labels of Wexler's robe, and shoved him hard against the mantel. "You have ten seconds to convince me you had nothing to do with destroying Ren's ship."

"For God's sake, man!" Wexler struggled to gather the rather voluminous skirt of his robe as it flirted dangerously with the fire. "Do you mean to catch us both on fire?"

"If you are responsible, it's no less than you deserve. You now have five seconds."

"Christ sake! I haven't a clue what you are going on about."

Henry shook the weasel. "Someone blew up the Mermaid less than two hours ago, and I am waiting for you to convince me it was not you."

"Me? Why the devil would I blow up that ship?"

"You tell me."

"I cannot because I did not. Now take your bloody hands off me before I have you arrested for assaulting a peer of the realm."

Henry ignored the threat. "I am not convinced."

"It is the truth, you bloody fool."

Something in Wexler's tone and expression rang true, and Henry released him.

Wexler cursed as he smoothed the wrinkles that had resulted from Henry's rough handling of his silk robe. "Why the devil did you assume I was responsible?"

Henry raked a hand through his hair and ignored the question as his mind raced. If not Wexler… He glanced around the spacious room, which was empty save for Wexler. "Where is Miss Parish?"

"Honestly, I haven't a clue. She announced a few hours ago she was in great need of fresh air, and when I tried to convince her to allow me to accompany her she became hysterical. Given her delicate condition"—he shot an accusatory look at Henry—"I decided it was best to simply let her do as she pleased."

"You allowed a pregnant woman of Miss Parish's young age to venture out alone at night in a town she is not familiar with?"

Wexler threw his hands up. "As I said, she was hysterical and being around hysterical women makes me rather nervous. Besides, I am quite certain she will go no farther than the inn courtyard."

"And yet she left hours ago," he reminded the fool, then shook his head before Wexler could respond. "Did she know where the Mermaid was anchored?"

Wexler frowned at Henry. "You cannot possibly believe—"

"Answer me."

"We discussed it, but I cannot imagine the location meant anything to her. Honestly, I was quite surprised by her questions, now that I recall."

"What sort of questions?"

Wexler's frown deepened. "Where is the ship? How large is the crew?" He snapped his fingers and crossed the room to a small writing desk. He lifted a piece of paper and extended it toward Henry. "She asked me to sketch it for her."

Henry took the drawing. Wexler had managed a more than passable likeness of the Mermaid. He had rendered her at a three-quarter angle, which showed a sizable portion of the large pained windows of the captain's cabin. He had even included a stylized depiction of the ship's name.

"She requested that exact angle," Wexler explained. "I did my best but I'm no artist."

"You did not find this request strange?"

Wexler shrugged. "The woman is with child. There have been a number of strange requests since she appeared here without warning."

"Such as?"

"Well, she requested a tour of sorts, claiming she wished to see where the most important member of local society lived. I do not need to tell you who that would be."

"My father."

Wexler nodded. "So, I drove her past the baron's house, but I refused when she all but begged we drop in for an impromptu visit. I explained it was not the done thing to simply show up unannounced and assured her I would secure an invite in due time."

Henry glanced at the drawing and everything snapped into place. "Get dressed," he ordered.

"Look, Westhaven, I'll not take orders fr—"

Henry dropped the drawing and drew the pistol he had tucked into the waist of his trousers. "Get dressed."

Wexler stared at the gun, then at Henry. "I have grown quite tired of having guns pointed at me."

Henry cocked the pistol. "Get dressed."

"You are all mad. You, that creature you married, Venton—"

"I will shoot you, Wexler."

Again, Wexler threw his arms up in surrender. "At least have the decency to tell me where it is we are going."

"To prevent Miss Parish from killing my wife."

Chapter Twenty-One

Ren stood at the large window in Henry's study and stared out into the night. The room was dark behind her, and she'd pulled the curtains all the way open. The moon, which still struggled to be seen amongst the thick clouds, provided occasional illumination for her to appreciate the view of the distant sea. Henry's home—no, *their* home had been positioned to allow all the rear facing rooms to enjoy an unimpeded view of the sea. Those rooms included their private bedroom, but she had wanted to be close to him in his absence, so she had taken up vigil in his study where his scent and presence surrounded her like a tangible embrace.

She leaned her forehead against the window glass and stared at the sea. The waves had grown angrier, but the threatening storm had yet to break. She had wanted to take a boat out to the Mermaid as illogical as she knew that action to be, but Henry had stopped her. He had told her over and over again there was nothing for her to do. Her men were safe but there was nothing she could do to save the ship. She had never felt so helpless in all her life.

A tear streaked down her face, and she swiped it away. She'd been crying off and on since the explosion, but they were silent tears that made her throat burn with suppressed emotions. Hysterics would prove nothing. The Mermaid was lost to her forever, and all she could do was wait for him to discover whether his assumption about Wexler's involvement was accurate or not. She had made Henry promise to bring Wexler to her if the man was guilty, and he had agreed with the condition she do the man no harm. She had refused his conditions, and he had walked out without a word, leaving behind a thick tension that only added to her misery.

Ren sighed and closed her eyes against the night view. In all honesty, she did not know if she possessed the willpower to do much more than smack Wexler across the face. Nothing would return the Mermaid to her. That part of her life was over, lying in burnt pieces at the bottom of the sea, and putting a bullet in Wexler or anyone, for that matter, would alter nothing. In fact, it would do more harm than good, because she would likely hang and spend eternity in hell with the knowledge she had disappointed Henry.

"Aww, are we mourning the loss of your precious ship?"

Ren jerked her head away from the window and spun around. Despite the darkness of the room, she had no trouble picking out the white of Miss Parish's gown. A chill crept down her spine at the ghostly illusion the young woman created, but Ren shook off the feeling and replayed Miss Parish's words in her mind.

"*You* were responsible?"

"Oh, yes," Miss Parish trilled and twirled around like a child showing off a new dress.

Ren scanned the top of Henry's desk. For a brief moment, the sporadic moonlight reflected off the handle of his silver letter opener. It was not an ideal weapon if Miss Parish had a gun, but it was better than nothing. The trick would be to reach it before being shot, but once it was in her hand, she did not doubt her ability to throw it with deadly aim. Henry had always teased that her skill with daggers nearly outshone her skill as a ship's captain. Perhaps with the Mermaid gone she would join a circus and throw knives at wide-eyed volunteers.

"After our encounter in the inn," Miss Parish said as she ceased spinning, "I decided your ship needed to be destroyed. I was *so* very tired of hearing about it." She flitted her way toward the dormant fireplace. "Algernon was quite unhappy at having to hand over ownership of the ship. I nearly went mad listening to him go on and on about how unjust it was to win something fair and square in a card game only to be forced to relinquish it." She spun around, putting her back to the mantel. "Perhaps I shall pay a visit to the meddlesome Earl of Cragmoor once I am through with you."

There was a sudden burst of frantic pounding on the study door. "Mrs. Westhaven?" Danvers yelled through the paneling. "Mrs. Westhaven, are you quite all right?" He pounded some more.

"If I do not answer, he will likely break down the door," Ren informed Miss Parish.

"Go on then. Assure him you are fine."

"All is well, Danvers." Ren's yell silenced the pounding. "Miss Parish and I are merely having a private conversation."

"Very well, madam," Danvers said after a few moments of silence.

Ren returned her attention to Miss Parish and her last comment about paying a visit to Venton. "Why are you so determined to avenge Wexler's loss of my ship?"

The soft rustle of fabric indicated a shrug. "He is to be my husband, and no woman wants to marry an irate man. He is quite put out over the way the earl bullied him into handing over the ship, but for reasons he will not explain, he refuses to demand satisfaction."

"Perhaps he realizes it is not worth his life."

"True, true, and he is already engaged to fight one duel, and dying for my honor is much nobler than dying over a ship. Not that anyone will die, of course," she added quickly. "Oh, no, no. I have given Algernon very strict instructions to make certain the duel ends with first blood. It does not serve my purpose to allow either of them to die."

Ren took a cautious step closer to Henry's desk and halted as she heard the unmistakable cock of a gun.

"I have a list of reasons why I wish to shoot you, Miss Teague, and I will add foolish if need be."

"Mrs. Westhaven," Ren corrected.

"Hmph! Soon you will be the departed Mrs. Westhaven."

"I admit I am a little confused, Miss Parish." She needed to keep the girl talking. To give Danvers time to fetch help. God willing.

"Oh, by all means, tell me what confuses you."

"If you mean to marry Lord Wexler, why does it matter if I am Mrs. Westhaven?"

Miss Parish laughed, and it was too easy to imagine the sound echoing through the corridors of an asylum. "Henry will never agree to share my bed as long as you live."

"I thought he was desperate to share your bed? Is

that not how you came to be carrying his child?"

Miss Parish laughed again. "Lies. Those were lies, you foolish woman. I am no more with child than the queen."

"It was part of your plan to provoke Wexler to challenge Henry?"

"Oh, yes, and it was brilliant, would you not agree?"

Ren said nothing.

Miss Parish huffed quietly then continued. "Algernon is so very devoted to me. Mama assured me if I satisfied him in bed I would have him wrapped around my finger, and she was right. Mama is seldom wrong about such things. After all, she managed my father like a strict nanny would manage a wayward child. Until he passed, of course."

"How did your father die?"

"Oh, he was thrown from his horse. Mama said something must have spooked the docile creature, and she assured me Father did not suffer. She was devastated, of course, to be widowed so suddenly, but Mama is a strong woman, and the estate and Father's vast fortune needed to be handled."

In that moment, Ren realized Miss Parish had come by her madness quite naturally.

"Provoking Algernon into challenging Henry was simply a way to prove his devotion to me, and a devoted husband is so much easier to live with."

"In other words, a devoted husband will turn a blind eye to his wife's affairs."

Miss Parish scoffed at that. "Affairs? No, no. It is only Henry I want, which brings us back to my reason for eliminating you."

Ren chanced another step toward the desk.

"Really, Miss Teague, I will shoot you if you continue to test my patience."

It occurred to Ren she likely made a nice clear target with the window at her back. "Do you truly believe killing me will make Henry love you?"

"He *does* love me, you little fool. He has loved me since the first moment he saw me, but then you came along and ruined everything with your seductive wiles."

"All of this could have been avoided if you had accepted his proposal."

"I could not accept," Miss Parish whined. "Mama would have been most displeased with me, and I cannot displease Mama. She becomes so very angry."

"And it is her wish you marry a title."

"Of course. That is the wish of every mother, is it not?"

Ren ignored the question, but she could not help but believe, that, had her mother been alive, she would have only wished for Ren's happiness. "Henry would never sleep with another man's wife."

"I understand you need to tell yourself that, Miss Teague, because you believe Henry loves you, but he does not. He loves me, and it will be me he turns to once you are dead."

"Henry and I have been in love for years, Miss Parish. He pursued you in an effort to forget me." It was dangerous to provoke the girl, but Ren could not remain silent in the face of such delusions.

"No!" Miss Parish's slipper slapped against the tiled hearth. "No! Lies! You have infatuated him with some sort of dark magic, but he loves me, and love is more powerful than anything else in the world. When you are gone, he will forget you."

"What if you are wrong?"

"Wrong?"

"Yes. What if you are wrong about Henry's feelings? What if you are wrong, and he does not love you?"

"He proposed to me," Miss Parish insisted.

"Oh, yes, I know he did, but did you know he proposed to me three years ago?"

Miss Parish inhaled sharply. "You lie."

"It is true." Ren took a deep breath and prayed the risk she intended to take was not a deadly mistake. "We were together on my ship, and after we made love, he proposed."

"Do not," Miss Parish warned.

"Do not what?"

"Do not speak of making love to Henry."

"Has he ever kissed you, Miss Parish?"

"Stop it!"

Ren saw the glint of the gun and realized Miss Parish had raised her arms to cover her ears. "Does that mean he has not? What sort of man makes no attempt to kiss the woman he loves?"

"I said stop!"

"Especially a man such as Henry," Ren pressed. "He is so very passionate—" Ren dove for the desk as the glint of the gun lowered. She palmed the letter opener and let it fly just as the gun fired.

****

Gunfire echoed through the house just as Henry and Wexler entered.

"Sir!" Danvers appeared before him like a damned ghost. "The study, sir."

Henry took off as if actual hell hounds bit at his heels. He skidded around the final corner with enough abandon to upset the rug, a small table, and the statue atop it. The latter crashed to the floor.

"Bloody hell, Westie! That statue was worth a small fortune." Wexler sounded a tad breathless as he pounded after Henry.

Henry ignored the imbecilic comment and finally reached the study. The door was locked, and he did not think twice before giving it a solid kick that crashed it open. "Danvers! A light, now!"

"One step ahead of you, sir." Danvers materialized at his side and held out an unshuttered lantern.

Henry snatched the light and stepped into the room. "Ren?"

"Henry? Is that you?"

He swung the light in the direction of Miss Parish's voice and saw the woman kneeling on the floor before the fireplace. Her blue eyes seemed to glow in the dark. How the devil she had gotten into his home would be just one of several questions he would ask later of Danvers.

"We can be together now, Henry."

Wexler shoved past him and moved toward the fireplace. "Annabelle, love, what happened?" He spoke in a tone one might use to cajole a wild animal, and Henry recalled the vicar's wife's story of the horse she suspected had been possessed by the devil.

"What are you doing here, Algernon?"

Wexler hunkered down before Miss Parish and reached for her, but she scurried away. "Don't touch me!" She gathered her skirts, climbed to her feet, and threw herself at Henry.

He barely had time to lift the lantern out of the way to avoid a catastrophe.

Miss Parish clung to the labels of his jacket and looked up at him with wild eyes. "I killed her. You are mine now."

He shoved her away and swung the light around the room. There was no sign of Ren. He looked back to Miss Parish. "Where is she?"

"What does it matter? I killed her, and now—"

"Where is she?" He did not yell, but the chill in his tone must have made Miss Parish realize it would behoove her to answer.

"She fell behind the desk when I shot her." She huffed and crossed her arms. "But it does not matter. She is dead, and you are mine now, and nothing—"

She yelped as Wexler grabbed her from behind and spun her to face him.

"You need help, Annabelle. You aren't well."

"Unhand me."

Henry left them to battle it out and moved toward the desk. He stepped around it and found Ren slumped against the window.

"Christ," he mumbled and fell to his knees beside her. "Ren?" He put two fingers to the side of her neck and felt the flutter of her pulse. "Ren?" Gently, he cupped her face and turned it toward him. "Ren, love. Can you hear me?"

Her eyes fluttered open. "Henry."

"Hush, do not talk. Let me search for the wound."

"No." She shook her head and winced. "She did not shoot me. She shot *at* me, and in the process of dodging the bullet, I slipped and fell and hit my head on the damned window."

Henry did not know if he wanted to laugh or cry with relief. "Better a bump on the head than another bullet." He held out his hand. "Can you stand?"

Before Ren could accept, Miss Parish's voice screeched through the room. "One more step, and I will shoot you, Algernon."

Henry sprang to his feet to find Miss Parish had the gun pointed at Wexler, who stood a few paces away from her with both hands raised.

"Annabelle, what has come over you? We are to be married."

"I do not want you. I never wanted you. I did as my mother ordered me to do."

"Are you implying—"

"I am implying nothing," Miss Parish interrupted. "It was all an act. All of it. I never wanted you to touch me. I *hated* it," she said with enough vehemence to make Henry wince in sympathy for Wexler.

"Westhaven is married, Annabelle." Wexler's tone had lost some of its gentleness. "Perhaps all you need is a restful stay in the country to clear your mind, hmm? Then you will realize the right thing to do is forget all this nonsense and become my wife."

Henry did not understand Wexler's willingness to go through with marrying Miss Parish, but then he recalled her sizable fortune. A man such as Wexler would overlook a great deal for money.

"I killed Henry's whore, and I will kill you if I must." Miss Parish waved the gun at Wexler. "I will never be yours."

"And Henry will never be yours," Ren suddenly said from beside him.

Miss Parish gasped and spun around to point her

gun in Ren's direction, and Henry stepped between them. "It is over, Annabelle. Put the gun down."

"Move," she yelled.

"No, Annabelle," Henry said. "Put the gun down."

"You are mine! Move so I can shoot her!" Her tone had become hysterical.

Henry felt Ren's hand on his back, but he did nothing to acknowledge it. If she believed he would actually move, then Annabelle was not the only crazy female in the room. He stared at the gun pointed directly at him. Annabelle had already shot at Ren, which meant she had one bullet left. He could charge at her and take his chances that the surprise would make her misfire, but her arm was alarmingly steady, and he did not doubt the crazed motivation behind her intent. She would probably shoot him simply so Ren could not have him.

His other option was to throw the lantern at her, which would result in the room catching fire, followed by the entire wing of the house. With the window at his back, he could easily get himself and Ren to safety, but what of the servants? He could not yell to Danvers to clear the house without alerting Annabelle to his plan, which meant it was no plan at all.

Ren clutched at his shirt and gave him a little tug. Her breath brushed his ear as she whispered, "Toss the lantern at her."

"Yes, I already thought of and eliminated that option."

"What?" Annabelle demanded. "What are you saying? Do not speak to her." She took a step forward and screamed when Wexler made a grab for her. She spun around and hit him across the face with the gun.

He stumbled in shock but caught himself against the mantel.

Henry used the moment to make his move. He placed the lantern on the desk and raced toward Annabelle only to come up hard against the barrel of the gun as she whirled around a split second before he could grab hold of her.

She blinked up at him. "Why are you doing this, Henry? Why are you pretending you do not love me? I know you do. You proposed to me. You wanted to marry me. Me! Not her. Me! We belong together."

"Put the gun down, Annabelle."

She shook her head and began to cry. "If I cannot have you, then neither can she." She raised the gun to the level of his heart. "Please do not make me do this," she begged. "Tell me you love me and that we will be togeth—"

Her words ended as a black mass struck her from the side and drove her to the floor. The gun fired and Henry braced himself against the impact. Something shattered and he knew the bullet had gone wide.

"Am I interrupting?" Venton's voice interjected itself into the chaos.

****

Ren's head still throbbed from the hit against the window, and the sudden chaos and light that erupted in the room made the pain worse. She pressed fingers to both temples, closed her eyes, took a few deep breaths, and prayed for endurance and a large dose of patience.

"What are you doing here, Bram?" Henry's question forced her to open her eyes. She took a good look at the scene, and if not for the pain in her head, she might have laughed.

Miss Parish sobbed like a child and was sprawled face-down upon the hearth with the largest dog Ren had ever seen seated upon her back. Wexler stood frozen against the mantel with a wide-eyed gaze that flicked back and forth between the dog and Venton, who wore an amused expression as he thumped a walking stick against his thigh. Danvers moved about the room lighting candles and wall sconces until the space blazed with brightness akin to the noon day sun.

"I was out walking Cerberus when I heard a gunshot," Venton answered.

"And you naturally assumed the shot originated from my house?"

"Oh, no, but Rus has a keen nose for gunpowder, so I simply followed him." Venton spread his arms. "And here we are, just in time, by the looks of it."

Henry waved away his friend's comment and turned to Ren. "Are you all right?"

"Fine, fine, but Miss Parish confessed to blowing up my ship, and I fear if you do not remove her from my sight, I shall kindly ask the earl to order that beast to eat her."

Miss Parish let out a terrified squeal that no one paid any mind to.

"I've sent for your father, sir," Danvers interjected. "I imagine he will know the proper course of action to take with the young lady."

In Ren's mind, the only proper course of action was a long walk off a short gangplank into freezing cold water, but the baron would likely suggest an asylum. Ren hoped it was one very far away.

A sharp pain lanced through the back of her skull, and if she did not lie down, she might end up falling

289

down again. "Henry?"

He whipped around so fast it made her dizzy. "What is it?"

"If my presence is no longer required, I would like to lie down."

He tucked her against his side. "Venton, I trust you can see to all of this since you seem keen to save the day?"

"Go, go." Venton's gaze found Ren. "I am sorry to hear about your ship. She was as beautiful and impressive as her captain."

Ren's throat burned with emotion as she acknowledged Venton's words with a nod then allowed Henry to lead her from the room. Neither of them spoke until they were in their bedroom with the door closed.

"I assume the duel is off?" Ren kicked off her boots and crawled onto the bed.

"I had forgotten all about it, but yes, it seems a safe assumption." Henry sat on the edge of the bed but, after a moment, stretched out alongside her and wrapped her in his arms. "I am heartily tired of you being shot at."

"I am heartily tired of being shot at." Ren turned within his embrace to bury her face against his throat. "At least this time the bullet missed." As did the dagger she had thrown at Miss Parish. She made a mental note to hone the skill of throwing under great duress. Perhaps Eirene would be game to join her. "I believe the bullet is buried in the front of your desk."

"Better than you being buried in the family plot."

She chuckled at that, then cursed. "Bloody hell my head hurts, and why the devil are your floors so slippery?"

"My floors? Oh no, my darling mermaid, you have

290

always been a bit clumsy on dry land," he teased and stroked her hair, then quickly apologized when his hand accidentally passed over the growing bump at the back of her skull. "Can you recall the details of what happened?"

"Rather vividly." She feared Miss Parish's eerie laugh would haunt her for years. She shifted closer to Henry. "I have no idea what I will do without The Mermaid."

"If you are determined to continue smuggling, I can halt the refitting of my—"

"No," she answered before he could finish.

"It is a damn fine ship," he protested.

"It is a *boat*." She smiled and smothered a laugh as he sighed against her hair. "Perhaps it is time for me to step away from the game." A thought struck her, and she pulled away to sit up. The room spun a bit, but she ignored it. "We should purchase a pub." The idea seemed more logical than joining a circus.

Henry rolled onto his back and crossed his arms beneath his head. "You wish to become a pub owner?"

"Why not? I could provide a safe haven for—"

"Smugglers," Henry finished for her.

"Of course."

"I can only imagine how proud this will make my father."

Ren rolled her eyes at Henry's sardonic tone. "It is not illegal to own a pub."

"No, but it is illegal to aid those who are actively breaking the law."

"Only if I am caught."

It was Henry's turn to roll his eyes. "My fearless mermaid."

"I thought I was your troublesome mermaid?"

He reached for her and hauled her atop him. "Oh, aye. You are fearless, troublesome, beautiful, loyal, intelligent, seductive, and incredibly irresistible." He cupped her buttocks and moved her against him so she could feel the proof of just how irresistible he found her.

Ren ground herself against Henry's erection and kissed his neck until he groaned for mercy. She lifted her head to look down at him. "Would it be inappropriate to make love right now?"

"Given the gathering in our study, you mean?"

"Yes." She nuzzled his neck again and moved her hips until he caught hold of them in a tight grip.

"I believe it would be cruel of you not to make love to me," he finally answered her. "But what of your head?"

"I shall remain on top." She kissed away any further protest he might think to make.

Chapter Twenty-Two

Dearest Readers,

Another Season has ended, and there is almost too much for me to report upon in one column, but I shall, as always, endeavor to do my best.

Rumor has it the oh so lovely Miss A.P. will be spending an unforeseeable amount of time enjoying the quiet solitude of the Yorkshire countryside following events that took place in Cornwall. Lord Wx seems mum on the matter but has stated to any who will listen that he is, once again, in search of a bride. One can only assume the wealthier the better.

As for the dashing, Mister H.W. and his ravishing, Miss T., rumor has it they are married and have decided to reside in Cornwall. It is this author's hope they will grace us with an appearance next Season and not become recluses like Lady R-W and her husband who have retired to the country to await the birth of their first child.

Ah, speaking of children. It seems the Dark Lord of the Nobility is in need of a governess due to the sudden appearance of a child no one had any knowledge of. Perhaps the child was conjured with a bit of magic, like his father before him. Nevertheless, this author hopes whoever answers the earl's advertisement for employment is a woman of very strong character.

I bid you adieu for now, dear readers.

About the Author

In addition to being an author of romantic, happily ever after stories, Lora Darling is also a photographer, rock drummer, and tarot reader.

~*~

Visit Lora at
www.loradarling.com

Also Available
from The Wild Rose Press, Inc.
and major retailers.

A Lady's Ruinous Plan
Rumor Has It Book One
By Lora Darling

Lady Eirene Rowe-Weston has inherited a great fortune and a great dilemma. Every bachelor in London wishes to marry her, but she has vowed never to become any man's bride. She has two choices, hide forever in the country or render herself unfit for marriage. She chooses the latter and hires one of London's most celebrated rakes to see to the task.

Viscount Adrien Benoit is not all he appears or is rumored to be. When Lady Eirene offers him an exorbitant amount of money to ruin her, he counters and offers her a secret guaranteed to destroy him. The lady accepts, plans are made, but the moment of her ruination doesn't quite go as arranged. Nothing ever does when love interferes.

The Duke's Decision

Dukes in Danger: A Haversham House Romance

By Carolina Prescott

While gathering research for the puzzles she sells to newspapers, Vivian, the widowed Viscountess Rowden, literally stumbles across the arrogant Duke of Whitley.

Whit, known to the ton as the Ice Duke, is spymaster for the Crown, and he has evidence of enemy agents using newspaper ciphers to send coded messages to Napoleon's army. His mission is clear—less clear are his feelings for the woman he may have to destroy.

While Vivian struggles to put the past behind her and find a future where her heart can be safe, the duke must decide whether the lovely and independent viscountess is friend, foe, or fate.

Thank you for purchasing
this publication of The Wild Rose Press, Inc.

For questions or more information
contact us at
info@thewildrosepress.com.

The Wild Rose Press, Inc.
www.thewildrosepress.com

To visit with authors of
The Wild Rose Press, Inc.
join our yahoo loop at
http://groups.yahoo.com/group/thewildrosepress/